The
BLUE KINGFISHER

The

BLUE KINGFISHER

a novel

ERICA WRIGHT

The following is a work of fiction. Names, characters, places, events and incidents are either the product of the author's imagination or used in an entirely fictitious manner. Any resemblance to actual persons, living or dead, is entirely coincidental.

Hardcover ISBN: 978-1-947993-26-6
eISBN: 978-1-947993-46-4
Library of Congress Catalog Number: 2018955209

First hardcover publication:
October 2018 by Polis Books LLC
221 River Street, 9th Fl., #9070
Hoboken, NJ 07030
www.PolisBooks.com

POLIS BOOKS

For Adam

ALSO BY ERICA WRIGHT

THE RED CHAMELEON
THE GRANITE MOTH

"...I think this is
the prettiest world—so long as you don't mind
a little dying, how could there be a day in your whole life
that doesn't have its splash of happiness?"

—MARY OLIVER, "THE KINGFISHER"

CHAPTER 1

The George Washington Bridge disappeared halfway across the Hudson River. More than six hundred feet in the air, the suspender cables and steel beams towered over me like some sort of robot giant, content to rest for a minute before crushing the land under its weight. But it had been resting since the Great Depression, and there was no reason to suppose a crisp April morning would drive it into action. Its bright lights strained against the fog, but the effort was no use. Here one minute then gone—poof. A neat magic trick, and one I often wished I could perform on myself.

Most of what I knew about the historic structure came not from a meticulous study of my city's landmarks, but from a children's book, *The Little Red Lighthouse* and *The Great Gray Bridge*. My mother had bought two copies, one for reading and one for decorating. From the second one, she cut out all the illustrations and taped them up in my bedroom, intending perhaps for the message to seep into my admittedly stubborn head: you don't have to be the biggest to make a difference in the world. I could be accused of a lot, but thinking myself the biggest—the best at anything— wasn't on the list anymore. I liked to call leaving the New York Police Department my retirement, but since

I had been a few decades away from a pension at the time, that particular lie didn't hold up under interrogation. I had quit, planning to never look back, planning to vanish.

The unusual darkness of the morning had driven me from my apartment early. This was my favorite spot, even more so on those lucky occasions when the trails were deserted. A recluse's paradise. I walked closer to the lighthouse, its diminutive size toy-like compared to the bridge. It wasn't any taller than the trees in Fort Washington Park, and its lantern only shone on special celebrity-filled occasions these days. The children's book had helped it get declared as a national treasure, and I remembered a single sentence taking up a full page: "Behind it lay New York City, where the people lived." That had never seemed truer as I looked around at the empty picnic tables. Mostly when I wandered there, I was wary of bicyclists flying down the paths. That day, the whole place was vacant, downright godforsaken, and I felt a thrill of ownership. Mine.

Of course, it was risky to ever have such a blasphemous thought. As soon as the city got wind of your possessiveness, she would close your go-to restaurant and put up a bank. It was a dysfunctional relationship, sure, but one that eight million residents knew all too well. I pulled a thick scarf over my nose. The calendar may have said spring, but it still felt like winter, another charming aspect of my hometown; she bullied spring, letting tulips emerge then snapping them with frost or sometimes a full-blown snowstorm. It happened every year, and yet the flowers would return, their optimism downright quixotic. To be honest, I could relate. After years of feeling useless—or feeling little at all, more accurately—I discovered that I rather liked solving cases as a private investigator. No safety net, sure, but no boss either.

My eyes watered, and my bare hands were pink. Even so, I was reluctant to break the morning's spell, and climbed up on one of the boulders for a better view. Up close, it was easy to see how well-maintained the lighthouse really was. Being called a landmark had its perks, not least of which was a fresh paint job. I had always wanted to see inside, but the gate was kept locked. As a teenager, I might have snuck in, maybe tagged my name on the side, but I followed the laws these days. Give or take a few illegal cars, a couple of incidents involving bolt cutters and duct tape.

I squinted up at the small watch room, imagining what it would have been like for a keeper to pull an overnight shift in the country's most populated city without a soul in sight. Peaceful, I decided, helping ships navigate their cargo to the docks then helping them return to sea. I blame that daydream for not noticing the arm at first, one hand dangling over the platform's edge. When I finally saw the body, I thought it was another trick of light, the strange mist making me mistake a broom for a ghost. But no, the sight was all too human, the tan flesh in sharp contrast to the bright red. Was there a darker stain as well? I yelled for help, knowing even as the words flew from my mouth that nobody would come.

Praying for reception, I pulled out my cell phone and dialed 911, hoping the dispatcher could understand me as I scrambled back down the rocks and onto the gravel path. I was panicked by the time my hands reached the metal railing, and I hung up on the woman telling me to wait for paramedics. Even with their fast response time, it would take at least fifteen minutes to navigate an ambulance to this hidden spot. I cried out to the person, but he was unresponsive and most likely injured. I understood the curiosity that led to his current unconscious state. That could have been me, I thought. Only a few years earlier I would have been foolhardy enough to break into the place just for kicks.

It was hard to maneuver between the spikes, but I managed to flipped myself over the bars, landing with a thud. My knees slammed down into the concrete slab, but I barely felt the impact. The door was within reach, and I used the handle to haul myself upright. I expected the entrance to be open since I was following someone else's path, but it was shut tight, and the padlock made me pause. Besides my phone and keys, I'd come empty-handed, not expecting trauma. I had on heavy winter boots, though, and adrenaline pushed me to act recklessly. I turned sideways and slammed my foot against the metal. I made a dent in the door, but the lock didn't budge. I would never get used to the jolt of using myself as a battering ram, but I regained my balance and struck again. Two somewhat steady kicks later, and a pop let me know I succeeded.

The stairs began immediately, and I ran up, grateful this wasn't one of those record-breaking monstrosities down in Florida. I wasn't sure about seventeen, but four flights I could handle. I was winded when I got to the widow's walk, and in the end, my rush was pointless. The victim was long past first aid, his skull smashed and limbs twisted into impossible angles. His body looked churned, as if caught in the claws of some great beast. His eyes were open, staring up at the bridge, and I turned to stare too, half expecting to see the monstrosity come to life and swoop down on us. There was no demon, though, only the solemn overpass and a few streaks of sun trying to push through the clouds. Neither heaven nor hell, it was just an ordinary day except for men falling from the sky.

I stepped around the pool of blood to get a closer look. The almond-shaped, caramel eyes were too familiar for my liking; I was looking at my apartment building's maintenance man, Tabor Campion. Rocking back, my throat constricted, and I gagged. Would I have felt less sick if the man had been a stranger? This wasn't the first time I'd stumbled across a dead man—my violent past intent on catching up with me—but it was the first time black spots swarmed my vision. I shook my head, forcing myself to look again at Tabor's face. He deserved whatever respect I could muster.

His eyes weren't his sole unique quality. He was the only Frenchman I'd ever met in my predominantly Dominican neighborhood. And while he was as slow to respond as any other super in a low-rent address, he'd also been kind to me on more than one occasion. Replacing my deadbolt when my paranoia peaked, for example, as it usually did once a season. It was hard to see him in this smashed-up state, even if we were more acquaintances than friends. I was sure he didn't even know my real name, Kathleen Stone.

My lease said Katya Lincoln, my preferred alias of a dozen or so. It wasn't exactly a blessing, being able to turn into Kat or Kitty or Katya, being indistinguishable in a crowd, but it had some benefits. My nondescript appearance was the main reason I'd excelled at undercover work, then it was my fallback plan when I left the police force to chase philanderers as a private investigator. I was three years into that gig and no closer to running away from my past. But that was a pity party for another day, I told myself, mumbling something about resting in peace over the prone body. If there was any peace to be had in such an ending, I wanted Tabor to find it.

When I turned away, I was surprised to find that I could see the other side of the river, now visible. I could see cars on the bridge, too, crawling toward work. Had someone watched him fall, I wondered? Had they bothered to report the incident? I called to let the police know the situation was no longer an emergency.

"A jumper," the dispatcher said. "I see."

This time, the woman hung up on me, and I started waiting for anyone with a badge. It wasn't the kind of vigil I wanted to last very long. I'd lived nearby when a bullied teen had made headlines with a social media post and a headlong flight into the water. He'd joined fifteen others that year. I'd only ever heard of ocean sirens, those winged creatures luring sailors to their deaths with pretty songs and prettier faces. Were there river ones, too? Were they calling now? All I could hear was the occasional honk from above and, finally, real-world sirens, nothing mythological about the piercing sounds of ambulances and police cruisers. Giants, beasts, ghosts, and mermaids. I knew better. The fog might make the landscape look otherworldly, but it was always people who did the most damage, sometimes even to themselves.

*

A couple of stringers nagged me for quotes, but I waved them off, refusing even the steaming cup of coffee one held under my nose. My commendation would be sent via post, I assumed. The milling cops were less interested in my story, jotting down a few notes, mostly asking me to repeat why I was outside so early in such "piss-poor weather." It turned out, not everyone had a beloved spot for reciting a laundry list of personal failures. When they asked for my name, my impulse was to lie, but obstruction of justice wasn't something I wanted to add to my resume (read: rap sheet) with the NYPD.

When I joined the force after college, my aspirations had been meager. I'd been using my real name at the time and Detective Kathleen Stone had a nice ring to it. To be fair, I did have that title for a hot minute. But after two years of brutal undercover work, a hand-to-mouth life as a private investigator made more sense at the time. Fast forward, and I was finally getting my bearings. A steady stream of referrals meant I didn't have to advertise, didn't have to wave even my fake name around, much less my real one. And since the biggest bad from my past life had already found me, what was the point of all the secrecy anyway? Flaunting wasn't really my style, but at least for once, it was an option.

The young officer asked again for my name, and I coughed up Kathleen Stone. I almost laughed when I saw him write down Catherine Stein. I didn't even have to try sometimes. This group was ready to turn the potential six o'clock news items over to the Parks Department and call it a day. I couldn't help but be bothered by their cavalier attitude, even though I knew they had other cases that needed their attention. It had been less than an hour, and medical personnel were already wheeling a gurney toward the ambulance.

"Wait," I called, surprising myself. One of the EMTs glanced at me, the visible veins in her eyes suggesting the end not the beginning of her shift. Tabor's body lay covered in front of her, a once imposing figure reduced to an unwieldy package. Rigor mortis must not have set in yet because he was in a more standard position than the one I'd found. They had straightened him out, and I didn't have time to marvel at the sangfroid of the team who had moved his arms and legs until they looked human again. "Wait," I said again, more forcefully this time.

"Lady, you can't see the body," the first paramedic said, stopping the cart to glare at me. She crossed her arms in front of her chest and widened her stance, making her already imposing self into a shield.

What kind of creep did I look like, I thought, momentarily forgetting my purpose. "No, I just want to ask if it's normal for jumpers to miss the water."

"Normal? Ain't nothing normal about making city employees clean your guts up."

Yep, definitely the end of her shift.

"Come off it, Delores," her partner said. He was younger, in his early thirties maybe, and looked only eighty percent ready to collapse. "Everybody gets desperate sometimes."

"Desperate, sure, but that's why God made pills. You make a mess, you make a mess in your own damn bathroom."

Delores wouldn't stand for being detained any longer, and the gurney wheels squeaked as she pushed them forward. I turned back toward the cops, wanting to be released and think over my uneasiness alone in my apartment. Not that I'd be able to enter the building again without seeing Tabor's dead, caramel eyes. And didn't that unnerving stare explain my qualms? I couldn't shake the feeling that rushing to declare his death a suicide was insensitive, but I was probably looking for trouble where there wasn't any. It wouldn't be the first time I stuck my hand in a mousetrap, and, eventually, we learn our lessons, right? After we lose a finger or two?

A park ranger joined the officers and gesticulated wildly at the lighthouse. I walked closer then stopped when I caught snippets from his tirade: "door" and "damaged" and "replacement." If the man was more worried about a dent than a dead human being, it was little wonder that he'd been assigned this solitary post. I took a few steps backward, as quietly as possible in my bulky boots, but was caught trying to escape.

"Miss Stein," an officer called, smiling at his own personal joke. "Perhaps you'd like to apologize for the property damage." His smiled turned into a laugh, and the others joined in, relieved perhaps to have a distraction—or a scapegoat.

"This guttersnipe?" He jabbed his finger into my chest but didn't take his eyes off the men in charge.

I'd been called worse, but his tone was little better than a sneer. Which was to say, politeness eluded me.

"I promise to use my key to the city next time," I said.

The man looked directly at me then, his expression as wild as his gray hair sticking up in one great tuft. Mr. Rhinoceros was past retirement age, and I almost excused his bad attitude. It was early and cold and his castle had been stormed by someone who—from a distance or with a little subterfuge—could be mistaken for a teenage boy. Keith was one of my better disguises, but I was mostly trying to be myself these days and clearly not succeeding. What did it mean to pass as yourself? I hoped to live long enough to find out. See? I was practically a ball of sunshine.

As if to prove my point, the laughing officer mispronounced by last name again and said I was free to go. I turned toward the path, noticing for the first time that the tips of tree branches were turning green. They looked dipped in paint, ready for their debut. Nature could come as a surprise in the city. Visitors sought out the bright canary of taxis, not the hawk-colored river. They might visit the botanical gardens, but missed the daffodils growing up Madison Avenue. "Chassez le naturel, il revient au galop," I remembered Tabor saying once while fixing a broken pipe beneath my sink. I think he was blaming spiders for what seemed to be a rusted gasket. Nonetheless, the translation he offered stuck with me: "Chase away what's natural, and it will gallop back."

The others were probably right, I told myself again. They were professionals. If depression affected fifteen million Americans each year, why not the man tenants called when their showers were clogged? And yet, there was that one pesky detail tugging at my mind, refusing to be ignored. If it was a watery grave you were after, why take the plunge over land?

CHAPTER 2

A steel door, lacking in vintage charm and dented without my help, greeted me in my building's hallway. I'd always been grateful that Tabor had replaced my old one with something that would require more than a boot to kick down, but had I been grateful enough? A bottle of wine might have been appropriate. Flowers, candies, Yankees tickets. Anything better than a cagey attitude and mumbled thanks, my normal response to acts of kindness. I paused to appreciate a man who pretended not to speak English very well if you called him after five o'clock—four on Fridays—but who could be counted on to show up eventually. Maybe not an epitaph for the ages, but a solid enough review in a world full of cheats and worse. It was the "worse" that made me reluctant to enter my apartment.

It had been four months since drug trafficker Salvatore Magrelli alerted me through his cronies that I hadn't been forgotten. No, a devil never forgot a bargain, and a man like that never forgot the upstart who finally got him arrested, even if the charges were mysteriously dropped. I'd been in my version of hiding ever since, switching cell phones and wigs in dizzying succession. If I were being honest, I'd admit to a certain degree of relief that I'd been found. After three years of self-imposed exile from a regular life, he'd offered me a deal: join him or—the "or" specifics weren't clear but didn't involve lollipops and puppies. Cement boots in a charming size eight, perhaps.

And now? I hadn't responded, so we were in what I thought of as our Spring Break phase. Bust out the cheap rum and beads! Holding my breath, I unlocked the deadbolt and walked inside. Everything was exactly as I had left it, right down to the Pop-Tart wrapper on the kitchen counter, calling out to cockroaches. My vacation from Magrelli's world of cocaine and violence wasn't over yet.

I threw out my leftover breakfast and made up the twin-size bed. The studio was small—one room for sleeping, living, and eating—but it beat the Bronx beauty I called home during my undercover life. Next door to that fire hazard of a questionably legal space, the Costa family lived in an equally dingy unit. The Costas had been my ticket into Magrelli's orbit. They may have been small-time, but their daughter, Eva, was destined for bigger fish, a prize worthy of taxidermy and wall mounting: Salvatore Magrelli himself. Eva's marriage had propelled her from neighborhood queen bee to proprietor of an exclusive nightclub for Manhattan's biggest socialites. It was Cinderella meets Scarface and ready for prime time. Oh, except for that time Salvatore killed his wife's favorite cousin. I wasn't sad to be missing Christmas dinners.

Looking around, I was a tiny bit apartment-proud, though anyone living outside of New York City would

have laughed at the three hundred square feet I considered worthy of bragging rights. At least here, water
rather than blood made the ceiling stains. The neighbors were an upgrade, too. They might not call the cops
for anything less than a three-alarm blaze, but they
didn't actively want to kill you either. I was pretty sure
Eva Costa's unstable sister or even her honey-tongued
mother wouldn't hesitate to take an axe to my neck.

As if they knew I'd been thinking fondly of them,
a few other tenants from my building started gathering
in the hallway. I could hear their murmurings, and I
wasn't surprised. They'd lock their doors for emergencies, but gossip? Gossip rousted even the most self-pre-
serving hens from their nests. The voices were too low
to decipher, and I couldn't see anything out of my peephole. All I wanted to do was collapse onto my loveseat
or maybe take a shower. As a compromise, I threw away
my boots, which were wet with what looked like mud,
but I suspected might contain some of Tabor's guts.
When I'd crouched beside his body, I hadn't been thinking about footwear. Suddenly, it seemed important to
know exactly how my super was being eulogized by his
tenants. Anything to get as far away from his bodily flu-
ids as possible.

I grabbed some old sneakers from the back of my
closet, glad I'd held on to a spare even if the heels were
frayed. When I stepped into the hallway, the group of
nosy neighbors stopped talking and stared at me like
the intruder I was. Depending on the day, they'd seen a
redhead, a brunette, and a blonde exit 3B. Since moving

in, I'd stayed in some sort of disguise most of the time, worried that there might be a small bounty on Kathleen Stone's head and therefore content to go by any other name. They probably thought I was running a brothel, or at least an illegal Airbnb. Self-consciously, I ran a hand through my short, cropped hair that never quite managed Halle Berry chic. I attempted a little wave of hello, but the gesture looked more like a twitch.

"Is something wrong?" I said, knowing full well that word of Tabor's death must have made its way to our hallowed linoleum halls. Perhaps the police had dropped by? An unlikely guess given their dismissive attitude at the park, but there was often paperwork to be filed, checklists to rush through. Someone could have made a half-hearted attempt at locating relatives at least.

An elderly woman I recognized from the mailboxes used her cane to gesture toward the stairs. Her thin nightgown revealed a lot of her sagging skin, so her gesture was as good an excuse as any to look away. Amador, I remembered, from the names on the outside buzzer. The space beside my apartment number was still blank, three years after moving into the building. Another Tabor favor. There were probably more that I would remember, more that would make me feel guiltier and guiltier over the next few days. I'd been so worried about myself that I'd hardly noticed the people orbiting around me, busy with their own worries. A whole planet of catastrophe waiting to happen.

"Mr. Campion," Señora Amador said, switching

the conversation to English. "He's not coming back to us."

The man from 3F laughed, his gut punctuating the sound with ripples. "No point confusing the lady, viejita. He's dead. He died."

"¡Debería darte vergüenza!" the woman replied, covering the ears of a small boy who had appeared and wrapped his arms around her legs. "Not in front of my grandson."

The boy in question clutched the corner of a stuffed frog. His eyes were wide, putting together "died" and "dead" in his mind perhaps. I guessed his age around two, but I didn't have much experience with toddlers. He was little enough to make my heart squeeze ever so slightly. I crouched down to his level and pointed at his animal.

"Does your frog have a name?" I asked. His grandmother turned away from us both to welcome another neighbor into the already crowded and noisy group. "¿Cuál es el nombre de su rana?" I tried again.

"Frog. His name's Frog," the boy replied in English, pulling the furry body closer and putting an ear in his mouth. The thing looked more like a chew toy than a stuffed animal from years of acting as a security blanket.

"No, Victor," his grandmother said, somehow fully alert to the child's gesture even though she'd been facing the other way. "That's dirty." She yanked the toy from him and tucked it under her arm while Victor hung his head.

I stood up, suddenly frustrated with this blood-sniffing crowd. What a bunch of sharks, I thought dismissively. I planned to go back inside my apartment, but a woman hovering at the edge caught my attention. She acted more shocked than the rest, looking for comfort rather than lurid details. She twisted a strand of her flat-ironed hair around her finger. When she saw me staring, she stopped and almost smiled. It was as close to an opening as I could rightly expect.

"Did you know Tabor?" I said, stepping toward her and keeping my voice low so as not to be overheard. The grandmother was shouting at another neighbor from the floor, so perhaps I was being overly cautious. The woman answered in a whisper, though.

"It's such a shame," she said, nodding. "A good man."

I agreed, hoping she would elaborate unprompted. How well did any of us really know our super? He'd been in all our places at one time or another, replacing broken radiators or re-caulking tubs. Tabor knew more about us than we knew about him, a perfect spy, albeit one with no ulterior motives. At least none that we knew about. When the young woman moved to speak to someone else, I blurted out the first thing I could say of Tabor. "So handsome."

It was true even though I was embarrassed to comment on his looks even now. Every time I had called for a repair, I worried he'd think I was flirting. And it wasn't just those unusual brown eyes now lodged permanently in my memory; he'd been tall and fit with a head full of shiny hair even in his forties. The French accent always made me think the universe was playing a cruel joke. Why was the man fixing toilets when he should have been starring in movies? Excuse me, les films. Replace his jeans with a tux, and he would have looked at home on a Cannes red carpet.

Much to my relief, the woman grinned, almost wolfishly, before replying, "There was that."

Mr. 3F was much closer than I realized, and he snickered. "That's one way to speak of the dead. His body's probably not cold yet if you girls want a go."

Señora Amador made a strangled noise and clapped her hands over her grandson's ears. The boy took that opportunity to snatch his frog back. If there was one lesson living in the Heights taught you, it was to take a chance when it comes along. Who knew when another one would bother showing up.

"What?" 3F said in response to the woman's eye roll in my direction. "Tabor had a sense of humor. He'd like that two broads were in heat for his corpse."

I noted that I'd gone from lady to girl to broad in less than ten minutes and couldn't help my revulsion at the man's cavalier attitude. Or maybe it was the sweat-stained t-shirt and baggy sweatpants he never seemed to clean. I was with Señora Amador either way; he couldn't shut up soon enough for me.

"A good man," the grandmother said, parroting back her neighbor's phrase. The assortment of characters nodded, in agreement on that point at least. Or maybe it was just the kind of thing you said about the dead, regardless of past behavior. One man nodded more vehemently than the others, though, and I suspected he believed those words. He looked all of eighteen, a kid really, and lived with a few other quiet teenagers. I'd seen them huddled on the corner, smoking cigarettes and eyeing the dominoes game that went on 365 days a year, rain or shine. A late-night gambling opportunity for nickel and dimers. As dependable as the post office and about as expensive as a stamp.

I made my way toward the teenager, hoping nobody thought it odd that I was interested in everyone's story after years of, well, avoiding everyone. "Was he a friend of yours?" I asked, watching the teenager fidget with coins in his pocket. He looked more upset than the others, almost afraid. He shook his head at my question, though I wasn't sure if he meant no or didn't understand me. An apartment door opened down the hall, and one of his roommates emerged. They stepped off to the side, and I tried to eavesdrop on their rapid-fire Spanish.

Mr. 3F delighted in his captive audience and regaled us with a story about that one time he found Tabor stargazing with a date on the fire escape. "Like it was a damn balcony," he finished, waving his meaty hands for emphasis. I had my doubts about the tale and wasn't alone.

"Stargazing in Manhattan?" someone challenged.

"You ain't seen stars," Mr. 3F responded with surprising force. "You ain't looking."

I glanced at the teenagers who were frantically gesturing to each other. I could only pick up a few words over the other conversations: "jobs" and "money" and "martín pescador."

I knew pescador meant fisherman, but I wasn't familiar with the phrase.

"What's a martín pescador?" I asked Señora Amador, leaning close to her.

Her grandson was opening and closing one of the hallway windows, and she was distracted by the squeaks. "Enough," she shouted in his direction.

I thought she might not answer me, and I considered who else could help. I'd been fluent in Spanish since I was a kid—not so hard if you grow up close enough to Spanish Harlem for cabbies to refuse to take you home sometimes—but the idioms could trip me up. There was one about darkness in the mouth of a wolf that stumped me no matter how many times the intent had been explained.

"Un martín pescador," Señora Amador finally responded. "A kingfisher. Like the bird. Someone who finds jobs for boys like them."

She didn't have to say "immigrants" for me to know what she meant. It was an immigrant building in an immigrant neighborhood, and I would always be an outsider with my American birth certificate and American job, never mind my family's stories. I was lucky that she'd told me that much, but I supposed she thought something along the lines of, What's the harm? Tabor's not getting into any trouble now.

"They're afraid they'll lose their jobs now that Tabor's gone?" I asked, looking at the teenagers.

Pulling her nightgown down as if only then realizing she might be revealing too much to strangers, she called to her grandson, affectionately this time. When the boy got close enough, she bent to kiss the top of his head, holding her back when it cracked loudly, resisting the movement.

"He was a good man," she said again, crossing herself. "Come along, Victor." The boy tucked the frog back in his mouth, and no reprimand followed. His chaperone was too distracted, her eyes filled with tears.

CHAPTER 3

Sammy Carter grimaced when he saw me enter my former precinct. I might have played a small role in getting him re-assigned desk duty. But hey, he hadn't been happier on the street, and I was sure his wife appreciated that he could only piss off a limited number of people if ensconced behind acrylic. On the corner of Atlantic and Nostrand? He could offend everyone from waiters on their smoke breaks to the bodega cats. He was a master of the faux pas, and to be fair, that was why I'd grown to actually like this mess of a human a little. When I smiled, he only grimaced more. The liking wasn't mutual.

"You know what your problem is?" he said, picking up on a conversation he must have been having in his head for the past few months. I hadn't seen him since November when he helped me break into a suspect's apartment. In my defense, I thought she was a victim instead of a murderer, so tomayto, tomahto. "You're like a beacon in a shit storm," he finished after a Tony Award-winning pause.

"Aw shucks, Sammy. I only want to shine as brightly as you."

He grunted and buzzed me into the bullpen, where I went in search of Detective Ellis Dekker. A few officers turned to stare as I scurried past their desks, and I refused to duck my head in embarrassment. In fact, I may have added a little swagger to my walk. A lot of good that did in my bulky parka and worn-out sneakers, but it made me feel more confident. In general, folks didn't pay a lot of attention to me, but an unescorted civilian in a precinct tended to make a uniform or two sit up. Never mind that a few of these law upholders had wanted to throw me in a cell and toss away the key a few months ago. What's a relationship without a little foreplay?

I survived the gauntlet and let myself into Ellis's office without knocking. He raised a nearly invisible eyebrow at me and gestured toward a chair while he finished up a phone call. His white-blond hair and pale blue eyes made him my opposite—as easy to pick out of a lineup as a purple muppet. There was also something about his bearing that screamed "cop," one of the good ones, unflappable in the pursuit of justice. Or so I would have sworn until I informed him that his brother was working for a drug cartel, and he hadn't pursued my tip. Family makes us, then makes us doubt ourselves. We hadn't talked about Lars since, and I wasn't going to dig into that wound today, especially since I needed a favor.

Ellis had been my best pal in college, the one I called on Mondays to recap our weekend adventures, and now we were working our way back to friendly, or at least civil. And if I sometimes thought about what he might look like with his shirt on my apartment floor, I kept that fantasy to myself. He hung up without saying goodbye, then made a few notes, waiting for me to speak first. It was a power play, one we'd both learned at John Jay College of Criminal Justice, so who did he think he was fooling? I may not have been valedictorian, but my diploma was the same size as his. Wherever that document was collecting dust these days.

"Martín pescador," I said, giving in. "You've heard the term?"

I watched him write another sentence, uninterested in my acquisition of new Spanish vocabulary. This time, I waited, resisting the urge to fidget until he answered. "A sort of head hunter for immigrants, documented and otherwise. Finds jobs, takes a cut."

"One was found dead this morning, supposedly a jumper off the George Washington Bridge."

"They dragged the river today?" He dropped his pen, worried that he hadn't heard about such a massive use of department resources. His eyes turned toward my face, but he didn't really see me, lost in speculation.

"He wasn't in the river. They found his body on top of the lighthouse. Well, I found his body."

Ellis removed his tortoiseshell glasses and rubbed his forehead. There were few people as dedicated to their jobs, and rumor had it he was up for another promotion. Assuming his brother's new extracurricular activities didn't create a giant red flag. Lars Dekker was front-page corrupt, at least below the fold. Me dragging in a non-case wasn't likely to make Ellis's day either, but he considered what I wasn't saying outright, probably for old time's sake. He didn't actually look pleased to see me in his office.

"Injuries consistent with a fall?" he asked.

"No autopsy, of course, but yeah. Skull smashed right in. Definitely not a baseball bat." I swallowed thinking that the unnaturally twisted arms and legs were the real nightmare fuel. I'd managed not to think too much about the scene, throwing myself into a make-shift investigation even as the rational part of my brain acknowledged that I was maybe just avoiding shock. Or maybe this was how I wore my shock. Stirring up trouble rather than rocking myself to sleep. All I had was conjecture and some unsalvageable shoes in my trash-can. Not exactly a case.

Ellis finally looked at me—really looked—and it was like being hypnotized. His eyes were too strange to be pretty; they were more like lie detectors, or those ho-cus-pocus paranormal sensors favored by ghost hunt-ers. I wasn't sure that I wanted to see what he saw inside of me. Thankfully, he kept his mouth firmly shut on the subject of my immortal soul.

"It's not too late for an autopsy," I said, intending to change the subject, then realizing we'd never left it. "If an investigation were opened."

Ellis didn't bother acting shocked by what I was asking. He'd known why I was there as soon as I said "body," but he shook his head, squashing any hope I'd hauled in with me. "You know the victim?"

"A little." Not as well as I should have, I added silently, hoping again that I wasn't confusing guilt with suspicious circumstances. Trust your gut wasn't exactly a helpful saying for someone as paranoid as me. If I trusted my gut all the time, I would live in my bathroom with a box of cereal and a switchblade and never think about leaving. "Tabor Campion," I said in case the name was familiar to Ellis.

"A French 'pescador'?"

"Weird, right? It's all weird."

"The fact pattern is odd, but an unusual profession and unusual place of death doesn't equal murder." I started to protest, but he cut me off. "I'll see if there were any spectator calls this morning. If you can bring me something else, something concrete, I'll take it to Sergeant Wilkinson. He won't listen to me now. You know that's true."

I tried not to bristle, but "more evidence" had long been my least favorite phrase. It was the response to every piece of intel I collected while living next to the Costas and risking my life to bust the Magrellis. "More evidence" meant "not good enough." And I was tired of never being good enough.

*

This time I decided "more evidence" meant "go on then, Tabor's apartment is not going to search itself." I'd never been in our building's basement past midnight when the laundry room closed, and I noticed how much colder it felt without a ray of sunlight pretending to add life to the damp, tar-stained walls. Without the dyers on, it was even more like a cave, eerily quiet except for dripping water. I checked for bats then checked to make sure nobody else was spelunking. Somewhat comforted by being all alone, I slipped out my lock picking kit. The knob didn't require much precision; a couple of bobby pins would have done the trick. I'd come prepared, but Tabor hadn't bothered with a deadbolt. I felt comfortable assuming that he didn't think anyone was trying to kill him.

Once inside, I stuffed the towel I'd brought into the crack under the door, then flipped on the lights. The decor greeting me was my first surprise of the night. I was expecting folding chairs and a cot, something to match the grim tone of the basement. Instead, I was standing in a tastefully decorated and well-equipped kitchen. Chef-worthy pots and pans hung from a metal rack over a rolling butcher's block. The dining room table in the corner looked custom built out of elm, and newly upholstered chairs were pressed next to it. The counters might not have been granite, but they were spotless, and the only smell was something like cinnamon wafting from a basket of potpourri. The scene looked like an advertisement for country chic, catalog-ready. I smiled thinking of Tabor preparing dinner, perhaps for the date Mr. 3F had mentioned. I added "decorator" to what I knew of the victim. Super, chef, charmer, decorator. If nothing else, I'd be able to fake my way through a eulogy before too long.

Shaking myself out of admiration because it was blasphemous to envy the dead, I started rummaging. The drawers were almost as neat as the rest of the apartment, although there were a fair number of flyers for jobs with hourly wages: movers, holiday fair booth attendants, dog walkers. I tucked them all into my bag and opened the refrigerator; the contents made mine look like it'd been scavenged by wild animals. Tabor had a stack of leftovers in matching containers plus enough ingredients for a spontaneous feast or at least a well-appointed picnic. There was a loaf of sourdough bread, a basket of strawberries, and four different types of cheeses. A man about to kill himself did not buy fresh milk and vegetables, but I doubted I could take that "evidence" to Ellis.

The living room couch was new, as was the flat screen mounted on the wall. I ignored those and made a beeline for the desk. It seemed like an antique—small and hand-carved—with enough drawers and levers for even the most fastidious collector. The contents were less impressive, and I grabbed a few more flyers before heading into the bedroom. When I flicked on the lights, I gasped and slapped my hand over my mouth. It wasn't the faces that bothered me, but their expressions.

Each mask hung midway down the wall, acting out exaggerated pain or pleasure. They looked too real, too precise, even though my brain finally processed them as art. After my heartbeat returned to normal, I looked more carefully at the closest one. It wasn't cartoonishly red, but I suspected that I was introducing myself to the devil. Its eyes were inhuman, painted full black with pinpricks in the middle, while the mouth was lush, leering at me. This one depicted pleasure, but its neighbor was grimacing, its unholy eyes little slits, its teeth bared for a silent scream. I reached out toward the hair, expecting harsh bristles but finding soft strands instead. Shuddering, I brushed them aside to see small horns embedded in the figure's forehead. That was when I heard rustling from the closet.

CHAPTER 4

The cat had the sleek appearance of a mouser, a pet adopted solely for the purpose of killing critters and not likely to welcome strangers. Her tabby coat needed brushing, but her green eyes were clear and bright. She crouched and peered at me like the trespasser I was. Her low growl of warning sent me scooting away from the closet door, and I tried my best soothing noises. A flick of the tail told me she was unimpressed, and I started to back toward the apartment exit. Which was not to say that I was scared of a ten-pound animal—not me! But still, a slash of claws to the face would rule out disguises for at least a few weeks. There was also the question of my little remaining dignity.

Not wanting to leave empty-handed, I grabbed one of the masks and tucked it into my bag. I turned to go, but a pitiful mewl stopped my retreat. I turned to see the cat had transformed. She must not have liked the thought of being abandoned and had adopted her most docile expression, a flawless come-hither stare with whiskers. Her hair no longer stood at attention, and she was rubbing herself against the bed, keeping me in her peripheral vision. I paused, and she approached, stopping at a distance so that I could pay my respects. I knew this particular dance because we'd had a cat growing up. A lazy alleycat my mom had brought home one afternoon, which my dad tolerated because Bootsy had no problem with Sundays on the couch watching football.

I sighed, knowing I couldn't very well leave this one to fend for herself. Who knew when Tabor's family would collect his things. Who knew if he even had family in the States. I found her plastic carrier easily enough and, steeling myself for a fight, scooped up the beast and slipped her inside. She meowed a few times, then resigned herself to being captured. I added a cat to my list of problems and raided Tabor's pantry for kibble and litter. It was a small miracle nobody saw me when I snuck back to my apartment. Cat burglar had a nice ring to it, but cat kidnapper? That was not a nickname I wanted.

Once in the safety of my room, I considered what to do with Penelope. Yes, it had only taken me a few flights of stairs to name my temporary roommate, and she didn't seem to mind. Trouble would have been more accurate, but Penny for short, I decided, and she flicked her tail in approval or disapproval or apathy. What had I gained from my break-in beyond a furball? I set out food and water for Penny, then spread the flyers on my kitchen counter, looking for links. The hiring companies favored cheap, often handwritten photocopies, and were vague about responsibilities. Ten dollars an hour was most common, but one boasted twenty dollars. I set that one aside to call in the morning. The mask was a more impressive discovery. I ran my fingers along the face, noticing the intricate patterns on the eyelids and mouth. The one I'd grabbed was of the pleasure variety, and I was glad I didn't have to study the other kind. This one made me feel woozy enough, as if it pumped out evil vibes. But that was nonsense, a trick of the late hour and lack of sleep. I realized that I had almost been awake for twenty-four hours, and a mission wouldn't keep me going much longer.

I flipped the mask over, expecting to see a "Made in China" stamp, but instead there was a small, illegible signature. Tabor had a collection of hand-painted sculptures, and I wondered if they could be his own creations. I hadn't noticed any supplies, but my super was becoming more mysterious as the night stretched into its darkest hours. Who's to say he didn't keep a studio across town, cavorting with the city's bohemians in Paris-style salons? Little would surprise me at this point, and I had only scratched the surface of his life.

Penny hopped onto my windowsill and stared into the alley. If you pressed your face against the glass and looked up, you could see the top of the George Washington Bridge, but the cat wasn't interested in those lights. Her ears twitched, and she watched something I couldn't see on one of the fire escapes. I rose and squinted in the direction of her gaze, but the shadows all looked the same to me. A rat, I told myself. It's always a rat.

In the morning, Penny proved herself to be a fine alarm clock, and by 7 a.m., I was pouring chicken-flavored niblets into a bowl and planning out my day. My head hurt from so little sleep, but it had been a while since I'd stopped by my office. While my assistant, Meeza, never worried when I didn't show up, it was unfair to leave her with a week's worth of paperwork and the inevitable dissatisfied customer calling repeatedly to complain. Too many people hired PIs to find out dirt they later wished to un-know. Short of recommending a lobotomy, we couldn't help them with that part of the process. I referred them to therapists and did my best to block their pain from my mind. The truth usually came out anyway; private investigators only hurried the process along. Or so I told myself.

Before I left, I crept down the hallway to where the teenagers lived, the ones Tabor had helped get jobs. When I knocked on their door, feet scurried inside, and I could hear belt buckles jangling into place. I waited, trying to make out the whispers, but soon there was only silence.

"Hello," I called. "I saw you yesterday. I wanted to make sure you're okay."

I looked directly into the peephole, trying to make myself look as nonthreatening as possible. Who me? I'm just your friendly neighborhood welcoming committee, bringing by my basket a few years too late and under suspicious circumstances.

"It's hard to lose a friend," I tried again. "If you need anything, I'm over there in 3B."

Sixth sense or a little real-world experience, I knew at least one of the teens watched me as I returned to my apartment. I waved toward their door before disappearing inside to collect my belongings. If I could talk to someone who benefited from Tabor's services as a martín pescador, I could learn how he operated, whether he took unnecessary chances, angered the wrong people. That seemed unlikely to happen soon, though, so I resigned myself to research. Based on the furnishings in his apartment, Tabor didn't want for much. I considered how much his side hustle brought in each month. Or maybe his maintenance responsibilities were the side gig, a way to snag free rent.

Taking a cat on the subway probably wasn't the best idea, but my fellow commuters acted no more annoyed by her meows than they were by the mariachi band. A sane person would have left her alone for the day, but I was living on borrowed time until Salvatore Magrelli decided to call in his debts. I didn't think I owed him anything besides spit in the face, but traffickers had their own sort of bloody logical. I wasn't coming home to a dead pet, even if this particular pet didn't belong to me.

When the train stalled underground because of a sick passenger, I had too much time to think about my past chasing "more evidence" on the Magrelli brothers. Frank was outgoing to a fault, frequenting the city's best nightclubs, buying bottles of Dom Pérignon for models and trying to end up in their beds. Sometimes his dreams came true, but mostly, he'd party himself into a blackout and one of his lackeys would have to get him home and clean the vomit from his pants. Salvatore was another breed entirely—the vicious not furry kind. I'd managed to make Frank's charges stick, and rumor had it, Salvatore was grateful to me for finally getting his brother out of his way. That logic was almost far-fetched enough to be believed, and I'd seen some far-fetched shenanigans starting with his twenty-million-dollar townhouse.

It made sense for him to own a whole building rather than a luxury penthouse with a doorman who might get suspicious of Salvatore's crew. He collected men like they were baubles, assembling a group of Ivy-league educated experts on everything from taxes to hacking to eighteenth century European art. Men, always men, in his upper circle. In the second loop? Well, there he might find use for a nobody like me with connections at the NYPD. Unless he only wanted to kill me. There was always that possibility. He'd shown an interest in my skills before, though I had no desire to repeat that particular meeting.

Penny meowed and scratched at the door of her cage, bringing me back to the reality of a hot subway car and frustrated travelers. A few glanced at the cat, but their expressions seemed to say, You and me both. I stuck a finger into one of the breathing holes, and Penny smashed her face against it. I stroked her chin as best I could and tried to decide if my encounter with Magrelli could help me understand his motives now, why he claimed to want me on his team. I lied to his face for two years—why did he think that I could be trusted? Or was this another psychological maneuver, a calculated risk? The word pescador had unearthed a memory I'd tried to repress. Even now, when I tried to look at the scene objectively, my palms felt clammy, all my hard-won bravado leaking out.

To be fair, it was the kind of monstrosity you'd expect in a drug lord's home. More Miami than Manhattan maybe, but eccentricity wasn't regional. In some ways, it was better than a snow leopard or an anaconda. At least the shark couldn't escape from the tank and eat me. All the same, as soon as I spotted the smooth hide and fearsome mouth, I tried to make myself as small as possible in a corner of the room, hoping Magrelli wouldn't notice that Zanna Costa had brought a pal along for their informal chat. Zanna hoped that the meeting meant some sort of step up the food chain, and I was there so that she could have immediate bragging rights, someone to harass on the way home. It wasn't exactly a healthy friendship, but she was my link to the Costa family, and the Costa family was my link to the Magrellis. That's how I found myself eyeball to vacant, pitiless eyeball with a blacktop reef shark.

Once I could move my gaze away from its eyes and teeth, there was something mesmerizing, pretty even, about the animal's markings. The end of each fin looked dipped in ink and its smooth skin glistened. I'm no shark psychologist, but it looked unhappy with its confined space. The tank must have held at least six thousand gallons of water, but it only took a few seconds for the five-foot shark to reach one end and swivel. The motion might have been called gliding, but there was something jerky and defiant about the turn. I was watching this ballet so intently that I didn't notice when Salvatore crossed toward me, and I usually knew exactly where he was. Never forget where the alpha predator lurks. The shark might have been intimidating, but I was no fool. I knew who the monster was, and he wore a tailored three-piece suit.

When Salvatore got near enough to touch me, I jumped. The last time he'd been that close, he'd used a knife to slit the inside of my thigh. The stitches may have been removed, but I was still healing. The violence was my punishment for disobeying him—I'd refused to shoot a teenager who knew the location of a coke shipment. My act of rebellion hadn't mattered. Magrelli killed the boy anyway, and it haunted me that I could never prove that he'd pulled the trigger. What would have happened if I'd stayed rather than run, been a more reliable witness? When the kid's younger brother confessed to the crime, my sergeant had thrown up his hands. What could he do? I'd had some time to reflect on that question, and the answer was something, anything to prevent another life from being wasted. The brother had gotten off with a lenient sentence, the judge unwilling to toss away the keys on a minor with no priors and a sob story about abuse. But the rewards and riches Salvatore promised the child? They never materialized. He'd made an alliance with his brother's killer, and no good would come from that. Zanna's plan was built on wishful thinking, too, and I hoped I didn't suffer from the same pipe dreams.

The subway train intercom crackled, and I

snapped my head toward the sound. Often when I thought about my history with the Magrellis and the Costas, the memories overwhelmed me. It felt like being back in the same terrifying circumstances, clinging to my identity as Khalida Sanchez, wanting to become her, replace Kathleen Stone, if it meant one of us got to keep all our limbs. After the conductor finished his announcement, I was right back in Salvatore's townhouse, watching a shark tank test the limits of her cage.

"Gray eyes," Salvator said after a pause too long for comfort. I'd been staring past his shoulder at the tank's clear water, but I forced myself to look at him.

Most people couldn't tell the color of my eyes, would swear they were brown or hazel or sometimes green. In the glow of the aquarium, I'm surprised they didn't look blue, and I shrugged in response. Standing out in any way when working undercover was dangerous. No, I wanted to be just another body in the room, faceless if at all possible.

"If you say so," I said when it seemed like he was waiting for an answer. That made him chuckle, a low sound that filled the cavernous living room.

"Zanna," he said, never taking his focus from me. "Give us some time."

My skin turned to ice, and I shivered, not wanting to be left alone. Never mind that paid staff members circulated on the other floors. My screams wouldn't bring them running. I would have bet my hat that the place was sound-proofed.

"Sir?" Zanna said, the most noncompliant answer

she was willing to try. In our neighborhood, she had a well-deserved reputation for being a loose cannon. She yelled at strangers and started fights with them for fun. If she'd been a man, she might have been useful as muscle for the Magrellis. An interrogator maybe if she could learn to control her temper. As it was, she wasn't going anywhere in the operation. Her star role consisted of being a liability. She'd tag along sometimes, mostly so that someone could keep an eye on her. Salvatore would make a few small concessions for his fiancée, Zanna's sister Eva, but she wasn't worth any full-blown disasters.

"There's some whiskey in the kitchen," Salvatore said in what sounded like a suggestion but was really a command. Zanna sulked, but moved toward the stairs. The kitchen occupied most of the first level, and we were on the fifth, a floor that could easily be called a ballroom, every inch exposed. Without the blackout curtains, light would flood the refurbished oak floor. In another era, perhaps flappers scratched the surface with their heels, spilled champagne into the cracks. Whatever twinkle the space once held drained away in the gleam of M-17s cradled by two security guards. Only the shark tank and a long table occupied the room, but two men patrolled anyway, earning their keep.

Magrelli didn't move, so I didn't either. My greatest fear was always being sniffed out as a narc. If Zanna's sex worked against her, it worked for me. Out of the one hundred or so undercover police officers in New York City, an even smaller number were female. I was more likely to be deemed a pest than a plant, but the fate of pests wasn't so nice either. A quicker execution perhaps. No elaborate "accidents" involving lye and bathtubs. I should be grateful for small favors and all that.

"What's its name?" I said, forcing myself to gesture toward the aquarium. Magrelli finally shifted from me, and I unclenched my throat, feeling slightly dizzy. He walked toward the tank, placing a palm against the glass, and his reflection swam beside his captive.

"Her name is Tesora. You know the word?" I shook my head, seeing the movement in the water. "Zanna thinks of you as a sort of pet, no?"

"I prefer friend."

He laughed again, and the shark darted away at the noise, only to come face to face with the end of her cell. There was nowhere to turn but back.

"Yes, of course. We all prefer friend. But how many care about us? Truly care, I mean. A couple, if we're lucky."

I wondered if he considered himself lucky to be marrying Eva Costa. She was the local beauty and smart to boot. If he'd run a casting call for The Kingpin's Wife, she would have won the role, but did she love him? I couldn't rightly say. She wanted out of her rat-infested building in the Bronx, and she wanted to take her family with her. Her sister, brother, and mother held the keys to her heart. Still, there was no sense denying that Salvatore could be attractive. Tall and imposing, he sometimes seemed like a giant among men. He was a man of moderation, too. Unlike his brother, Frank, he never overindulged, never even tested the product. There were chemicals and test tubes for that, more precise than any nose. And I'd never seen him angry. Even when he cut me, the point was clear: punishment. No more, no less.

"Tesora doesn't seem much like a pet," I said, shoving my hands into my pockets so that they didn't linger over the scar. No sense giving away more than I had to.

It struck me as odd that Salvatore would have this impractical animal. His accommodations were luxurious, sure, but there were no gold toilets or diamond-encrusted televisions. The whiskey Zanna was no doubt chugging rather than sipping, probably cost a few hundred dollars a bottle, but other extravagances were hard to spot. Based on the tasteful decor, he valued quality over gaudiness. Except for Miss Teeth over there studying us through the glass.

Magrelli agreed with my statement about Tesora. In fact, he liked my appraisal and stepped closer to pat me on the back. I tried unsuccessfully not to flinch at this act of approval.

"No, not a pet," he said. "An investment. Would you like to feed her?"

No, I would not, a voice hollered in my head. But I found myself with a fistful of shrimp anyway, standing on a bench and dropping them in one by one. She eyed them suspiciously before swallowing. Well-fed, I thought, which seemed like a good sign. Magrelli took care of his own, but I knew that before I'd set foot in his townhouse. I didn't need a demonstration. As long as your loyalty was never questioned, there was an endless supply of shrimp. A shark's paradise, if you didn't mind confined spaces.

"Not greedy, then," I said, trying to make something like small talk. You'd think I would value a few minutes alone with my target, despite my anxiety. But Salvatore hadn't asked for privacy so that he could reveal company secrets. Angling for the biggest fish took patience and precision, and I wasn't sure that I had both in endless supply. My dizziness didn't subside as I ran through the possible reasons for our tête-à-tête. I was still weighing the options when he suggested that I touch her.

"It's safe. I assure you."

I let the last few shrimp fall and watched as Tesora found each one and ate it, almost daintily. But she ate them all the same, and I wasn't keen on the experiment Salvatore proposed. My mind raced as I tried to figure out his motives. If I knew why, I would have the right answer, how to say no in way that wouldn't be brushed aside. It seemed like I'd been playing games with Salvatore since we'd met, and I'd never once won.

"If you're trying to scare me, I'm there already," I admitted.

Salvatore waved off this answer, climbing up on the bench beside me. He was too close, and I felt the blood in my cheeks drain away. "Oh, you're scared. You've been scared from the beginning. What I'm trying to determine is why you're still here. As I say, Zanna doesn't care for you. And your indifference to her is obvious."

Was it? I'd tried hard to hide my disdain for the woman. I wanted to believe that Salvatore was bluffing, that he assumed I didn't like Zanna because, well, she was unlikable. But the man didn't really gamble. Risks were assessed and sometimes taken, but they were never unknown. I was standing near enough to tell if he was sweating, and he most certainly was not. He didn't smell like anything, as if he repelled all traces of the world.

"There must be something you want from me," he continued. "You'd like to pet Tesora, yes?"

Did he really expect for me to stick my hand into shark-infested waters without a fight? I could try to run. I'd done it once, but he'd caught me then and would catch me now. The NYPD hadn't been keen on removing me from my assignment before. This time wouldn't be any different. Was I being offered an opportunity with this initiation ritual? I could show my loyalty, see what hush-hush intel might fall my way. While I was trying to make a decision, Salvatore decided for me, grabbing my elbow and thrusting my hand in the water. I hardly felt the cold, but my whole body started convulsing. Tesora was drawn immediately to the ruckus as I fought against Salvatore to remove my arm. Water splashed onto our faces and shoes, but his grip was strong. The shark looked at my fingers with the same curiosity she'd shown the shrimp, and I closed my eyes, bracing for the pain.

CHAPTER 5

The train lurched back into motion, and I snapped back into the present, wiping sweat from my brow with still intact hands. Penny had quieted, but when I looked through the cage bars at her, she hissed. "You got that right," I whispered, and it was New York, so nobody thought it was strange that I was talking to a cat, or at least not stranger than the woman clipping her toenails onto the floor.

Penny and I transferred to a bus, then walked the six blocks to my office. Reminiscing about my days with Salvatore had made me jumpy, and I stared at everyone who passed me, trying to tell whether I should be worried. Was that teenager in red sunglasses being paid to spy on me? What about the dog walker? Would you say that two Labradors, two mutts, and a dachshund was a normal quantity of pooches? More importantly, was that Red Sox cap trying to hide a man's eyes from me, or did he want to be heckled? I only stopped my inspections when black spots clouded my vision. They would pass; they always did. By the time I arrived, I suspected I looked near enough to normal for Meeza. She started cooing at my sidekick before I even unlatched the carrier door.

"Aap khubsoorat hain," she said. "What a beauty!"

She scooped Penny up and started scratching her ears. The cat purred in response, rubbing her face against Meeza's. It was hard to tell which one was more delighted. My assistant plopped down on the futon and let the cat curl up in her lap. Penny went straight to sleep, as if Meeza's lap had been her life goal all along. I shouldn't have been shocked. There was something about my friend that drew people toward her; it was no wonder an animal would follow suit. It wasn't just Meeza's long, glossy black hair and doe-like eyes. She was beautiful, but she also glowed when she smiled, genuinely pleased with the world. She was smiling then at Penny, one finger hooked under her chin. "You should bring pets to work every day," she said.

At "pets," I remembered Tesora, but I pushed the thought away before it could show on my face. "I imagine a few persnickety clients might object."

"Who are these persnickety clients? Nobody ever comes here."

In her gentle tone, the comment came across as observant rather than insulting. She was right, of course. I'd taken pains to hide my business address, preferring to meet suspicious husbands and wives on their own turfs. Not exactly a power play, but it prevented a lot of crying scenes from being acted out in my sad little rented space. Not so sad anymore, I reminded myself, looking around at the improvements Meeza had made piece by piece. Her changes appeared gradually until the room looked brighter, as if it had promised to make more of an effort.

For starters, the lone fern I'd bought on a whim had been brought back from the dead and was—I was almost certain—about the burst into blossom. The lavender curtains wouldn't have been my first choice, but sometimes the sunlight through them winked at me, a reminder that Meeza was a short commercial break shy of magical. Somehow, the place smelled better, too, a combination of my assistant's rose-scented soap and my increased efforts to not sleep on our futon as much. I sniffed inconspicuously, pleased not to detect an undercurrent of coconut hair gel. Meeza's boyfriend, V.P., was partial to the product, and I was partial to him catching a one-way flight to Antarctica.

When cataloging my mistakes, introducing Meeza to V.P. ranked pretty high on the list. Not that I had intended to play matchmaker. V.P. provided a unique service to criminals and people like me who didn't have credit cards and preferred aliases to nicknames. He rented cars—presumably stolen—to the shadier denizens of New York and New Jersey. I wasn't surprised that he'd taken a fancy to Meeza. The harder question was what she saw in V.P. As a small-time crook, he should have been beneath her notice. Now he was trying to move up in the underworld by latching himself to Salvatore Magrelli, parasite-style. Pointing out the dangers of her association had almost made me lose my friendship with Meeza, so I was keeping my mouth shut for a while, careful not to say anything that might make its way to unfriendly ears. It wasn't ideal, but it was better than the days when we weren't speaking. There was little chance that Meeza actively spied on me, but I knew well enough that her good nature could be manipulated. What she saw as a charming work anecdote might be valuable information for V.P. to pass along to his boss. I hadn't given up on separating her from V.P., but I needed a better plan than repeating what Meeza deemed gossip. Not that I could speak from personal experience, but I had witnessed the downsides of seeing the best in everyone.

"Where did she come from anyway?" Meeza had somehow produced yarn from her purse and was dangling it in front of Penny, who batted at the yellow thread, yawning but willing to humor her new favorite human. Before long, the cat would be sitting on command and sorting the mail for us.

When I told her about Tabor, Meeza's eye filled with tears for the man she'd never met. If ever a woman was less cut out for our demoralizing business, I was looking at her. Or rather, looking slightly above her head so that I didn't have watch her sniffle and generally be a better person than me. Cut out for private investigation or not, she was determined to do something more interesting with her life than answer phones, and she'd been taking classes to obtain her license. Any day now, she'd become my partner, and I worried about whether her sunny disposition would suffer.

"Where did that come from?" I asked, pointing at the yarn to keep myself from unhappy speculation.

"Oh, I'm making something for my niece." Meeza rummaged in her bag, then pulled out two perfectly symmetrical knee socks with matching yellow bows. Penny took a swat at those, too, and Meeza clucked at her.

"I found something else at Tabor's apartment besides your new furry friend."

"I can keep her?" Meeza asked, her voice shaking slightly in her excitement. Penny seemed happy about this development as well, and flipped over to let Meeza rub her stomach, a sign of instant loyalty. If nothing else, I had one win on my record for the day.

I brought out the mask I had swiped and held it up to my face. The eye holes were too small to see much, and I could detect a nauseating lacquer. Based on the smell, it must have been a new acquisition for Tabor, but new or not, it wouldn't be going into my disguise bin. Call it art if you liked, but it gave me the heebie-jeebies.

"Ever seen anything like this?" I asked.

Meeza paused, thinking of something nice to say, I assumed. She didn't disappoint me and commented on the precision of the details. "Quite interesting, the fake lacework at the edges."

I turned the mask toward me and ran a finger over the design Meeza had noticed. She was right. It was surprisingly intricate, the kind of markings that could only be made with a very fine brush.

"I think this may be a research day," I said as I reached over Meeza to grab our shared laptop. We were finally operating in the black, but neither of us planned an early retirement. "Do you need to check anything first?"

Meeza had returned to making kissy noises at Penny, but I knew she heard me. She kept her face turned away from mine, and I put the laptop down to give her my full attention. I may not have the sensitivity of a cat, but my hackles were raised.

"Plans today?" I tried again.

"Just an appointment in Queens."

"For your parents?"

Meeza shook her head, and Penny pawed at strands of her hair. "No. At a gun range."

My heart sunk, but I didn't say anything. I'd had a sweet little Smith & Wesson for my first two years as a PI. Ellis had confiscated it, and I'd be lying if I pretended not to miss the feeling of security offered by its weight. I'd never fired it at anything other than a paper target, and I wouldn't be a hypocrite. At least not today. There was also a part of me that thought she might be safer around her boyfriend if she were armed. It wasn't that I thought he planned to hurt her intentionally, but he wasn't exactly staying out of trouble these days. And where V.P. went, Meeza followed. At least for now.

"A travel agent," I said after an awkward silence.

"Pardon?"

"You'd make a great travel agent."

Meeza grinned, a blinding expression of instant happiness, and I couldn't help smiling in return. "If there were any travel agents left in the world, I would join their merry ranks. In the meantime, I have a date with a pistol."

When Meeza scooped up her new pet and sashayed out of the office, I dug out the job flyers that I had snagged from Tabor's place. One number was disconnected, but the other two were answered by harried women who didn't want to talk. "Who sent you?" they both asked, shouting an address and telling me to stop by next week. I looked up the addresses on a map, noticing that they were across the street from each other, about as far west in midtown Manhattan as you could get without falling into the river. I'd walked there before and noticed the employment agencies, single-room spaces catering to Chinese restaurants. Workers would be bused out, sometimes hundreds of miles from the city to cook buffet entrées or clean floors, whatever was asked, in exchange for wages well below the federal minimum. If employers provided housing, it was shared rooms and bathrooms, dormitories for adults. It seemed doubtful that Tabor was honing in on the services these employment agencies provided. They were well-oiled machines, impervious to meddling. More likely, he sent his most desperate clients there.

A Google search on the mask gave me thousands of hits, and I narrowed them down by looking for versions with horns. A view of the image results showed several pieces with similar expressions. This style typically came in pairs, pain and pleasure. Some novelty stores sold them as gag gifts, the insides covered with a special, never-drying ink that would leave their wearer marked. I wiped my forehead, but it was clean, thankfully. The first results were brightly colored, but didn't match the quality of Tabor's collection. It took some digging, but I finally found one with the fine lines Meeza had noticed. It was for sale at a pawn shop in my Washington Heights neighborhood for two hundred dollars. Its mouth hung open in a loose O, and its eyes were half closed. Lightning bolts had been carved into the forehead, an exploding storm, and I hoped the artwork wasn't prophetic. Fortunetellers had a tendency to run away from me, and I liked it that way.

*

A bell announced my entrance into Ángel's Treasures, and I suppressed shudders at family heirlooms mixed in with bric-a-brac at the store. If desperation could be bottled, this was the source. Artisanal Melancholy, $0.99 and Up. Along one wall, the owner had hung a row of guitars, and I could only imagine the abandoned dreams they represented. Here a rock star, there a songwriter. The chinaware looked like nothing so much as divorce relics and didn't inspire much nostalgia either. I avoided eye contact with the dolls in the corner, dodged an armoire, and approached the glass counter that also served as a display case. The engagement rings sparkled in the artificial light, but I wasn't fooled by their optimism. I called out, "Hello," before my nerves failed me.

A grunt from a hidden room returned my greeting, which I took to mean, "I'll be right with you, miss.

Please make yourself at home." I glanced down at the earrings and collector coins, trying to spot a diamond in the rough. Not that I knew the difference between cubic zirconium and the real deal. The silver loops were pretty, though, and I traced my fingers on the glass above them.

"No smudges!"

I jumped as a man emerged from a doorway I hadn't noticed before, flapping his arms at me and yelling, "Don't muck up the glass!"

When he got closer, I could see that he wasn't the old curmudgeon I expected. A curmudgeon, sure enough, but young, around my age with outdated glasses and black hair that ringed his head like a mane. He used his sleeve to polish away my fingerprints.

"Excuse me," I said. "I was interested in the bracelets."

"Interested? Bah. You want something. I can smell it on your sweatshirt."

I pulled at the garment in question, impressed and uneasy but also caught, so I dug out the mask and held it out to him. He snatched it from my fingers and held it up to the light. He flipped the face over and peered closer as if looking for something. A signature, maybe? Some sign of authenticity?

"Twenty-five dollars," he said, dropping it onto the counter and making me wince. I didn't exactly like the thing, but I didn't want to make it mad either. Who knew what curses it might belch out.

Twenty-five dollars. The unfair amount sank

through my superstitions. If the man was selling his own for two hundred dollars, that was quite a markup. I swallowed my pride, though, and explained a modified version of my so-called real reason for barging into his store. "No, I want to buy a companion piece. I saw one on your website that looked similar, but I can't know until I see it in person."

He cocked his head and looked at me as if for the first time, wary of my interest. I forced my hands from where they had drifted to my hoodie's zipper. I'd worked for years to avoid having any tells, at least any obvious ones. "I'll give you thirty dollars," the man said, unmoved by my careful poker face.

I glanced down at my outfit to see what vibe of distress I was putting off and realized that my worn-out sneakers probably didn't scream "art collector." What I really wanted to ask was where these masks came from, if he knew Tabor Campion, and if Tabor painted them himself or brought them over from Paris. But we were a long way from those questions, and I couldn't see a path there. I heard footsteps in the backroom, slow and laborious. There was a sound like glass jars rattling against each other, then those shuffling shoes again. A stock boy or maybe someone more important.

"Are you the owner?" I asked, wondering how I could get the conversation moving forward at least.

He grunted again, his version of yes. "Ángel López. Thirty-five dollars."

"Where I can find more like this one?"

"Forty dollars. Final offer. You won't find a better one. Nobody likes these things. I've got a regular, Carla. Over in Marble Hill? Thinks they're evil. Calls to make me promise I don't have one before coming inside. Thinks they're voodoo or some such."

"But not you?"

"Evil? Voodoo? These are the gold star of babies. The patron saint of pregnancy. I sell them as soon as I get them." He realized that he'd contradicted himself and glared at me as if his mistake was my fault. "Okay, they sell, but don't think I'll go higher than forty dollars."

I pretended to consider his final offer, but I really wanted more information about his clients, people who thought this ugly mug might lead to children. Demon spawn, more like, I thought, moving aside the mask's hair to see the horns again. I'd heard of fertility rituals, old folklore for women who couldn't afford in-vitro fertilization. But I'd never heard of them involving expensive art options. Some olive oil maybe and a pacifier. A little ground beef for the diehards. The point was to bolster spirits for a few more months, stave off depression. "One hundred dollars," I said, absentmindedly, trying to keep Ángel talking.

"Forty-five dollars," he countered. "But that's it."

A crash from the backroom jerked his attention away from me, and he shouted at the person making such a ruckus.

"Careful, Dante! We got three more boxes of that junk."

Dante learned around the doorframe, his height

and broad shoulders surprising me. When he grinned, I knew he must be more friend than employee, not bothered by Ángel's grumpiness. An eyetooth protruded slightly from his lips, puffing up his lips and making him look like an overgrown chipmunk, approachable despite his size.

"You know me, all thumbs. Hello," he said to me, nodding, then stepping more fully into the room. "I know those masks. My wife has one."

His expression grew even softer, and Ángel all but rolled his eyes.

"Forty-five dollars, that's it," he repeated.

I paused before replying, trying to put together what these men might have in common with my super. Maybe Tabor had simply pawned one of his masks here. He had plenty, at least a dozen in his apartment. On the other hand, ignoring gentrification—the influx of young families looking for more affordable rent, the doctors and nurses wanting a shorter commute to New York Presbyterian Hospital—Washington Heights was a tight-knit community. Tabor and Ángel probably knew each other. Was the link simply that both men dealt with people desperate for money? Tabor found immigrants jobs and Ángel took their grandmother's tea kettle? I tried out a theory and told Ángel that forty-five dollars sounded good, but that I'd rather have somewhere to work.

"No chance you're hiring?" I said, glancing at Dante, then putting the mask back in my bag. Ángel's eyes followed the movement, and I realized that his pupils were dilated. It was dark in the dusty space, but not dark enough to warrant the black holes I found myself considering. His eyes gave him away, telling me that I'd hit on his weakness: greed.

"Not hiring," he said, and I shook myself away from whatever spell he was casting over me. Had it always been that cold in the shop? I pulled my sleeves over my hands and started to thank him for his time. It didn't seem like I was going to get any more information, but when I turned, Ángel reached out and grabbed my arm, harder than I would have liked. "Not me, but there's a place."

I resisted the urge to shake off his grip and instead tried to make myself look eager. "I'll do anything," I said.

Ángel tapped his fingers on my arm as if testing out my bicep. I knew that he would be disappointed with his investigation and hoped he didn't reconsider his offer, whatever that was going to be. "Men," he said. "I usually work with men."

I didn't like the sound of that, but I kept my expression hopeful, praying that I hadn't wandered into a makeshift prostitution ring. I couldn't imagine anything less sexy than afghans and grandfather clocks, but who knew what went on in the back room. Dante didn't look like a gigolo, though, and he didn't seem worried about whatever his friend was about to suggest.

Finally, Ángel released my arm, holding up a finger to tell me that I should wait. He disappeared from view, tugging Dante along with him, and I fought down my impulse to run and never look back. There was something unholy about this place. Pawnshops always made me uneasy, but this one was more sinister than others, Ángel more suspicious than the typical bored cashier. Instead, I rocked back and forth and did as I was asked. When the owner returned with a flyer for a boating company, The Blue Lagoon, I snatched it from him, my eagerness not entirely fake. A photo of an impressive yacht was surrounded by advertisements for tours, specifically deep-sea fishing excursions. It definitely matched one I'd found in Tabor's apartment, down to the contact information circled at the bottom.

"I usually work with men," Ángel said again to let me know he was doing me a favor. "But tell them I sent you. Five percent finder's fee. Hank will know."

I imagined myself slinging fish guts overboard and started to say no out of some last vestiges of self-respect. It was too much of a coincidence that Tabor had been a martín pescador and that Ángel seemed to be in the habit of handing out manual labor jobs. For a cut, of course.

"A one-time fee?"

The man laughed, a wheezy sort of sound, unhealthy for a young man. "Every payday."

I paused to consider what this meant for the forlorn folks who stumbled into this place needing to make a decent living. Ángel hadn't asked me for any identification, so maybe he assumed I was a citizen or had a work visa. More likely, he didn't care. Had Tabor been making similar cold-hearted deals? Did someone get tired of forking over cash every week for the equivalent of a phone call? Or was Ángel new to this business, taking over my super's territory before his body hit the ground? Excuse me, hit the lighthouse.

I needed to talk to someone Tabor had helped, and The Blue Lagoon seemed like a good bet. I took a final look at the flyer then forced myself to thank Ángel for his personal brand of generosity. As soon as I stumbled back into the daylight, I took out one of my disposal cell phones and dialed, reminding myself to ask for Hank. And to sound like being on a boat would be a dream come true rather than a reason to buy Dramamine in bulk.

There were still a few piles of dirty snow piled up against the curb. It hadn't snowed in weeks, but that didn't deter the most stubborn patches from sticking around. I wondered when it would warm up properly and hoped it happened before I was in the middle of the Atlantic Ocean, elbow-deep in some tuna. A woman answered on the third ring, asking for a preferred reservation date before I even said my name.

"I'm calling about a job," I said. "Ángel said to ask for Hank."

"Hank? Hank don't do shit. You need me, and, honey, sure enough, I need you. You got clean clothes? Khakis or something?"

"I have something that will work," I said, figuring I could spare some pants from my Kate Manning disguise. My version of a soccer mom had never been my favorite cover anyway, but maybe she was about to come in handy.

"Praise be, I'm about to birth this baby right here on this linoleum, but you think they care? You know how they say shit for brains? I say shit for hearts. Eight o'clock tomorrow morning work for you?"

Chapter 6

The Blue Lagoon office did indeed have linoleum floors, bright blue and glittering like a ten-by-ten lure. The fish might decide to jump through an open window, no rods and reels required. The floor's sparkle was nothing compared to Leesa Almy, though, whose lips were covered with the shiniest pink gloss I'd ever seen. She was wearing a bedazzled cape over bare legs and bare feet, and when she caught me staring at the words "Goddess in Training," she whooped in disbelief.

"Some Goddess," she said, "But I'm not spending another damn dime on maternity wear. This baby either crawls out of me this weekend, or I'm going up there after it. As soon as you can put people on hold, I'm getting my hair done and my nails done, and I'm gonna jump up and down in my living room until somebody shakes loose. You ever been knocked up?"

She didn't wait for an answer, but gestured for me to follow her to the desk. It had a glass top, and if you peered from above, you could spy a model of the place's lone yacht. I'd yet to see the boat in person, but was assured by Leesa that it was the most punctual one around. Other perks included a sunset schedule for honeymooners and free coffee on board. The thought of cream and sugar on a rocking boat made me want to put my head between my knees preemptively, and I thanked my lucky stars that The Blue Lagoon needed a temporary receptionist/travel agent. See? They do still exist, Meeza. I imagined gloating when I made it back to my own non-glittering office. I started to smile, then stopped myself when I thought of my assistant firing rounds at a paper human. Was there a flesh and bones human she was worried about? Did his name rhyme with "Tee Pee"? Grown adult or not, I had no problem associating V.P. with toilet paper. I'd thought of worse insults that wouldn't fly on a first grade playground. Sixth maybe, if the teachers weren't around.

"The tours, they sell themselves. Nobody's calling or coming in here unless they're ready to make a reservation. Nobody needs to be convinced," Leesa said, flipping on the ancient computer and showing me how they kept their records. It was a mom-and-pop sort of operation, and I made an educated guess that paying their employees under the table helped them avoid a higher tax bracket. I'd yet to be offered a W-9 and thought paperwork unlikely.

The front door opened, and Leesa let out a low growl, but the beefy man was holding up one hand in the universal sign of "I mean no harm." The other hand was holding a box of doughnuts, which Leesa grabbed from him. "Don't think this makes me hate you any less, you son of a bitch," she said, sliding out a pastry covered in blue icing.

"Your mother-in-law thinks you're special, too, hon," the man said, extending a hand to me. "Hank

Almy. You've met my beautiful wife, I see."

"Bite me," she said, but it sounded less venomous with her mouth full of frosting.

Hank grinned even more and pumped my hand. "If I'd known you were starting today, I would have bought an extra one."

I glanced at the dozen doughnuts, but didn't dare question his logic. In fact, I couldn't remember saying anything other than "hello" since arriving. I cleared my throat and introduced myself as Kay Moroz. I hadn't done anything to hide my natural appearance. I felt exposed without a wig, but Salvatore Magrelli had already found me. That much effort seemed pointless. Nonetheless, I wasn't about to go around announcing myself as Kathleen Stone, drawing unnecessary extra attention. I didn't want the happy couple to suspect that I was a private investigator before I'd had a chance to ask around about Tabor. I knew that Detective Dekker would keep his word—if I could find any evidence of foul play, he would open an investigation into Tabor's death.

"Moroz?" Hank said, and for a moment I thought he didn't believe me. His face lost its easy-going expression, and I got the sense that I wasn't the only one hiding a secret. It was more of a gut reaction than a psychological evaluation, like recognizing like. After a pause, he forced another smile for my sake or his wife's. "My queen over there said Ángel sent you. We don't know Ángel so well."

I considered whether that meant Ángel had always been Tabor's rival or whether he'd taken over the operation when my super's body was found. Either way, he had a tidy little motive, complete with dollar signs.

"Yes. I knew Tabor, though." Dropping his name into the conversation so early was a risk, but I didn't want to waste time. The more days that passed between a death and an official case, the more time killers had to cover their tracks. One in three. The number of murders that went unsolved in the U.S. You could bet the NYPD wasn't eager to add another body to their already overworked desks. But Ellis would do the right thing, I reminded myself. The faster I brought something concrete into the hallowed, fluorescent-lit halls of my former precinct, the better the chances that Tabor's murderer wouldn't walk free, cruise around my neighborhood with a song in his heart and blood on his hands.

I waited to see if Hank recognized my super's name and wasn't disappointed. "Tabor and Ángel working together? You tell me when the locusts arrive."

He laughed at his own joke, and I hesitated to dim his good mood. Here was a man ready to be in love with the world—or at least his hormonal wife. There was no point delaying the inevitable, though, and I let the couple know they wouldn't be seeing Tabor anymore. Leesa gasped, swallowing the last of her third doughnut.

"Oh no, not Tabor! He was one of the good ones," she said, fat tears rolling down her face. She let them drip onto her cape, not bothering to wipe her cheeks.

Hank didn't seem stunned by Leesa's reaction, and I got the sense that tears were part of the daily routine. "Honey, it's alright," he said, crossing to his wife and tucking her head under his chin. It was difficult with her protruding belly, but he managed. He made noises that might be used to calm a horse, and I was impressed by their effectiveness. Leesa wiped her nose on his shirt and straightened up.

"We didn't see him that much," Hank said, rubbing Leesa's back. "But you could count on him. He was a man who would show up."

"Maybe not on time," Leesa adding, hiccuping. "But he would show up."

That had been my experience as well, and I nodded. Leesa's crying spell didn't last long, and she was shooing her husband out the door before I could apologize for springing the bad news on them. When I'd called The Blue Lagoon, I had wondered if Tabor ever visited the places where he sent workers, but that fact was clear enough now. He showed his face sometimes, built relationships. I made my way around the desk and stowed my purse, glancing over the notes I'd taken from Leesa's haphazard orientation. Emails, phones, and flyers. Locking up after shifts. That about covered the job description.

"Not yet," Leesa said, pulling me from the chair I started to claim. "You got to know the product to sell it." There was a wicked gleam in her now dry eyes, and I didn't want to know what that meant. She shoved a man's XL parka into my hands, then lead me back to the door. "Morning tour leaves in half an hour. I'll see you after lunch."

I found myself standing on the corner of Sea Breeze Avenue and Ocean Parkway with sounds of the Coney Island amusement park whistling and whooping behind me. Across the street, a seafood restaurant prepared to open, waiters shaking out plastic, checkered tablecloths while men from two different delivery companies carried fish and beer into the kitchen. At 9 a.m., the popular tourist area was starting to wake up, prepare itself for a small crowd. April wasn't the most profitable month, but it was warmer than the day before, and there were always people who wanted to pretend summer could arrive any day. I zipped up the raincoat and pulled the hood over my ears. The office was strategically located near foot traffic, but the actual boat was parked a few blocks away.

I walked along the boardwalk as far as it would take me, watching the hotdog stands turn into Russian bistros when I neared Brighton. I was close to Vondya Vasiliev's shop, where I bought wigs and tried on personalities for size. I missed those other voices shouting in my head and felt stuck as Kathleen Stone, though she had grown on me during the past few months. Any other time and I would have stopped by to see Vondya, bask in her reprimands, but I figured I would be missed if I tallied.

There were a few people on the beach, wearing long sleeves and flying kites. It may not have been warm enough for sunbathing, but it was ideal kite weather, the brightly colored fabrics soaring in the sky and swooping when strong gusts hit them. I tried not to think about how the winds might affect my boat ride. Before I could worry too much, I found myself blinking up at The Blue Lagoon, a yacht from the '80s that had been gutted to make room for chairs, fishing nets, and tackle. It looked more glamorous in the photos than in person. There didn't seem to be any paying customers around, and I worried that I had misunderstood Leesa's instructions. Maybe this was some sort of first-day hazing ritual.

Then familiar hairy arms gripped the side of the boat, and Hank yelled down to me. "Moroz. You ready?"

*

The waves splashed higher over the side the farther we journeyed into the Atlantic. I had no sense of nautical miles, but the shore disappeared, and the water turned an unfamiliar shade of blue, almost black. There were three other passengers on board, and they looked like extras in an updated, made-for-television version of *Moby Dick*. Their RayBan sunglasses were at odds with their gray beards and matching scraggly hair. The men's faces were permanently red—from windburn or alcohol, I couldn't tell. Either way, it struck me as odd that this group didn't have their own ocean-faring vessels. More surprisingly, my stomach was holding up, but my fingers were numb from gripping the rail. We hadn't passed another boat in a while, and I wondered how often the Coast Guard patrolled.

Hank's spirits dimmed with every passing minute. After welcoming me on board, he'd criticized my black dress shoes as inappropriate, and I didn't bother to explain that I'd been hired for a desk job. It seemed unlikely that he had forgotten I was replacing his wife. Without that woman in sight, he was almost a different man altogether. He shrugged when one of the passengers mentioned that the buckle on his lifejacket was broken. I checked my own, now with a new source of anxiety. The plastic looked flimsy on closer inspection, and I tightened my belt even though it was already pushing the parka's nylon uncomfortably against my stomach. All-in-all, I was glad when Hank retired to the lower level and let Captain Barrera take over hosting duties.

Freckles and liver spots crowded Captain Barrera's tan skin, and when he squinted into the sun, the deep lines around his eyes became even more visible. He smiled to himself a lot, as if making private jokes in his head. He didn't share any of these with me, but he did offer me a canned ginger ale, a sign of impending friendship, I decided. He opened one for himself, and we clinked the aluminum together, toasting. Hank had introduced me as the "new Leesa," a term that made him cackle. When he'd shown up with a box full of doughnuts for his wife, I had been inclined to like the soon-to-be father, but now I wasn't so sure I wanted to be alone on a boat with him. Not alone, I reminded myself, glancing around and acutely aware that I was the only woman on board. Nobody seemed like an active source of trouble, but still, you could never tell.

"Este no es su primer viaje," Captain Barrera said. "Nobody's first trip."

"They're all repeat customers?" I asked. I wasn't

paying close attention, focusing more on the inflatable raft and calculating how many could fit inside. I'd seen *Titanic*, and I was no Kate Winslet. I doubted anyone would give up their space for me.

Captain Barrera laughed again and told me that the tours were very successful. I glanced around skeptically, wondering if summertime business made up for excursions like this one. I doubted three paying passengers would even cover costs. Today's trip was most likely operating at a loss. I mentioned my informal calculations, but Captain Barrera waved them away.

"It's a fine day for sailing," he said, gesturing to the clouds marching above us.

I didn't know how that applied to our situation, considering there was an engine and all, but I nodded, then tried to follow his train of thought as he told me about how oranges could cure gout and how the best meals in Brooklyn were the cheapest ones and how ocean swims helped a man live to one hundred. He winked when he made the final proclamation, and I hoped that he wasn't hinting that I should test the waters. When his curls fell into his eyes, he tugged them back with unflagging optimism that this time they would stay in place. He had a glass half full attitude about most subjects—those clouds would blow over, his wife was joking when she called him a "pirate-faced jerk," that one passenger who'd fallen overboard had enjoyed the experience. I prayed he wasn't in charge of the fuel tank and vowed not to stand up until the boat had come to a complete stop. I was starting to wonder if that would ever happen, though, or if we were going to cruise on up to Maine for lobsters because Captain Barrera had heard that they were delicious.

The man's positive attitude was in stark contrast to my own. Sure, it wasn't as cold as the day before, on that front we could both be happy. But Captain Barrera told me that he didn't know Tabor very well and explained that he had gotten his current position through more traditional means, i.e., family connections. I had seen a few other Blue Lagoon employees, but they were all back at the dock. It didn't seem likely that I was going to have a long talk with anyone who Tabor had helped, at least not on my first day.

The dark waters looked ominous, and I didn't want to think about what monsters might lurk beneath the surface. Even though my brain kept identifying dangers, it was unfair to think of animals as evil—instinctual but never evil. I'd survived my shark encounter at Salvatore Magrelli's. Tesora hadn't so much as nipped my fingers. She had brushed against them, but I suspected that was an accident caused by her small space. Salvatore had let go of my hand, shaking the water from his custom-made leather shoes and greeting Zanna with fake brotherly affection when she stumbled back onto our floor, drunk on his best whiskey. I'd left as quickly as possible, dragging Zanna with me and not even caring that she had to stop a few blocks away to vomit in an alley. I felt like vomiting, too, but knew that wouldn't bring any relief. The questions in my head would make me sick for a good long while: What had

Salvatore meant to teach me with that stunt? I got the sense that he was grooming me, but for what purpose? What skills did I have that might interest him? "Below notice" was my life goal. Part of me—the part that understood Captain Barrera's desire to make arsenic into lemonade—thought there might be a way out of my current standstill with Salvatore. I couldn't join him, but what if I could appease him? If he was genuinely grateful that I'd gotten his brother out of the picture, maybe there was something else I could give.

I'd tried to make myself as inconspicuous as possible during my undercover time, and perhaps that was the appeal. Salvatore didn't have someone on his team who could disappear in a crowd. My talent wasn't exciting as, say, cracking safes, but maybe it had value in the shadowy world of drug trafficking. Wringing Tesora's water from my sleeve, I had wanted to disappear completely once and for all, but, unfortunately, being nondescript wasn't magic, not by a long shot. Instead, I had to haul myself back to my fake apartment in my fake building and fake smile over pabellón criollo with the Costas. My favorite pastime during those years was dreaming about the day when I could be myself again. By the time I got out, I wasn't confident "myself" even existed.

CHAPTER 7

The boat's deceleration caught me off guard, and I slipped down the plastic seat, grabbing my lifejacket panels as if they could save me from falling. Nobody noticed my unease in their excitement. The three old men acted years younger, leaping to their feet and high-fiving in anticipation of their big catches. I couldn't imagine the crew of the Pequod being quite so jubilant over some cod, but then again, I'd never reached the last pages of Moby Dick. Ellis told me how it ended, and I received a perfectly acceptable C on the final exam.

Our friendship had always been a little uneven, me needing Ellis more than he needed me. Perhaps that's why he resented my absence so much; it broke with tradition. Not that he would have held a grudge over me going undercover, at least not for very long. While disapproving of my unsafe plan, I knew part of him respected the mission. He'd wanted an undercover assignment himself, but he was too blond, too well-mannered. Some signs of a blue-blood youth couldn't be washed off with Dial soap. He'd never quite gotten the hang of cheap socks and cheaper lunches. But even if he approved of my desire to rid the city of dangerous elements, he wouldn't forget that I had avoided him for years afterward, intent on becoming someone wholly new, someone a kingpin wouldn't notice if she jaywalked in front of his Escalade. Three years wasted, I thought, then shook myself out of self-pity. It wasn't a good color on me.

Lost in thought, I hadn't noticed Hank emerge from below deck, a bit wobblier on his feet, and I didn't think his lack of grace was due to the waves. When he got close to me, I thought I detected beer on his breath, but it was hard to say for sure. I was more certain that his attitude had gotten worse, and that the boat seemed awfully small. There were six rows of seats, but I couldn't hide underneath any of them. Hank was too much of a businessman to harass his paying customers, but he didn't seem too worried about my Yelp review.

"Do I have a rod for you," he said, holding a fishing pole between his legs. I was as offended by the lameness of the joke as I was by its crudeness and didn't respond. A major perk of working for yourself was not worrying about ass grabbers. Well, at least not in the office. Anything could happen on a crowded train. Hank mumbled a slur and threw the equipment down at my feet. It was hard to believe he was the same man I had met in the morning. Did he always keep up an act in front of his wife? Leesa wasn't exactly a shrinking violet, so perhaps he saved his worst behavior for other women. Lucky us.

"Will it be tough running the business without your partner?" I asked, deflecting. Who would process my sexual harassment claim anyway? Mine was a solo mission, and one that could be concluded quickly with the right intel. A little hard evidence, and I could hand this case over to the capable hands of the NYPD. An overworked bunch, but one with a lot more resources than me.

"Who? Leesa? This is my business, and mine alone." Hank spat over the side to emphasize his point, then joined Captain Barrera at the wheel. So much for my interrogation.

Growing up, my experience with the great outdoors consisted of visits to Central Park. I had run around the Great Lawn and once almost gotten lost in the Ramble, an artificial wildness that spanned a few acres. But there were always hotdog vendors nearby, ready enough with relish and sodas. I'd never had to catch my own food. I'd seen people fish in movies, though, and figured I could imitate the other passengers until someone gave me permission to sip my ginger ale and stare at the horizon. It was lonely on the water; there was no other word for the utter isolation. I understood why whole crews lost their minds sometimes, so far from home, so far from land of any kind. There was something cruel about being surrounded by water that you couldn't drink. Like mirages or disco music, another mean prank of the universe.

My line was tangled, purposely by Hank I suspected, and I tried to find a knot that looked manageable. I kept my nails trimmed short, adding fake ones when an identity needed that sort of thing. Today, I wished I had the long, manicured talons of Kennedy

S. Vanders, my socialite alter ego, but then again, she wouldn't be caught dead on this rinky-dink piece of driftwood. Frustrated, I used my teeth instead, accidentally biting through the line. This presented a new dilemma, and I picked up the hook from where it had fallen to the ground. Did it matter that it was rusted? The thought of such an old needle slicing through the mouth of a fish made me queasy, but I supposed the fish wouldn't be happy either way, shiny new hook or old used one.

Captain Barrera watched me with an amused expression. He caught me staring and apologized, his eyes still twinkling. When he approached, he didn't seem daunted by the mess I'd inherited and then made worse. Instead, he took the line into his calloused hands. He untangled the knots with impressive speed, then checked my handle and guides.

"When I was small, I liked the bait best. All those worms and chapulines. I wanted to keep them and would slip them into my pockets."

"Where was this?" I asked, keeping my eyes on his fingers as they restrung the pole and tied a new hook onto the end. It was larger than the previous hook, and I knew that people paid for these excursions so that they could have trophies, swordfish and the like. I wasn't sure that taxidermy really matched my apartment decor, and I was certain that Meeza wouldn't allow such a monstrosity into our shared office space. Maybe it didn't really matter that there were knots in my line. I planned on pretending to participate anyway. I could fake enough enthusiasm to not lose my fake job.

"Jalisco. Do you know it?" Captain Barrera finished his work, then set the pole into a custom-made slot on the side of the boat. I was confused that I didn't have to hold it the whole time. I thought I would need to demonstrate feats of strength and endurance like I'd seen on old episodes of *Matlock*. Instead, I simply had to wait, demonstrate feats of patience. That was in my wheelhouse at least. The other three passengers had claimed multiple spots, and I didn't blame them. They might as well take advantage of this semi-private trip. Would there be more customers when the weather warmed up? It didn't seem possible that The Blue Lagoon could stay in business with such a meager showing. Leesa had said that the tours "sold themselves." Was today an anomaly, or did Hank keep the truth from his wife? He'd made it clear that she wasn't a partner, so perhaps keeping secrets from her wasn't hard.

"Yes. I've never been to Mexico, though," I finally responded. I didn't want to tell Captain Barrera that I knew of his home state from vice training. The Los Zetas cartel had a heavy presence there, and the Sinaloa was rapidly expanding. Mostly, they fought against each other, their rivalry leading to torture and beheadings of lower level players. But there were always civilians caught in the middle as well. I tried to think of something positive I'd heard about the region and mentioned coffee. This answer delighted Captain Barrera, and he told me about growing up near San Sebastián, a mountain town that still attracted tourists who wanted to see where the cocoa beans grew. It was clear that he was proud of his background, and I asked what had brought him to the States. His expression clouded briefly, but he smiled when he answered.

"This is a good job."

I recognized a partial truth when I heard one, but I couldn't say what Captain Barrera was hiding. Had he been fleeing from the violence in his region? Was he sending money back to a family? Those were the reasons typically given, but New York was an unusual destination for Mexican immigrants. They mostly stayed in the Southern states and California. And many had returned home during the recent recession, taking their chances with an improving economy in their own country.

My pole jerked, and I jumped, startled by how quickly the line was unraveling into the ocean. I looked at Captain Barrera for help, and he told me to grab the handle and start reeling in my catch. The three other passengers cheered for me, hollering out their conflicting advice. "Give it some extra line!" "Don't let it get too far!" "Stop fighting!" "Start fighting!"

I tried to turn the lever toward me, and my hands started to burn immediately from the effort. The fish was strong, not to mention angry, and the combination of the two created a force I couldn't control. "Plant your legs!" "Use your back!" "Don't hurt your back!"

I tightened my grip, pulling up and trusting my equipment not to break. It must have been built for wrestling with whales. And that was surely an orca on the end of my line. What else could have such force?

"Looks like she's got a tuna out there," said one of the men behind me. They'd all come closer to watch my epic battle. Tuna were big, right? I wouldn't be embarrassed by my struggle with something housecats ate as a treat.

"She'll lose it, wait and see." Hank's voice sounded bored and maybe slurred. Adrenaline had flooded my system, and I didn't notice too many details. The water looked alive, as if rooting for its own rather than me. White caps sparkled in the bright sun, casting their spells. I managed to turn the lever two full times and let out a whoop of excitement. All at once, I understood what brought people this far out into the Atlantic. It was a hero's journey, this push and pull. I was Jason of Argonauts fame! I was Jonah and Ahab at once! I was having fun.

A more urgent tug caught me unaware, and the line slipped back out. I started to reel again, ignoring advice to be calm, and felt my arms snap forward. The rod slipped from my fingers, and I lunged after it, off-balance. The fish breached, and I glanced toward the splash dizzy with excitement and panic that I might lose, that this one would get away. One of my knees slammed into the side of the boat and pain shot through my whole leg. I tried to stand again, but a sharp jab from behind made me slip, smacking against the rail. Then the rod flew out into the ocean, my body not far behind. I had a second to scream before I plunged into the water.

CHAPTER 8

The lifejacket didn't prevent me from slipping under, but I reemerged quickly, trying to cough up what I had swallowed. My teeth began chattering—from fear or cold, I couldn't say. At first, I was only about a yard from the boat, but the distance quickly grew more pronounced as I drifted away, caught on one of the giant waves I'd been so recently admiring. My parka made it difficult to swim, but I didn't want to remove my lifejacket and risk losing it. Treading water without help, I gave myself ten minutes tops in those turbulent waters. I tried to move toward The Blue Lagoon, losing sight of it when another wave roiled in front of me. The white caps were a lot less magical up close, and I forced my mouth closed even though every instinct told me to keep screaming, pray for rescue.

Something brushed against my leg, and I kicked more frantically, worried about sharks and revenge-minded tunas, not to mention undiscovered monsters of the deep. There were an infinite number of ways to die in the ocean, I realized belatedly. None of them sounded particularly appealing, and I kicked off my shoes before attempting a breast stroke, trying to move forward but also conserve energy. My arms started to ache from the effort, and the boat drifted farther away. The frantic voices of Captain Barrera and the others faded, but I kept my body directed toward them, the boat quickly becoming toy-sized in my vision. The Atlantic seemed hellbent on showing me her powers. I'd only been overboard for a few minutes, but already I was growing frantic. Two waves converged near me, and I was buoyed high before being tossed back down.

When Captain Barrera finally got the boat started, the motor sounded like celestial music. I waved my arms, trying to make myself more visible as another creature brushed against me, seeing if I were edible, presumably. I doubted these wild animals were as well-fed as Salvatore's Tesora. Given the chance, they'd do more than wait for me to hand them shrimp. I didn't blame them, but I hoped that I smelled enough like synthetic fabric to make them hesitate at least long enough for help to arrive. And help was on its way; The Blue Lagoon crept toward me. I'd understood later that Captain Barrera didn't want to accelerate too quickly lest he accidentally run me over, a consideration I appreciated only in retrospect. At the time, I wanted to curse the snail-like speed.

When the boat got close enough, Captain Barrera killed the engine, and I kicked as hard as I could toward the three paying customers reaching out toward me, their long, flowing gray hair seeming majestic, and I was sorry I had ever thought of it as scraggly. I reached up as far as I could, but I couldn't get high enough for them to grab me. My hands were touching the fiberglass, but I couldn't climb up. The next time something brushed against my leg, it didn't stop with casual interest, and pain shot through my ankle. It felt as if a brand were being held against my skin, and dark spots clouded my vision. I shrieked, inhaling more water as I smacked my palms futilely against the boat.

A tool that looked like a harpoon appeared beside me, and I reached for it, holding on with all my remaining strength as Hank yanked me out of the water. The others grabbed my clothes and finished the job, pulling me over the side and depositing me in a coughing, crying heap onto the floor.

"Peligro," Captain Barrera said, and I added hysterical laughter to my one-woman soundtrack. Hank scowled, not bothering to hide the drink he made himself this time. If I were thinking generously about his behavior, I'd admit that my survival did deserve a toast. Everyone else started laughing when I thanked them. We were all high on relief. It wasn't every day that a person outmaneuvered death, even with a team. I was overjoyed to be wet and cold but alive in the middle of the Atlantic with this lot of strangers.

Then the pain sliced through my ankle again, and I clawed at my wet socks, pulling them off to see the damage. The swearing that came from Hank and Captain Barrera didn't offer any comfort, and my skin did look awful—swollen and lumpy with an angry, red line lacing through the mess.

"Jellyfish got her," I heard someone mumble behind me as Hank called for the first aid kit. I screamed again as the poison pulsed through my leg, and I ripped my pants trying to push the fire away. The black spots receded from my vision, and I looked up in time to see Captain Barrera unlatch a red tin and spill gauze bandages onto the floor. When I tried to ask him if I needed those, the words came out as a gasp, and I watched his black curls writhe and hiss, each one a viper turned toward me.

I scooted away, my injury less important than escaping the nightmare in front of me. When hairy arms restrained me, I twisted and kicked, anything to get free as the sky turned green and cracked open. From the center, a train flew down, blowing its horn and dragging ropes behind. They formed lassos and came for me, unmanned outlaws wild with fury. Horses followed, snorting and pawing the air. Rainbow confetti streamed down from their stampeding, then pooled around me. The slips of paper formed shapes on the floor, a prophecy in jagged symbols I couldn't decipher, but knew by heart—a warning. Even in the festive colors, a promise of ambush. I watched the horses swoop closer as Captain Barrera grabbed my feet, his snakes flicking their tongues, trying to steal the vinegar as Hank poured it over my ankle. When the bottle was empty, they curled their bodies back into a nest, patient killers, every last one.

"How long will the hallucinations last?" Hank asked, and I tried to hear the answer over the hammers that beat against my skull. The noise became a whistle, then a tornado's shrill cry, and I passed out before I could see what maelstrom followed.

*

"They must have one hell of a legal liability waver." Dolly was applying fake eyelashes with tiny LED lights at their tips. He wasn't performing for another half hour and had given me his full attention as I regaled him with my heroic escapades, namely peeing my pants as I was saved.

"Oh, sugar, if the fish do it, why can't we? Pee away, I always say," he said, waving off my embarrassment. My friend had a way of brushing off my more neurotic concerns, preferring to save his energy for my genuine emergencies. There had been plenty in our brief acquaintance, what I liked to call our "whirlwind friendship." It was hard to explain how my bond with Dolly had formed. When we met, I had been avoiding all personal connections, worried that Salvatore Magrelli would find me through an informant. But when you're looking to your right, the punch always come from the left. Naturally, it was my professional connections that had gotten me into trouble. Car thief V.P. was a fight best left for another day. I'd survived near drowning and maybe the apocalypse. I was determined to bask in my relief at least for an hour or two, though my brain couldn't help dwelling on the jab I'd felt before being pulled overboard. Had Hank pushed me? And if so, why'd he try so hard to save me after?

"A muscle cramp?" Dolly asked. "I get them when I'm dehydrated."

That was a logical explanation, especially since nobody had mentioned anything to me during the long ride back to shore. The swelling went down in an hour or so, but the visions pestered me until we docked. Clock towers with teeth. Trees with saws instead of branches. It was as if my subconscious had declared a holiday, letting loose all its metaphors for fear in one giant purge.

I watched Dolly flip on the eyelash lights to check the battery, and his handsome face was illuminated. With a bit more blush, a bit more contouring, it would morph into beautiful. He was the biggest draw at The Pink Parrot, an entertainer without equal in the drag circuit, and he was treated as such. His boss, Lacy "Mamma" Burstyn, made sure he got the biggest paycheck and the biggest dressing room. More than that, she treated him and all "her boys" like family. They'd lost two members of their close-knit tribe a few months earlier, and there were still reminders. Increased security. A row of candles at the club's entrance. Dolly's burn scar. That particular souvenir would be visible on his forehead until he pulled on his custom, hand-made pageboy wig, a work of art if you asked me or the artist herself, Vondya Vasiliev. She was a master craftsman and didn't bother to feign humility.

I looked down at my ankle where I'd attached the Hello Kitty band-aid I found in Dolly's first aid kit alongside Neosporin, gauze, and condoms. Everything a PI gal might need for a night out on the town. Or a night in, more likely, since I wasn't planning on leaving the comfortable settee. It had been my on-and-off camping spot ever since I'd discovered that Salvatore knew who and where I was. Not that the frequently busted front door to my Washington Heights apartment didn't inspire confidence, but I was overly fond of the two security guards Mamma Burstyn hired to watch the club's front door and patrol the facility. Earl and his cousin had even taken a sort of kid sister liking to me, and I wasn't about to take their good will for granted. There were too few people in this city who still enjoyed my paranoid company. My personality now included the added charm of not being able to distinguish a sequin from an eyeball, but the internet assured me that the hallucinations were temporary.

Around 3 a.m., Dolly would take a town car to his doorman building in Tribeca, but by then, I hoped to be unconscious, forgetting my unseasonable swim and enjoying nightmares in my sleep where they belonged. The thought of returning to face Captain Barrera and Hank in the morning didn't hold much appeal. On the one hand, the whole incident screamed "lawsuit waiting to happen." On the other, I didn't think they were worried about being sued. They supposed I was in the country illegally, or at least working under false pretenses. Either way, I wasn't likely to lawyer up. By the time The Blue Lagoon docked, I had managed to convince everyone that I didn't need an emergency room. If they suspected that I didn't have health insurance, they didn't say anything. And I didn't say anything about how the boardwalk appeared to be made of bones and jellybeans instead of wood, so we were even. I had picked up a pair of cheap, plastic sandals and made the trek to SoHo.

Returning to the office in the morning assumed that I still had a job waiting for me. Answering phones and handing out flyers weren't exactly irreplaceable skills. But I would show up, as eager as I needed to be for a second chance. I still wanted to chat up some of the workers Tabor had helped. Was there only gratitude, or did some of them resent the finder's fee? I could imagine a few weeks of indebtedness, but every time that five percent got taken, feelings of goodwill would fade, wouldn't they? Bit by bit until the name Tabor Campion was synonymous with greed.

"Ten minutes, Mr. Rodriquez," a voice said through the closed door, knocking softly.

Dolly pinned his hairdo into place, completing his Ovid-worthy metamorphosis, at least in appearance. He was Dolly on stage and off, effortlessly navigating his personas. He threw a silver boa over his shoulder and sauntered out into the hallway, sending waiters scurrying out of the way. They watched until he was out of sight, and I couldn't blame them. There was something magnetic about Dolly. I shut the door behind my friend, then curled up under a cashmere throw and watched a caterpillar smile and wink at me from the ceiling. Maybe not so real, I decided, but at least not dangerous. I closed my eyes and considered if I'd learned anything useful since I found my super's body.

The riskiness of Tabor's occupation—or side hustle—offered the most obvious explanation. Maybe Ángel at the pawn shop wanted to expand his client base. Maybe somebody found out about Tabor's illegal activities and blackmailed him. I trusted Blue Lagoon owner Hank Almy about as much as I trusted a crocodile, even if he had helped save me. He and his wife acted well-acquainted with the victim, but, surely, I'd be safe behind a desk? Dry feet and dry pants didn't seem like an unrealistic goal for the next day.

My ankle gave a throb, and I admitted to myself that sleep was unlikely. Sitting up, I flipped on Dolly's laptop and shook my head that he hadn't added a password even though I'd made the suggestion more than once. "Then how would you join those spy chatrooms?" he'd said, leaving me to guess that he didn't have anything to hide.

"It's just you and me, buddy," I said to the caterpillar as she settled down in my lap. "You're pretty cute at least."

"I'm freaking gorgeous," she said with a yawn, a hallucination with an ego.

A quick search for Tabor Campion gave me a brief article in a no-name online news source about his death, called a suicide by the anonymous reporter. There was a blurry photo of the little red lighthouse, and I wondered at the lack of professionalism. Why even bother to run a news site? Ad revenues weren't exactly goldmines. Behind the lighthouse were a few smaller blurs. A line from *The Little Red Lighthouse* and *The Great Gray Bridge* sprang to mind: "What would the boats do without me?"

CHAPTER 9

The flowers were a nice touch, a motley arrangement of hyacinths and carnations and some unfamiliar white tuffs. Captain Barrera had written the card in Spanish, assuming that I was bilingual or that "I'm sorry" needed no translation. It didn't really make sense for him to apologize. He hadn't been standing near enough to prevent my fall. Plus, there was no way he could have predicted my wild reaction to hooking a fish. I still wasn't sure what had possessed me, why I'd been so excited. Even if someone had pushed me, he wouldn't have been able to send me flying if I hadn't already been poised at the edge. Perhaps Hank and Leesa Almy should consider safety guards. They could childproof their boat for their new baby and for grown adult women who let themselves be pulled overboard. Not "they," I reminded myself. Leesa worked for her husband, he'd been quick to assure me.

Leesa had left The Blue Lagoon desk well-organized for me, brochures on the right, laminated photos of tuna—my new nemesis—on the left. The morning was quiet, not too much foot traffic in early April. The day was disturbingly bright, though, as if the city had woken up on Ritalin. As a lifelong New Yorker, I knew it was a ruse. Spring would take her sweet time, as always, waiting until we were all ready for the loony bin before offering us daffodils and, if lucky enough to find ourselves outside Grand Central Station, tulips. I held Captain Barrera's bouquet up to my nose and was pleased by the smell. Maybe I was feeling grateful that he'd helped haul me out of the water, but he seemed like a kind man. Not the boisterous captain that might be prized in the sunset cruise community. I couldn't see him stepping in for the DJ or mixing Mai Tais, but I trusted his navigation skills. Maybe a little of his optimism had rubbed off on me.

Around 11 a.m., Hank shuffled through the front door, looking chagrined. His eyes were bloodshot, but he was freshly shaven and wearing clean pants. He swung his arms around nervously, his bulky coat making a match-striking noise with each pass.

"Didn't think you'd show up," he said, looking at me, then looking away.

"A gal's gotta eat."

He nodded, accepting my explanation, but kept up his shuffling routine. He commented on the warm weather, then complimented my swimming skills, saying he was impressed that I "didn't panic." That's how I knew the drinks must have dulled his memory. "Most folks," he continued, undeterred by my skeptical expression. "Most folks give up. But you? Nah. You fought, really fought."

If the man's personality shift the day before had confused me, it was starting to make sense through the lens of Bud Lite with vodka chasers.

"Drown or be drowned," I said, not knowing exactly what I meant, but sensing it was true.

"Flowers. That was smart. I should have bought flowers," he said.

"One bouquet is plenty."

Hank fiddled with the yellow ribbon that had been tied around the wrapper, and I tried to guess why he had come to see me. Was it to apologize? If so, he hadn't said the words yet.

"We're having a girl," he said after the pause had stretched too long to be comfortable.

"Congratulations."

"I mean, we've known for a while, but…"

When he fell silent again, I considered whether his guilt might help me gain information and jumped into the lull. "I'll tell you the truth, though, I thought Tabor was arranging house-cleaning gigs. Maybe dishwashing. I didn't think I'd be doggie-paddling in the ocean with a bad-tempered boss laughing at me."

"Did I laugh?" Hank sighed as if he genuinely couldn't remember. He ran a hand over his hair and then his face, pulling down his cheeks, then letting them snap back into place. "Tabor liked tourist work. Nobody keeps tabs on us much."

"Yeah, that became pretty clear to me yesterday."

"Where you from anyway? You sound pretty American to me, no offense."

I'd knew this question was coming and had developed my story. Faking an accent was risky. For starters, consistency was harder than you'd think. Then there was the possibility of running into someone from the same region. I'd considered Canadian, but I figured the more far-fetched my story, the harder it would be to factcheck. Not that this was the crossing their t's and dotting their i's kind of operation.

"My grandparents were in Cuba in 1960. After the embargo, they were stuck."

"No shit," Hank said, his eyes widening.

I shrugged as if I didn't want to talk about it. Hank had different ideas, his mind obviously reeling at the possibility that I had been born in Cuba. I had my escape story ready to go, but we were interrupted by Captain Barrera peeking his head through the door.

"¿Estás bien hoy, señorita?" he asked, holding his baseball cap in this hands.

"Sí, señor. Estoy bien."

I thanked him for the flowers, and he waved off my gratitude. He needed Hank to double-check the new equipment. They'd bought new lifejackets and a larger first aid kit in my honor.

"Triple-check, you mean," I said.

"Triple-check, I promise," Hank said, crossing his fingers over his heart. For a moment, the movement made it seem as if his shirt ripped open, but I clamped my mouth shut in protest. It hadn't quite been twenty-four hours, and I was still struggling to distinguish between real and imaginary. At least my caterpillar friend had decided The Pink Parrot's accommodations were more her style than a dingy office. I'd left her snoozing on a throw pillow.

The door jangled shut behind the two men, and I flipped on the desktop computer. An unfinished solitaire game greeted me, and I wondered if Leesa would make it through the day without a hospital visit. I didn't know much about pregnancies, but if the baby knew what was good for her, she'd make her appearance on her mamma's schedule. The internet connection was weak, stolen from an account named biglipsbigfun, but nobody had cleared the history. Leesa had been shopping for a stroller and fishing nets. Maybe she was having a mermaid instead of a girl. With this family, they might be pleased.

The map searches caught my attention only because there were so many. During the past month, someone had looked at maps of the Atlantic Ocean. Mostly the images were close to shore, but a few went a hundred miles out or more. Was someone planning new routes? Day trips? I tried searching for inhabitable—or at least visitable—islands near our bay, but there were no results. Moving on, the Excel accounting document didn't tell me anything I hadn't already suspected. Captain Barrera and myself weren't listed on the payroll. In fact, there was only one employee with official status: Mr. Almy.

I closed all of my open windows and walked over to the doorway to look out at the street. The shop wasn't directly on the boardwalk, but sat a couple of streets removed from the action. Still, the scene was livelier than I expected. A two-seater bicycle was decked out like a mini spaceship and blasted David Bowie from a boombox. Two topless women in their seventies argued about what movie they should see later, flaunting New York City's lenient decency laws. There were kids, of course, including a couple in t-shirts, making the sunshine seem warmer than its fifty degrees. I could hear the occasional shriek of delight coming from Luna Park, the newest incarnation of the old theme park. My parents had taken me here every summer, and I had begged to ride the Cyclone. My father wasn't much of a thrill seeker, so that particular chaperoning duty fell on Mom. I think they were both grateful when I could go alone. In fact, I couldn't imagine climbing aboard now. Classic wooden rollercoasters looked great in photographs, but were hell on your tailbone. I rubbed my bruised knee and breathed a sigh of gratitude that my injuries from yesterday were minor. On the other hand, I hadn't made much progress on my case.

I hoped for some inspiration in the scene, wondering what had lured Tabor away from the life in Paris he delighted in describing. Smoking in cafés was a particularly fond memory, though I'd never seen him with a Gauloise or even a Newport. Wine bottles cluttered our recycling bin, but I didn't think he was the only drinker in our midst. I'd added a few cheap specimens myself. If I were being honest, I'd never thought about my super that much before finding his body. He had acted happy enough, always ready to make conversation in the elevator. Maybe it wasn't his body's landing site that made me doubt the "suicide" label. It was his easy grin when we passed in the hallway. If the rumors could be believed, he'd snagged his maintenance position as a plucky teenager. He may have been hard to catch on the phone if your toilet was leaking, but he always helped Señora Amador with her groceries. Always helped Señora Amador with her groceries? I made a noise of disgust at myself. It was clear I didn't know enough about Tabor if all I could remember were the kind of platitude acquaintances rolled out when caught off guard by widows. What made someone look ready to die anyway?

I passed out flyers to a few people on the street, nodding at a brightly dressed woman doing the same a few stores down. She waved and even took a step in my direction, then changed her mind. A few people stopped to chat about the tour and one couple came inside. I think they just wanted to use the bathroom, though. I wasn't supposed to let anyone besides customers into the facility, but I wasn't too worried about losing my job after talking to Hank and Captain Barrera. I'd get a pass today at least.

There was no convenient excuse for me to visit the dock, but I went on my lunch break anyway. I took a different route this time, passing by the aquarium and admiring a mural that celebrated conservation efforts. A giant, happy eel towered over an orange Ferris wheel and that infamous sea dweller, the dairy cow. The building blended into the larger-than-life attitude of the area, the rush toward escaping regular life whether through rides or funnel cake. Inside the aquarium, though, I'd always found it peaceful, screaming children notwithstanding. The carefully staged tanks illuminated beautiful creatures we rarely had a chance to see. And the chlorine and other chemicals smelled crisp and clean in contrast to the urine-soaked sidewalks outside. That is, I'd always found the place peaceful until Salvatore made his shark into a psychological torture device. I hadn't returned to the aquarium since and wasn't keen on being reminded of my trial by teeth. The new shark exhibition wasn't opening for another few years, but I didn't even fancy seeing advertisements. Out of my periphery, the eel wiggled toward me, but when I turned, there was only paint.

Tesora may have spared my hand, but after our introduction, I still prayed that I would never see her sleek, gray skin again. My prayers went unanswered, though, and within a week Zanna and I had been summoned to Salvatore's lair—I mean, townhouse. Zanna again thought that she might be promoted, and I was amazed by her bravado. How she thought finishing half a bottle of Lagavulin would endear her to a cartel leader was beyond me, but she was more action than thought. Without a reason to beg off, I followed her up four flights of stairs and into the former ballroom. I let Zanna get ahead of me as she shook her future brother-in-law's hand, and I scurried toward the darkest corner like the little mouse I was. Salvatore never looked at me, and I hoped that I would be ignored this time. At some point, he'd tire of playing with me, right?

I wasn't the night's entertainment, which was soon clear when a stranger was led into the room, gagged and blindfolded. Two large men with the kind of job Zanna wanted dragged the victim behind them. The bound man struggled, pulling against his ropes and kicking into space, but his efforts were pointless. Whatever was happening, I didn't want to see, but there was nowhere to hide. The man slumped in the middle of the room, meek until his gag and blindfold were removed and he saw Tesora. His yell was silenced by a quick punch to the stomach, and I managed not to cringe. By then, I'd almost grown accustomed to bursts of violence. I expected them at least.

Tesora's pace never faltered. Back and forth she swam, dignified in her containment. Since she hadn't eaten my hand when she had the chance, I'd decided we were allies if not friends, and I wished I could save her from this madness. If Disney ever green-lighted a Free Willy reboot, I knew where to find their star. While Tesora was ready for her close-up, the stranger was bugged-eyed and sweating. I didn't blame him, but I knew now that the shark served as a scare tactic, not a real threat.

"Do you have any inkling as to why you're here?" Salvatore asked in a polite voice that made my skin crawl. Always calm, always calculating.

The stranger started crying, mumbling something about not knowing anybody was skimming, about paying back the missing money, about doing whatever Salvatore wanted, "sir." Always "sir." My undercover world could be divided between the Sirs and the Not Sirs. When in doubt, the sign of respect was recommended. And by respect, I meant intimidation. Tesora served her purpose, and the small part of me that wasn't scared was angry that they'd use her in such a way. A magnificent animal like that should be cruising through the ocean, leaving havoc in her smooth wake. Daydreaming wasn't recommended when on the job, but if I had the time, I was sure I could have devised some outlandish rescue attempt involving pulleys and watering cans.

The two muscle men shoved the stranger onto the bench I'd occupied only a few days before. I knew how this would go. He would be forced to stick his hand in the water, too. He would try not to piss himself and promise loyalty until his dying breath. At least, that's what I imagined. When they threw him inside the tank and slammed the lid back in place, I may have gasped and taken a step forward, not as jaded as I thought. A quick glance around the room told me that I was the only one shocked. And the only one not smiling about a man about to meet his maker.

CHAPTER 10

The Blue Lagoon was parked in the same spot as before, a few letters in its name peeling off. The boat would soon be "he goon," which didn't have the same romantic ring to it. Passengers disembarked, and I counted four. One better than yesterday's attendance, but still not enough to keep the lights on. Was Hank worried about losing his business, trying to raise a family while being unemployed? When he emerged on deck, I tried to see from a distance whether he was sober. He waved, then ignored me, so I couldn't be sure. Captain Barrera was friendlier, slapping me on the back as I thanked him again for the flowers. He wasn't eager to dawdle either, though, and shifted his weight from foot to foot impatiently as I explained why I was there.

"I think I left my sweater on board yesterday," I said. I'd come up with the lie on my way over, but Captain Barrera didn't seem to think it strange that I'd walked over. He gave me one last pat, then headed toward a seafood restaurant across the street, Manny's Catch. "Man y's Cat" actually, but in daylight I could see the letters with burned out bulbs.

Two other Blue Lagoon workers tied up the boat without supervision. I approached them and introduced myself, calling myself the "new Leesa," but they didn't respond to that joke, and I questioned whether they'd ever met Hank's wife. Maybe she didn't visit the docks. I couldn't imagine her descaling a grouper.

Even though it didn't seem warm enough, the men were shirtless, their young bodies somehow impervious to the cold. I tried not to stare at their thin but well-toned chests as I remarked on how calm the bay looked. One of the men grunted in response, but the other didn't look at me. They could have been brothers, their thick black hair falling past their shoulders. They had clearly worked together for a while, their movements synchronized as they wound rope around the dock anchors. I mumbled something about my sweater again, but neither acknowledged the comment.

Once on board, Hank avoided me, and I pretended to search for my lost garment. There were fish in crates below deck, and I was impressed that four passengers had managed such a haul. At least twenty glassy eyeballs stared at me, and I blamed yesterday's jellyfish sting for the way they seemed to follow my steps. At least I wasn't permanently crazy, I reminded myself. That was the last positive thought I had, though, because my trip had been a bust. The workers who most likely knew Tabor wouldn't talk to me. Their reticence was frustrating, but not surprising. Curious strangers often meant trouble for immigrants, documented or not. The past year had seen an uptick in hate crimes, a few hundred more, each with a name and face missing from the FBI's pie chart. A few of the attacks were often the result of what you might call bubbling anger, unemployment rates being used as fodder by wealthy politicians. It was a story embedded in American history like a stubborn splinter that festers until the whole finger, the whole hand, is an angry, red welt.

The odds were against me that I'd get useful information from men who wouldn't talk to me. Failure made the walk back seem longer, but it gave me time to consider who had known Tabor and, more importantly, who might be willing to chat. I formed a haphazard plan, not expecting it to succeed any better than my first one, but glad at least to know where I was going after my shift ended. Reluctant to sit in an empty office, I detoured by Vondya Vasiliev's wig shop, disappointed when I saw a "Closed" sign on her second-story window. I climbed the steps anyway, peering through the glass at the row of mirrors and barber chairs. Even with Vondya haranguing me, this remained one of my more frequented spots in the city, a room where I could forget who I was and even who I had been. At least for half an hour. And sometimes if I had a thousand dollars to spend, I could bring home my amnesia in the form of a new identity, Katya or Kitty or Katerina.

When I saw Vondya's familiar form, I brought my hand up to knock, then paused, not ready to intrude. She was wearing a chestnut hairpiece I hadn't seen before, much more elaborate than her usual selections. It was pinned into curls at the crown of her neck, more appropriate for a prom-bound teenager than a senior citizen. Vondya stared blankly at her reflection, the wrinkles on her forehead and around her mouth seeming deeper than usual because of her expression, like a woman looking into her past and not liking the view.

I slipped my shoes off, backing noiselessly down to the street. Seeing Vondya so dejected shook me, but we all had our secrets. She could keep her own.

*

The Madigan's Happy Hour offered three-dollar beers, and Ángel was a few deep by the time I slipped inside. This was the third place that I had tried, and luck of the Irish was finally on my side. The bar was crowded, but I spotted the group easily enough. There were a few places like this left in Washington Heights. Watering holes that had been around before *The New York Times* called the neighborhood the Montmartre of New York City and realtors started bothering to show clients around the dilapidated brownstones. I'd called it home since 2010, but didn't socialize enough to be a regular anywhere. Well, the Chinese takeout owners might recognize me. Maybe Rio at the pizza shop. Then again, I'd rarely gone into either place without a wig and matching persona. I wouldn't be that easy to pick out in a lineup.

Ángel was in the corner, laughing at a joke someone had told. My favorite pawnshop proprietor had taken off his unfashionable glasses, but he'd tucked them into the front pocket of his wrinkled dress shirt. His hair was slicked down as well, and I wondered if the night was a special occasion. They toasted the friend I recognized from Ángel's stockroom, and Dante shook his head at their praise or ribbing. I was too far away to tell and uncertain how to approach such a raucous bunch. Then Ángel caught my eye, and I wondered if he'd recognize me, if I'd be called to the carpet. But no, instead, the man who had haggled with me over Tabor's mask winked and blew me a kiss. Balking at the gesture, I decided that he couldn't see much without his glasses. No sense in letting myself grow vain—my figure must have looked vaguely female-like from his blurry perspective.

Even without a costume, my face can be immemorable. Not exactly a source of confidence when I was a teenager, but I came to think of my changing appearance as a gift. Tonight, though, I needed Ángel to recognize me and hoped that his mistake could be rectified by a pair of spectacles. I smiled and sashayed in his direction, watching him run a hand over his already smooth hair.

"I found a pair of khakis," I said when I got close, waving a hand over my attire. Ángel's expression shifted from leering to confused to peeved. I had only expected the last category and wasn't unsettled by his gruff address.

"What do you want? Answering phones too good for you? How'd you find me?"

"A happy accident."

Ángel pulled his glasses out and jammed them onto his face as if I'd personally outed him as near-sighted. Or come to think of it, maybe all his friends didn't know that he was a martín pescador, that he'd most likely looted a dead man's business. They stopped to stare at me, pausing in their celebrations. Dante stood in the center, his chipmunk cheeks flushed. The stereo kept blasting Hall & Oates, but the group reacted as if a record had screeched to a halt. Kat Stone: Life of the Party.

"What's the occasion?" I said, hoping I wouldn't have to explain myself. "Are we toasting Tabor? I'll need a drink."

The men glanced at each other, silently electing a spokesperson in Dante. It was his party after all. I waited to see whether they thought it was strange that I would bring up Tabor. My gut said they knew him, or at least Ángel did. Sometimes my gut confused dairy with intuition, though. I've never been called dainty, but I felt small surrounded by the group of men, aware that it'd been a few years since my last self-defense class. Their silence made me feel more uncomfortable, and I was relieved when Dante finally spoke.

"Nothing like that, may he rest in peace," he said, crossing himself. He looked me up and down, not exactly checking me out. More curious than lewd. I returned the favor, noting his chapped hands and stained pants. The others watched our interaction, waiting to see if I was going to join them. I definitely got the feeling I wasn't welcome, but I hadn't expected bear hugs and free shots. I wasn't going to waste an opportunity to gather information because of a few curt words. If you shook enough bushes, you got some critters.

"No, let's toast to Tabor," I said, turning to order

a beer. "I lived in his building, and he did me a favor, sending me to Ángel. For weeks, I've been looking for work. Then I find you all here at my favorite bar? That must be a sign."

It was a gamble, I knew, mixing truth with lies. It might be hard to remember fact from fiction later. Most undercover work is about waiting, letting informants come to you. I didn't want to waste time, though. Expediting the process meant taking risks, throwing out some lines and seeing if anyone took the bait. Maybe that wasn't the best metaphor given my last fishing attempt, but I had better results this time. I could almost sense the men relax, happy to at least have figured out how I fit into their lives. Another desperate person trying to pay rent in a city with a billionaire's club. They could relate, and that bought me a few minutes at least.

"It's happy hour," Dante said. "Get two."

I grinned and held up two fingers to the waitress who brought over Buds in bottles. They were cold, and I wasn't lying when I said they tasted good. It was packed at Madigan's, men and women trying to forget about the chores or relatives waiting for them at home. Not everyone looked like they were having a good time, faces red from alcohol or body heat. It was too early in the year for the owners to turn on the A/C. That sort of expense wasn't part of the operating budget. I raised my glass to Tabor, and the others followed my lead. I said something about his being my hero, and Ángel snorted.

"What a freakin' ingrate. I got you that job. If Tabor's a hero, then I'm a bona fide God's helper. You see my wings?"

One of his friends slapped him on the back of the head. "More like horns, if you ask me."

"Who asked you?"

I had hoped my comment about Tabor would spark some fond recollections, but nobody responded with their own praise. I would have settled for insults, but the men were already distracted.

"Geez, Dante, you'd think fatherhood would soften you up."

The men all raised their glasses again this time in Dante's direction. He waved off their congratulations, but his smile implied that he liked the attention. His hulking appearance grew on me even more.

"Boy or girl?" I asked.

"Baby girl," Dante said, grinning. "Due next month."

"You sure your wife wants you out on the town?"

"You kidding me?" Ángel said, answering for his friend. "She wants him out of her hair for a minute. You'd think she's dying not pregnant. What, she can't get the remote herself?"

Dante tried to hide his embarrassment by taking a long pull from his drink, and I resisted the urge to say that his doting was sweet. I doubted that was the kind of comment that would be received well. I thought of Hank trying to please his wife with doughnuts then turning sullen as the hours passed. Did he go home angry? The men were around the same age, though Dante's marital bliss had led him to pack on a few pounds. Sweat showed through his shirt and clung to his forehead. If I weren't there, maybe they'd all be talking about getting laid, but I was there and meant to make the most of my interruption. I'd also finished the first beer too quickly and was feeling bolder than I had when I walked inside. Did intoxication play nice with hallucinations? There was a worrisome crack in the ceiling that seemed to be turning into a lightning bolt.

"You picked a name yet?"

"Fleur. After my mother."

It was loud enough that I didn't think anyone would hear me if I stayed close to Dante. I said that I was sorry Tabor wouldn't get to meet the little one, and that had the desired effect. Dante's mood dimmed, and he shook his head. What followed was a longer speech than I thought any of the men were capable of delivering. A bona fide monologue on Tabor's good qualities.

"Don't listen to Ángel," he started. "He's just missing Tabor. He was our friend. Or close enough."

I had my doubts that Ángel wasn't grateful for his new revenue stream. Being a martín pescador had its peril, but it seemed like an easy way to make money otherwise. I looked over at the pawnshop owner and wasn't surprised to see him watching me. He was wily, that one, knowing a deal from a voodoo mask. He didn't look away when I made eye contact, wanting me to know that he was watching me, that I was watched. I glanced at the lightning bolt to make sure he wasn't controlling it, but it had turned back to plaster damage.

"Three languages," Dante was saying. I refocused

and nodded in admiration as Dante explained that Tabor had spoken English, Spanish, and French. "He talked about learning Chinese, too. Can you imagine?"

"That bullshit again?" Ángel said. He had taken a step forward and stood close to Dante and me. I could smell his deodorant, cinnamon and strong. "You want to hustle in this city, you got to have talents. We all have talents."

I nodded, thinking that his attitude was annoying but true. Keeping a business open, even in a lower rent area of town, took more than luck. And with leasing options in higher and higher demand, Ángel had to be clever about how he managed his shop. His brand of cleverness made me think of V.P. and his questionably legal car renting operation. I was on my second beer, but I still shivered, certain he had ratted me out to Salvatore Magrelli and wondering when my time would run out. Shark tank wasn't some flashy television show in my world.

"True enough," I said, trying to keep my attention on the conversation. If I had any hope of proving that Tabor hadn't killed himself, I would need this colorful crew. Fingers crossed, they didn't already think I was nuts. "Even so, sounds like he had a lot going for him."

"A lot going for him. Where you from, lady?"

Ángel laughed when he asked, but it was dry and humorless. I wondered if his talents extended past finance and into fists. He wasn't as imposing as Dante, but he was sturdy enough.

"Away from his family, though," Dante said. "I don't know if I could stand it."

The quietest member of the grouped punched him in the shoulder. "Shit, we won't have to. You think ours would let us go farther south than 125th Street?"

"Speak for yourself," Ángel said, slipping off his glasses and putting them back in his pocket. His face wasn't handsome, but it did look better without the thick lenses. A few pockmarks, but lively eyes that darted around the room, looking for a lone gazelle. "And he was headed back there in any case for a couple of weeks."

My heart leapt, and I tried to keep my voice nonchalant. "He was going to to Paris?"

Ángel shrugged. "That's what he told me. It's how I knew about the gig I sent you. He wanted me to take over for a little while. Must be why he sent you my way. Before."

It could have been a fabrication, Tabor's generosity. Still, if I could prove that Tabor had purchased expensive plane reservations, I could push for an investigation, a real one that didn't involve me ruining dress shoes with fish guts. It wasn't a golden ticket, but it was more than I had before walking into Madigan's. The quiet man of the group gestured at a waitress who nodded at his request for shots. I wasn't included, but I didn't mind. When I turned toward the exit, I doubt they noticed. The mass of people inside wanted more than a stranger. Most days, it was hard to say exactly what they wanted. Some vague notion of a better job, a better place to live. It was the American dream, or rather, where people went to forget about how that dream was a garden in drought, weeds more likely to grow than lettuce and rhubarb. The American dream could never feed everyone, and yet people kept coming, turning from their own countries toward the poetry of our forefathers. Those founders had sold their schemes too well.

CHAPTER 11

I took out my phone and dialed my old precinct, holding for Ellis as I made my way down Broadway. An ambulance flew past, headed toward the nearby hospital. A local bodega cat glanced up, then went back to licking her paws, unfazed by the sirens. I wondered how Penny was making out at the Dasgupta home and assumed she was being spoiled with chicken biryani or murgh makhani. Meeza's family cooked elaborate meals, and I couldn't imagine her generous mother and father denying a retired mousing cat her fair share of treats. If only all of my problems could be solved by passing them along to some doting parents.

People shuffled home from work, congesting the sidewalks. Restaurants spilled out onto the streets, their outdoor tables occupied by optimistic customers in coats and scarves. At 173rd, I took a left toward Fort Washington Avenue, getting away from the noise before Ellis picked up. If he ever picked up. Most likely he was single-handedly bringing in a batch of bad guys while I wondered if the stray cat I'd found was liking her new home.

"Detective Dekker," Ellis said finally, and I pictured him hovering over his desk, his collar undone at the end of his shift, but his posture ready for another lead. A case addict. Our class at John Jay had some smart cookies—today's forensics hotshots—but nobody worked harder than Ellis Dekker, the heir to a fortune he resented. "Who's this?" he asked, and I realized that I had been daydreaming.

"It's me. Kat," I clarified, not confident he would still recognize my voice. Our daily calls were a distant memory. "Could you verify a purchase for me?"

"This about the jumper, Kathleen?" Ellis said, and the name sounded strange. He was the only person who used Kathleen after Mom and Dad died. Most people I knew didn't even ask about my real name, much less feel comfortable using it after I introduced myself as Kat or Katya. I never missed the old me until Ellis reminded me that she had existed.

"Yes. Tabor's friends say he was planning a trip to France. Had already bought the tickets."

I passed the J. Hood Wright Park, impressed by the kids racing around the playground equipment in short sleeves, unfazed by the chilly air. A boy ran up the slide, jumping into a girl at the top before they both tumbled down with screams that sounded more hurt than happy. But the adults nearby didn't glance up from their conversations, and what did I know? I couldn't imagine being as excited as Dante about a baby. Terrified, yes, but excited? I'd reached an age when a grandparent might hassle me about a biological clock, but there was no white-haired old lady to convince me that I had maternal instincts. If I had any at all, they told me not to put a child in the kind of danger a drug cartel could create in its spare time. I wasn't likely to pass an adoption background check.

"You want verification?" Ellis asked.

After September 11th and the Homeland Security Act, passenger information was relatively easy to access for law enforcement officials, but I didn't have the airline Tabor had booked. Without a warrant, the NYPD couldn't look into anyone's credit card record, and without an official victim, a warrant was unlikely. Ellis didn't balk at my request, though, asking me to spell Campion, then putting me back on hold. He would make a good father, I thought, then flushed, glad I had called instead of stopping by his office. The beer must have gone to my head.

The wait gave me time to consider when Tabor had moved to the United States. Before the attacks on the World Trade Center, immigration reform looked like it was going to pass. It was generally well-supported on both sides of the aisle. Then xenophobia fueled a push for tougher laws. While the media focused on mosque protests, Congress passed a series of bills intended to keep foreigners out, even those fleeing the very groups we were fighting. As a New Yorker, it had felt at the time like the government was an embarrassing and dangerous suitor, calling for duels on the city's behalf when she hadn't asked anyone to fight for her honor. Quite the opposite, in fact, based on the demonstrations that swelled throughout the boroughs. "En garde!" was met with "Oh hell no," but that response went ignored. Despite the legal intimidation techniques, as a European, Tabor could have gotten access to a visa without too much of a hassle. When Ellis returned, I would ask if my super had been a full citizen, a more challenging accomplishment.

"A one-way ticket was booked on March second for Mr. Campion. Direct, JFK to Charles de Gaulle," Ellis said, coming back on the line.

I wanted to high-five myself, elated that I was on the right track. Ellis heard the eagerness in my voice and advised me not to get my hopes up. He'd worked hundreds of more cases than me, and I knew he meant well. Disappointment was cruel, but I couldn't help grinning. My mood dimmed when I noticed the George Washington Bridge in the distance. It glinted in the sunlight, as if winking, keeping secrets that might help me. Why was Tabor even up there? While walkable, people didn't bike or run like they did on the Brooklyn Bridge at the other end of the island. For starters, the GW shook, creating the sensation of falling even though there was no way to accidentally slip over the side. Even so, the landmark was my favorite part of the neighborhood, at least it had been when I could look at its beams without also seeing a broken body.

"It's not proof, but I don't see Tabor buying a thousand-dollar ticket and not planning to use it," I said, nodding even though Ellis couldn't see me. I started walking more quickly as I got close to my home, ready to kick off my dress shoes and trade khakis for sweatpants. The commute from Coney Island to Washington Heights was about as long as you could get in the city. My head ached behind my eyes from a combination of stress and alcohol. "Plus, why one-way unless he was running away from something?"

Another block, and I stood in front of my apartment building, checking to see if I had been followed, mostly out of habit. I liked that the facade of my building looked like all the others down the street. Five stories of brick, blackened with rainwater over the years. Small, rectangular windows on every side matched the oncs across the street and across the alley around back. Some of the neighbors were more entertaining than television stars, but I kept my curtains closed most of the time. Today, the front doors were propped open by moving boxes, and I wondered if someone else had died. Not the cheeriest notion, but there were a lot of older tenants clinging on to their rent-controlled units until their dying breaths. I hoped to be among their number some day, eighty-five and paying a pittance or at least a manageable amount of money each month. In a way, you could say that I was as equally ambitious as Ellis with his eye on a chief of department rank. Maybe commissioner, though he'd never admit to wanting that much power.

"He's made no other travel plans recently that I can tell." I could hear Ellis typing over the phone, looking for anything that might help me. He mumbled something about flying AirFrance.

Sometimes I took the stairs to the fifth floor because the elevator had a fickle streak, as likely to stop between floors as on them, but my feet hurt and I took my chances, pulling the metal grate closed. The machine groaned into action, and I crossed my fingers. Luck was on my side, at least for a minute, because I was deposited to the right place and walked down the hallway to my apartment. When I put my keys in the lock, I knew that my luck hadn't lasted long. It never did. The door wasn't locked, and there were telltale scratches that hadn't been there when I left. The lines started to wiggle and form shapes, but stopped when I ran my fingers over them.

"Tabor had been a U.S. citizen since 2007," Ellis said above the low buzzing in my ears.

I turned my keys to make certain, panicking as I fumbled to remove them. I wanted to be quiet, but every action echoed, announcing my arrival to whomever or whatever waited for me behind my door. Before Ellis could tell me the date of Tabor's swearing in ceremony, I was sprinting back outside.

*

The streetlights flipped on moments before Ellis climbed out of the taxi, slamming the door behind him and stalking toward me. Off-duty or he would have used an unmarked cruiser, requested backup. It had taken him twenty minutes to get from the Upper East Side to my neighborhood, giving me time to assess that I probably wasn't in immediate danger. If a boogeyman had been waiting for me, he knew that I had tried to get in and changed my mind. From down the block, I had watched the front door, checking for anyone suspicious. The only strange face was the new tenant, a young blonde woman in tight yoga pants and a ponytail who struggled with box after box. If I had been a different person—Meeza maybe or Dolly—I would have offered to help. But no, I was waiting to see if someone wanted to kill me.

"Don't ask me if I locked the door," I said, studying Ellis for signs of irritation. The last time I had called him for apartment-related help was more than five years ago when a water bug the size of a squirrel wouldn't come out from under my radiator. It was hard to imagine ever being scared of an animal after what I'd seen humans could do with a little imagination. Then again, it was a big water bug. Today, Ellis only seemed alert, emotionless, if anything.

"I wouldn't dare," he said, but he didn't look at me. He scanned the street for vehicles with tinted glass or no tags. He glanced at windows to see if anyone peered out behind the curtains. After the military acknowledged that some soldiers have more intuition than others, Ellis started training himself. When the NYPD finally offered sixth sense training, he would be first in line to teach the class, directing his staff to spot an out-of-place trash bag, stray wires, or strange shadows. In most ways, Ellis had always been a superior officer to me, but anxiety excelled as an instructor. I'd already checked and double-checked my surroundings. I could tell you the color of every awning. I knew which kid owned the rusted scooter even though he let the others borrow it. There was a "Be Happy" grocery bag stuck on a tree branch. Five buses had parked at the terminal, and four had left. My neighbor Mr. 3F and his baggy sweatpants were at the corner deli buying a lotto ticket, and when the new blonde tenant got back to the street, she'd pick up box number fourteen.

Ellis finished his own scan, then we entered the building together, repeating our separate surveillance. He asked me if the front door had been propped opened when I arrived, and I gestured toward the woman moving into the building. She smiled at Ellis, pink from her efforts or from the sight of Ellis's cheekbones, I couldn't say.

When we reached my floor, Ellis knocked on my apartment door, pounding loud enough to pique the curiosity of my nosy neighbors. Señora Amador poked her head in the hallway, and I waved at her. I hadn't seen her since the morning of Tabor's death, and she hadn't magically warmed to me in the ensuing days. She grunted in greeting, and I didn't ask for anything else. Her grandson was laughing in the background at a robot cartoon, but he turned to see if my problem was more interesting.

"You can never be too safe," I said loudly, wondering if having a handsome man in dress clothes confirmed her suspicions that I was running a cathouse out of 3B. Thankfully, if your apartment was rent-controlled, you looked the other way for anything less than signs of the apocalypse. I hadn't shown up with horsemen yet, so I was in the clear.

"Sí, you can never be too safe," Señora Amador

repeated, shutting the door. I suspected her eyeball was glued to the peephole, but there was nothing I could do about her spying. Ellis turned the knob and stepped inside my place. Since I lived in a studio, all rooms except for the bathroom could be seen in a glance. There were few places to hide besides the small closet, which I yanked open, relieved to find it empty except for shoes and a couple of wigs. I kept most of my costume supplies at the office where they would be safer. I expected a ransacking, strewn clothes and books at the very least. Instead, the space was exactly as I left it, right down to the cereal bowl in the sink, except for one small addition: a brunette pageboy on a mannequin head propped up on my bed.

Most of my mannequin heads had been slashed while working a previous case, but this one was brand new with demur, half-smiling lips and overdone blue eyes. She stared vacantly at the opposite wall. I forced myself to walk toward her, bending down face-to-face with the doll. "Intruder," I hissed.

Ellis checked the bathroom, then watched me run my hands along the fake hair. It was high-quality and stylishly cut, but not human and decidedly not one of mine. My wigmaker was the best on the Atlantic seaboard, and this wasn't up to her standards. The scalp part was too even, too pale. The brown dye too uniform, too manufactured. Somebody had left me a gift, but I didn't think it was meant as a sign of affection.

"We can dust for prints," Ellis said, assuming by my reaction that the head hadn't been there before. He rested his left hand near his hip, telling me that he carried his gun. I considered asking him to shoot the smile off of my visitor, but that wouldn't solve my problems. And someone might actually call my landlord about gunshots.

"No need," I said, clearing my throat when the words came out in a dry croak. "It's a warning."

"Damn creepy," Ellis said after a pause.

"Damn creepy," I agreed, though I'd gotten used to the sight of fake faces and hair. When Ellis wrapped his arms around me from behind and pulled me toward him, I leaned into him, glad I didn't have to explain that I had pissed off the leader of a drug cartel or that he wanted me to join him or wanted me dead. Six of one, a half dozen of the other—it was all the same to Salvatore Magrelli. That Ellis's daredevil brother had gotten involved in the operation made the situation more strained, but we'd never discussed it after one brutal argument in which Ellis accused me of lying. It still hurt, his lack of faith in me, but his lips at my temple felt nice, and I let him hold me. When I circled toward him, he stared over my shoulder. The faint smell of sweat calmed me, my pulse returning to normal. His pale blue eyes made him look like a prophet, but maybe he'd been a wizard all along.

Ellis sighed, and I knew the moment had passed. I wrapped my arms around myself while he pulled away. He tugged on leather gloves and lifted the head off my bed. The wig slipped off, revealing a message in big, handwritten letters: Time's up. —S.

CHAPTER 12

Sleeping in Ellis's guest bedroom had sounded like a good idea, but when I heard the coffee pot gurgle the next morning, my stomach flipped. I should have gone to The Pink Parrot instead. Not that it wasn't thoughtful of Ellis to invite me, but after a restless night, I knew that I'd come to a decision he wouldn't like. He may have uttered the words "witness protection" on the way home, and I may have ignored him. My guilt increased when I saw the bag of fresh bagels from H & H. He must have made a special run while I was still dreaming about masks and mannequin heads coming alive in order to warn me about slippery sidewalk conditions. I didn't know what the last part meant exactly, but I planned to watch my step all the same.

Ellis's West Village two-bedroom apartment was the kind Iowa kids imagine before they move to New York City and realize that a thousand dollars a month gets you a windowless closet in a place with a couple of roommates. The mice come free of charge, though, if you're into disease-carrying pets. I stood at his bay window and studied 9th Street while I sipped my coffee. A woman walked her be-sweatered dachshund, stopping in front of a flower shop because the owner had set out a water dish shaped like a giant tulip. People had dogs in my neighborhood, too, but they were usually pit bulls and preferred to go au naturel. Call me unimaginative, but I couldn't picture a dog named Slayer in argyle.

"I have some numbers for you," Ellis said. Fresh from a shower and a shave, he looked younger, more like my old friend than a decorated detective. His suit told me that he had work and didn't have time for me to pretend I hadn't received a summons from a dangerous criminal. Still, I'd hoped to process my first jolt of caffeine before this conversation. I sat down across from him, surprising myself when I held eye contact. His tortoiseshell frames made him look a little like a college professor, but there was definitely something cop-like about his intensity. If he could turn off that part of his personality, he'd never tried. Nobody was handing him an undercover assignment unless they wanted him to get killed. He didn't exactly blend into his surroundings. My inverse, and I kept waiting for our magnets to flip over, to feel pulled together rather than apart.

"That's sweet, but I'm not looking for love right now," I said, responding to myself as much as to his offer of numbers.

"Kathleen."

I winked at him, feeling myself slip into old, teasing patterns. I hated to admit this flaw in my character, but it felt good to irritate him. Delivery of The *New York Times* was one of his charmingly old-school habits that I liked, and I pulled the front section toward me. Possible signals from Flight 370's detector provided new hope for the lost plane. I scanned the article for more information, then flipped past the U.S. sending warships to Japan because of concerns over North Korea. With such bleak stories, the novelty of having ink and paper under my fingers quickly lost its appeal. Before I could switch to the Arts section for movie reviews, an op-ed on immigration caught my eye. The gist was that the president tried, but didn't do enough, a response I could only assume was inspired by the multi-city demonstrations calling for Congress to pass some sort of reform. That didn't seem likely since fear-mongering was the hot, new trend in politics. Would you like some racism with that t-shirt?

"Did you hear about yesterday's protests?" I asked, glancing up at Ellis to find him still staring at me. He didn't answer right away, but when I didn't flinch, he nodded. We would return to the question of my safety, but he could be sidetracked for a minute or two. I knew this particular bargain all too well.

"Less aggressive deporting. Passing a bill with more paths to citizenship," Ellis said, summarizing what the protestors seemed to want, at least the ones in the middle of the conversation rather than the fringes.

"What's the name of the representative who's ring-leading the opposition? The one upstate?"

Ellis pushed back from the table to pour his coffee into a traveling thermos. Stalling, I assumed, while trying to decide if convincing me to hide was a winnable fight. I hadn't touched the phone numbers he'd placed between us like an ultimatum. I'd decided there had to be another option than the unpalatable ones laid out in front of me. If I could offer Salvatore something in return for being left alone, I wouldn't have to die or hide. I didn't exactly know what sort of information I had—or could find—that might buy my freedom, but something flitted in the periphery of my consciousness. A shadow of a shadow of an idea. Unfortunately, I wasn't sure when my time would run out. And if Salvatore found me before I had any concrete evidence for the NYPD, Tabor's killer would walk free. No pressure or anything.

"I doubt a senator is offing building supers, if that's what you're thinking. He wants campaign donations, not investigations," Ellis said.

"Not him, no, but his speeches have been creating a frenzy. Those people are taking your jobs! Those people will murder you in your sleep! Those people have laser eyeballs and chainsaw hands!" Ellis didn't laugh, and I didn't blame him. "He must have devotees is all I'm saying."

"The numbers," Ellis said, sliding the paper closer to me and nodding his approval when I pocketed it. He pulled on his jacket, freshly dry-cleaned, I knew. For all his "of the people" attitude, some wealthy habits died hard, and coffee-stained, wrinkled clothes were a precinct fashion statement that made him balk. "Tabor Campion, may he rest in peace, was small time. Beneath notice."

I cringed at Ellis's characterization, feeling guilty again that I hadn't really noticed Tabor before he died. I'd thanked him for repairs, been grateful for the new doors. But in the three years I'd lived in his building, I'd never asked about his family, his hobbies. How could I argue with Ellis's rough logic when my indifference proved his point? I wasn't indifferent now, though. Didn't that count for something?

"Did you check on callers? Did anyone see him on the bridge before he fell?" I asked.

"No reports. In the dark, though, it would be hard to see anything beyond your headlights."

Ellis and I walked out of the building together, pausing when we got to the corner. Spring had decided to arrive, and my coat was too warm. I slipped it off, holding Ellis's arm for balance, or so I told myself. Every time we were together, I found some excuse to touch him. This time, he pulled me close, and I had to lean my head back to look at him.

"It's easier not to feel anything, I get that. But you're starting to thaw, and I like it."

Ellis paused, glancing around to make sure nobody was listening to his speech. I glanced around, too, knowing that he was right. For the first couple of years after my undercover assignment, I'd been numb, like my body was releasing its own sedatives. And it was tempting to stay in that hollow state, not caring about anyone, least of all myself. But I could smell Ellis's soap, and it made my insides flutter in something that felt like anticipation. I wasn't empty inside, even if I wanted to be.

"Going after Magrelli now that he's on to you would be a mistake. Maybe a fatal one," he continued.

"I agree," I said quietly, and relief flooded Ellis's

face. He even smiled a little as he stepped away and raised his arm to hail a cab. I smiled, too, and turned toward the subway. A couple of blocks away, I looked back to see that Ellis was gone, then took out the list of numbers. Three in neat, handwritten rows. Three new lives waiting for me like the prizes in a gameshow. Choose a door, win a one-way trip to Sacramento. Before I could lose my nerve, I crumpled the paper and threw it in the trash.

*

If awards were given for water pressure, Dolly's shower would win a blue ribbon. He would also place for Best Bath Products, and I lathered up with something called The Heavenly Glow. I wasn't lying to Ellis when I agreed that going after Magrelli was a mistake. I had been a reluctant vigilante in the first place, and I didn't need anyone to remind me of the man's cruelty. What was that saying about the path of least resistance? Nice work if you could get it. My plan was flawless in its simplicity: I would ignore the problem for as long as possible. Salvatore had more pressing matters than little ol' me. And while he was setting up new farms in Venezuela or knocking off rival cartel leaders, I would dream up a way to get back into his good graces and be left the hell alone.

Dolly was meditating in his dressing room, or at least that's what he called listening to Beyoncé and stretching. It was a rehearsal day, so he wasn't in costume. I could hear him singing along to Spotify when I turned the water off and stepped onto his pink bathmat. Looking in the full-length mirror, I slid my hand over the four-inch scar on my inner thigh. The ER doctor had done a nice job with the stitches, and the line was impressively straight. It was bright white in comparison to my tawny skin and puckered like a topographical map. The night Salvatore cut me, I put in my first request to be extracted, assuming my wishes would be honored. "More evidence," my handler insisted instead. I hadn't softened toward that particular mantra.

"Hey, Dolly, I need something that says I work for a fishing company," I said, raising my voice so that he could hear me.

"I got you covered, honey."

No hallucinations so far that day, and my ankle looked normal. I peeled off the Rainbow Brite band-aid and pulled on a robe worthy of The Carlyle Hotel, then opened the door to find Dolly dancing to "Single Ladies" and removing a black, sequined skirt from his closet.

"A wardrobe essential. The kind of piece that will transition from the office to the club," I said as he handed over the shiny garment along with a thoughtfully demur cardigan.

"It won't show the blood and guts."

I nodded at his wisdom and wiggled into the items. Dolly held out a familiar blonde wig that I thought of as Kiki, and I took it so that I could feel closer to the brazen character for a moment. There was no point in disguises anymore, though. I'd spent years fooling my-self that the Magrellis and his charming in-laws, the Costas, couldn't find me if I wasn't, well, me. While not resigned to my fate and whatever shallow grave it might include, I wasn't trying to fool myself anymore. Prog-ress was for the ones who got up in the morning. And I was up, wearing a skirt that dared strangers to look at me.

"No Kiki today," I said, handing back the wig. "I can't imagine she'd let her manicure anywhere near a tuna anyway."

I hid my hands behind my back before Dolly could inspect my nails. His were intricately painted with a night sky, and the symbols couldn't have been more appropriate. He was the star of The Pink Parrot. Mamma Burstyn might like me, or at least my access to criminal records, but I knew that I was allowed to use this place as a second home for one handsome, five-shows-a-week reason only: Darío "Dolly" Rodriquez.

I sat down at his vanity mirror as I pulled on my black flats, grateful at least that the color was appro-priate if not the style. Dolly had taped up an array of signed headshots from fans, mostly celebrities, but one politician I'd noticed before.

"Isn't Senator Jackelson retired now?"

"Leaders with power. Once they have it, they don't let go until the good Lord says Boo. Even then, some of them are clutching riders in their fur-lined cas-kets."

I thought of politicians making the news lately,

stirring up their donation pots with incendiary rhetoric about Arab immigrants. The catchphrase "patrols for the people" circled in my mind, and I didn't pretend to understand all the subtle insults hidden in those four words. A militant attitude appealed to a certain contingent that worried about their children's safety, thought keeping people out of the country would keep bullets out of their sons and daughters. With no kids of my own, I couldn't understand their fear, and wasn't that the problem? For politics and PIs alike? How do we understand people we've never met before? Motives are slippery, hard to hold in our hands unless they belong to us.

These thoughts nagged at me even though Ellis was right when he said that Tabor wasn't the kind of person to grab the attention of a television-ready senator. The problem with my list of suspects so far was that everyone seemed to genuinely like Tabor. Ángel benefitted financially from his friend's demise, but if he was telling the truth, Tabor had already handed over some of his business. He'd certainly handed over a few masks. Maybe Tabor had planned to stay in Paris, explaining the one-way ticket. There were definitely folks who would resent that Tabor had been helping immigrants find work. As far as I could tell, his role as a martín pescador wasn't a well-kept secret. Everyone in my apartment building knew, apparently. Tabor's friends might as well have called him Robin Hood.

"Who hates Robin Hood?" I said aloud.

"The Sheriff of Nottingham. Mad because he can't

pull off tights, I always figured," Dolly said. My non se-
quiturs never threw him. In addition to choreograph-
ing all his own numbers and baking a mean zucchini
bread, his talents may have extended to mind-reading.

I used Dolly's laptop to Google the protests, un-
surprised that there was another one in a couple of days.
I thought about skipping my shift at The Blue Lagoon to
research any naysayers to the demonstrations, but I still
hadn't managed to find anyone who'd actually been offered a job through Tabor's unusual headhunting skills.
That seemed like my first priority. And if the tourist
company's office was as far away from a compromised
apartment as a lady could get on the A train? Well, that
was definitely a bonus.

CHAPTER 13

The warm weather brought in more potential customers, and I spent the morning talking up the sunset cruise. Not having a bar on board deflected a lot of casual interest, but a few folks were placated by our BYOB policy. I made a few jokes about being flung out to sea and left for dead so that I felt better about selling tickets. Hey, I'd warned them, hadn't I? Everyone knows that humor is mostly about telling the truth. I got a break around noon and flipped over the "Closed for Lunch" sign before walking over to The Blue Lagoon. Captain Barrera was finishing his mechanical inspections as Hank detangled nets.

"Any news?" I called to the expectant father.

"She's stubborn, you can bet on that. I love her already."

Hank hadn't yet begun his daily transformation from doting husband and almost dad to half-lit jerk. I grinned at his remark and held my hand up against the sun's glare. I hadn't noticed how the boat's paint sparkled before, the whole length a giant lure. I stepped on board, aware that Dolly's skirt wasn't exactly made for clambering, but determined to make at least some conversation about my murdered super before chatting up tourists became my permanent job and Meeza took over my PI business. Or, you know, I was ended by a drug lord.

"Is your wife taking a full three months off?"

"Already worried about money," Hank said, but his tone suggested sympathizing rather than cajoling.

"I'm no psychic, but Ángel doesn't seem to have the same connections as Tabor."

Hank nodded, sawing his knife over a particularly stubborn knot, grunting at the effort. "I'll tell you if I hear anything."

"Sí, señorita, we're like a family here." Captain Barrera joined us on the deck, looking at me only long enough to raise his eyebrows at my wardrobe. A few of the other workers on board noticed as well, snickering into their palms. I resisted the urge to pull down the hem of my skirt and draw further attention to the sequins.

"Did Tabor help anyone else here?"

It was the wrong question, and Captain Barrera busied himself with checking the navigational system even though I'd seen him do that already. Hank shrugged, noncommittally, holding his knife between his teeth as he ripped apart a small section of the net. Any more holes, and I doubted the material would hold anything smaller than a whale. I tried to make eye contact with the other men on board, even finger waving at the one with a long braid down his back. If Dolly had dressed me like a flirt, I might as well act like one. I approached the young man, holding out my hand for him to shake when I got close enough. His grip was limp and hesitant, as if he were afraid of me. That ritual complete, he turned his attention back to the crates he was repairing, nailing a broken piece back together.

"You have a talent for that," I said, starting with flattery. He mumbled something in Spanish under his breath, and I switched languages. He wasn't impressed, shaking his head in disgust and asking why if I spoke English I worked for a fishing company. A fair question, and, improvising, I said that I hoped to enroll in classes soon. "Accounting," I said.

When he still didn't respond with any sentences directed toward me, I introduced myself, getting a curt "John" No Last Name in response. He was as much a John No Last Name as I was a Kay Moroz. I tried batting my eyelashes when I responded, "Pleased to meet you," but batting eyelashes wasn't my best skill. He probably thought I had a bug in my eye. It didn't seem like I would make any more progress, so I climbed back onto the dock to find some food.

My options near the office were of the hotdog and funnel cake variety, so I resigned myself to fried foods and stopped for pickles. The walls of the trailer were decorated with colorful advertisements for the aquarium. Hurricane Sandy hadn't brought much good news, but I'd read that every animal had survived the storm, the attraction's marine biologists having a much higher success rate than Noah.

Fried pickles and a giant Diet Coke in tow, I headed back to the office without a plan. Maybe if my shift ended early enough, I could try to meet up with Tabor's friends again, but two visits to Madigan's pub might be suspicious. Or in that skirt, Ángel might think I was trying to seduce him, the worse of the two possibilities. His shop gave me the heebie-jeebies; I didn't want to find out if he slept in a Scrooge-style canopy bed or on a bed of nails. Neither would surprise me.

"Yoohoo," someone called as I tried to get out my keys while balancing my well-balanced lunch in the crook of my elbow. "Can I help you, pickle lady?"

I looked toward the trilling voice to find the woman I had seen before handing out brochures for her own business. She was dressed in head-to-toe lime green, her breasts defying gravity in some sort of halter top-corset hybrid that resembled a torture device. It was hard to miss the pink lipstick on her teeth because she was smiling broadly, arms open to save me from a culinary disaster.

"Thanks," I said as she took the soda and followed me inside.

"It's my lunch break, too, but I prefer the liquid variety." The woman pulled out a flask and took a long pull, then held it out to me. I shook my head, and she slid the metal container back into her pocket. "Suit yourself. If you can handle these clowns without a little rum, more power to you."

A young couple tried to enter the shop, and I mumbled something about coming back in five minutes.

"Closed!" the woman shouted, startling me as I tried to pull two chairs out from behind the desk. "Shoo, scram!"

The couple fled, and I couldn't blame them. I doubted they'd be back to talk about reservations, but I didn't mind that much. Probably safer for them anyway, I rationalized. They hadn't looked like strong swimmers.

"I'm Esmeralda, by the way. I own the parasailing booth two doors down. I haven't seen you." She'd waved at me before, but I wasn't surprised that she didn't recognized me. She took a couple of pickles, then passed them over. Grease made the container soggy, and I slid some napkins underneath. I'd ruined enough of Dolly's clothes for one friendship.

"I'm new," I said, wondering if Esmeralda spied on everyone and if that might be useful. She took another healthy swig from the flask, and I couldn't help but ask if she drove the boat herself.

"Who me? Hell no. I reel them in. One of the boys takes them out."

I pictured a flotilla of tanned young men in lime green speedos responding "Yes, Miss Esmeralda" to her commands.

"It must be slow this time of year," I said, trying to forget the image.

"We stay busy enough March through October. You wouldn't catch me in that water this early, but people are stupid. You takin' over for Leesa?"

I couldn't place Esmeralda's accent beyond loud, but if she wasn't a New Yorker, she'd adopted the attitude with a side of confidence I could only envy. I was born and bred here, but could only manage sassy on my very best days.

"For a few months, then it's back to knocking on doors."

"You ever drive a boat?"

I shook my head, grateful for her offer none-theless. Dolly's skirt must have been bringing me luck because Esmeralda's helpfulness didn't end there. She brought up Tabor without so much as a hint.

"That handsome Frenchman get you this gig? The one with the eyes and the ass?" She fanned herself, and I noticed that her long nails were decorated with mermaid tails. She could have been a Coney Island am-bassador, and I was sorry to dim her spirits by telling her that Tabor was dead. "No shit! A jumper? Him? I never would have guessed."

She paused and crossed herself, taking another pickle from my lunch. The news had finally made her quiet, and I mentioned that Ángel had gotten me the job, hoping for some gossip.

"Ángel? That his real name? Never heard of him. He cute, too? It's hard to fantasize about a dead guy, though I guess I could try."

"Tabor was here a lot?"

"Every other week or so, he stopped by. Not al-ways for business. I think he liked hanging out with the crew. They're alright, Hank and Leesa. Barrera, too."

"Pardon the question, but how'd you know Tabor got jobs for people?"

Esmeralda looked me up and down, a new skep-ticism darkening her eyes.

"You worried I'm gonna turn you in? I look like a snitch to you?"

To prove her point, she adjusted her breasts and straightened the ten or so bangles on her wrist to make herself into a human wind chime. She rang like a video game sound effect, the hero opening a portal.

"Sorry," I said, holding out the last pickle as a peace offering. "I'm paranoid is all."

Esmeralda sniffed, then patted my thigh. "Sure, sugar. I get it. You got a job most would die for. Most of these shit-paying gigs? Not worth the hemorrhoids and early death. Tabor did okay by folks, but there are limits. Making shoes in some windowless basement. Cleaning rat guts out of apartments used to belong to hoarders. This city, you hear me? This may be a city for hiding, but if you're hiding, it's the shadows or nothing."

Somehow, I knew all this before she told me. That below the poor in the city, there were the hopeless, people who'd come for a better way of life and found themselves in a hell they couldn't escape. From what I could tell, Tabor was one of the good guys, at least in comparison to other headhunters, the ones unconcerned about four men sharing a single mattress on the floor of a flophouse. I'd heard the stories but had been too worried about keeping my own neck on my own shoulders to care. Even now, as I was feeling sorry for the faceless people Esmeralda meant, I was thinking about my own version of hiding, wondering how to escape my past.

"So you're saying I should learn how to drive a boat," I said, not bothering to pretend her honesty didn't give me shivers.

"Drive a boat, give massages, change diapers. All I'm saying is, that skirt won't get you desk jobs forever."

Chapter 14

After the afternoon cruise set off for adventures unknown, I packed my bag and locked up the office. The lights from The Wonder Wheel caught my eye as I made my way to the train, and I paused to consider who did the repairs on the giant Ferris Wheel. In general, the more dangerous the job, the higher the union wage. I'd heard rumors about window washers that made me question why I sent in my PI licensing fee every year. But there was another option, of course. Give the dangerous jobs to people who can't complain about them without risking deportation. To be honest, Esmeralda had shamed me a bit. I knew a few talking points from the news about undocumented workers, but I thought of them toiling on tobacco farms in Alabama, not cleaning porta-potties at my favorite amusement park. A "them" problem, not an "us" problem.

I knew one grandparent had immigrated during the 1940s, but he'd died before I could ask about the transition. The rest of my lineage was a bit hazy, and my parents weren't that interested. As a teenager, trying to figure out whether I was more of a CBGBs or a Limelight gal had been my primary focus. Now I wondered what exact combination had led to a woman who could blend into a variety of crowds, who could disappear in plain sight. Of course, I was doing a pretty poor job of disappearing that afternoon if wigmaker extraordinaire Vondya Vasiliev could recognize me from across the street. She usually reserved her attention for more important clients than me, but she was hollering my name and waving her shopping bags in my direction.

Her enthusiasm made me expect a warm welcome, but this lady was volatile if nothing else. She started berating me as soon as I was close enough for a lecture. She handed me her groceries and marched toward her shop, knowing I would follow, even though her Brighton Beach neighborhood was a ten-minute walk away. I shuffled after her, ignoring the ache in my feet from working all day. I was happy that the expression I'd glimpsed on Vondya the day before was well-hid, and I was only partially embarrassed by my accidental spying. The teenage prom hairdo was nowhere in sight now. She kept her black bob tucked under a brightly colored silk scarf.

"Like a boy," she was saying, shaking her keys in the air. "You think you get a huzband with Army hair?"

"The skirt's nice, though, Vondya. Isn't it?" I knew I shouldn't tease her mid-harangue, but I couldn't resist. Once she got up to full speed, there was something charming about her well-intended abuse. If nothing else, you had to be impressed by her volume. She never ran out of insults. I'd been keeping my hair short for years to occasionally pass as a teenager named Keith. I figured sharing that tidbit with the woman yelling at me wouldn't help matters, though. "It's growing out a little,"

I said to placate her.

"Bez truda, ne vitashish i ribku iz pruda." Vondya paused to mumble to herself, then whirled around to face me. "Youth isn't much. Gone before you know it."

She let that sink in, then whirled back toward her destination. Vondya always moved at a brisk pace, and we were climbing the stairs to her second-story space before I had time to wonder how she'd roped me into checking out her latest wares. I knew I couldn't afford her prices, especially since I'd been neglecting my other open cases to focus on Tabor. It wasn't unexpected to see Dolly sitting on Vondya's couch, flipping through catalogues. He treated her shop like his second home, an open tab from The Pink Parrot making the place even cozier. In fact, this is where I'd met my most famous friend. He'd talked me out of a chin-length brunette and into a red bob. That hairdo had once spent an unpleasant few days in an NYPD evidence bag, but Vondya had managed to untangle the mess—the one related to coiffures at least. I remained her work in progress.

"Hiya, kitty kat," Dolly said, standing to take the bags from me. I couldn't tell what Vondya's staples were, but they were as heavy as bricks. I was surprised the paper sacks hadn't busted onto Neptune Avenue, but grateful nonetheless. Somehow, that would have been my fault, according to Vondya, and I didn't fancy chasing oranges through the layer of litter and general funk that deserved its own PSA.

"Vodka," Dolly mouthed at me, fake-straining under the weight. He was Vondya's best customer and could tease without fear of reproach. I aspired to making quips without being berated.

"Kitty kat? Cats. Drowned ones." Vondya laughed at her own joke. She patted me on the cheek, then changed her mind at that mild greeting, squeezing me in her fleshy arms. The hug felt nice, and I squeezed her back.

"Now, why were you coming to see me?" She held me away from her, rubbing a piece of my hair between her fingers.

I was confused for a second—thinking she had caught me at her window yesterday— then I realized Vondya assumed that my presence on the Atlantic seaboard must be because of her. I didn't have the heart to correct her. For all her bluster, I knew she was the sensitive type, Russian poetry running in her veins and all that. She'd once recited a half hour's worth of Anna Akhmatova during a fitting, only bothering to translate a few key lines. "You're sad for her?" Vondya took the bobby pins out of her mouth to consider how to convey the poet's meaning in English. "But better than that. Something like you're so sad for her?" she continued, flapping her hands in frustration. It had seemed important to her that I understand. "She doesn't much matter. / But I never say no in my heart. / Because...No not because. I don't know. Because she died for turning around."

"That's lovely, Vondya," I had said, but her face had clouded.

"Iz in Russian, yes. Very beautiful."

For all her frustrations with me, Vondya was patient when my mind wandered, which it did more often than I liked. When I forgot about our previous poetry lesson, I found her staring, waiting for a response to her question.

"I never pass up a chance to see you," I finally said, but she snorted and moved toward her back room where she kept supplies and also—I'd come to suspect—lived. That space was off-limits, a non-negotiable policy.

"You still got gun in purse?" she called.

"No, ma'am," I said, expecting her to approve. Dolly shook his head with a wry smile, knowing that was the wrong answer even if it was the truth. I paused to consider if Ellis might return my confiscated weapon, seeing as how a drug trafficker probably wanted to kill me. But I wasn't thinking about that today, was I? There wasn't much time, but maybe there was enough to save my skin.

Vondya emerged carrying three glasses and a bottle of Stoli. She pointed at me with the vodka then suggested that I had a hunted look and needed to protect myself.

"Whatever works," she said, setting down the glasses and filling them up. "You don't come to Coney Island for nothing."

If Vondya thought about me at all when I wasn't in her shop, it was to pray that I met a nice man and got married. She'd never spoken about children of her own, but she'd mentioned me having kids as if procreating were inevitable. And for most people, I suppose it still was the path, however much the term "brood mare" made me see red, no jellyfish stings required. When I signed up for an undercover assignment, I'd just wanted to escape the reality of being an orphan at twenty-two. I didn't think much about sacrificing a normal life. There had been a five-minute lesson on the mental health dangers of the job, complete with a dated PowerPoint and a handout. Something about sky-high suicide rates and drug addiction. But the words were more like those rapid-fire warnings at the end of prescription commercials. May cause difficulty urinating or night terrors.

I was moving forward, not looking back, I silently reminded myself. *But she died for turning around.* I'd known the poem was about Lot's wife even though I hadn't heard the story in years. Some days, I thought my fate might be pretty bleak, but at least it didn't involve dissolving into a pillar of salt. I took a sip from the glass, grimacing as the vodka slid down my throat.

"When did you move here, Vondya? Did you come straight to Brighton Beach?"

"Everyone from Moscow came here. We could read the signs. Get borscht. And wind from this ocean? Iz nothing."

"How old were you?" Dolly asked, and Vondya frowned, draining her glass to the bottom and refilling it. I didn't think that she was going to answer and shifted uncomfortably while Dolly waited patiently.

"A girl. Fifteen. Sixteen. What am I saying? I know exact age. Fifteen. It was a long trip, you see. We lost good women along the way. Good men, too."

I took another drink, not minding the burn as much this time. Even though my glass wasn't empty, Vondya refilled it before sitting down on the couch and crossing her legs at the ankles. She clasped her hands in her lap and looked up at Dolly and me.

"What else you want to know?"

She let herself fall back into memories she clearly hadn't unearthed in a while. She talked about leaving behind her sweetheart. How an aunt had refused to make the trip, and they'd never heard from her again. She recalled one night on the ship when they'd stayed up singing because it was too cold to sleep. A girl, "a new friend" she called her, was dead by the next morning.

"And what about when you got here. Was it difficult to find work?"

Vondya shook her head.

"No, plenty work. Hard work. My fingers still hurt."

I'd noticed her arthritis before but had assumed it was a natural part of aging. Dolly took Vondya's hand and rubbed the knuckles gently as she finished her answer, explaining that getting a job was easy, but everybody worked twelve, thirteen hours a day and still struggled to pay rent. Everybody shared beds, one rising to work when the other came home.

"A place like this," Vondya gestured with her free hand. "But ten people, not just one old lady."

"You're not old," I said, and Vondya smiled then

glared at me, changing her mind about the compliment. I should have known that my pandering wouldn't be welcome, but I couldn't help picturing her in the wig of ringlets I'd caught her trying on for size.

"How'd you build this empire, then?" Dolly said.

"Empire," Vondya repeated, laughing and leaning toward him. She refilled our glasses again and we toasted. The room started to spin slightly, but I tried to pay attention, knowing her answer might be important.

"The answer's always the same," she said, shrugging as if she wasn't revealing the secret to success. "Somebody helped me. We do nothing—nichego—alone."

CHAPTER 15

If we had dinner, I didn't remember it. There may have been some leftover baklava lying around. And the potato chip crumbs on my fingers meant that someone had gone out for snacks. Had I stumbled down Brighton Beach Avenue or had Dolly? My head had swollen to the size of a basketball, I was almost certain, and when I touched my forehead, I winced. The throbbing wanted to eject my eyeballs, and I squeezed them shut, believing that another half hour on the couch would save me. The sound of aspirin being shaken tempted me, but I resisted for as long as possible.

"It's eight thirty, kitten," said Dolly in his softest voice. It still sounded as if he were using a megaphone, and I groaned. "Your shift starts soon."

I sat up gingerly, taking the aspirin and water glass held out to me, too sick even to be irritated that Dolly looked ready for a photo shoot. His winter skin was paler than usually, but there was still a glow underneath, a side effect of being Dominican or Floridian, I wasn't sure. The burn scar on his temple was partly hidden by the clever haircut he'd designed and popularized himself, a sort of drooping faux hawk that managed to look more fox than rooster. I knew several of his co-stars had request the same look. Dolly didn't seem to mind the copycats. He was generous that way, and I tried to remember that I liked him even though I'd rather he left me to die that particular morning.

I drank the water, smelling alcohol on my own breath and trying not to gag. If I missed work at The Blue Lagoon, I would be replaced without a second thought. In fact, Hank and Captain Barrera were probably wondering why I hadn't quit already. But I still hadn't talked to anyone who might have been helped by Tabor except perhaps John No Last Name, and he hadn't been exactly forthcoming. A large part of me didn't care and only wanted to go back to sleep, but the nagging, truth-seeking part wouldn't let me lay back down. I'd slept in my clothes, and the sequins had smashed into my skin, leaving scales in their wake. Even so, the skirt would have to suffice. It was a long train ride back to my apartment, and there was some reason I didn't want to go there anyway. My mind worked slowly to remember. Oh yeah. Death threats. "Time's up. —S."

Not quite, I said to myself, praying that was true. A few days more, and that idea turning in the cloudiest part of my brain might make itself known. Vondya hurried into the room, grumbling at the sight of me, but holding out a lunch bag all the same. I hugged her spontaneously, regretting the sudden movement when a sharp pain zigzagged down my forehead. My reward was a small pat from my wigmaker who recommended the red pageboy she'd made for me.

"To distract from the rest," she said, shooing me out the door. There was nothing I wanted more than to don the hair in question and pretend to be socialite Kennedy S. Vanders for the day, but it was Kay Moroz who was due at The Blue Lagoon. I stopped for gum and deodorant on the way there—like a professional— and was unlocking the office door with two minutes to spare when Esmeralda appeared like a fairy godmother. Which is to say, she was wearing head-to-toe pink and holding out a cup of coffee.

"You're a saint," I mumbled.

"Sure enough. Hope he was worth it," she said, sauntering back over to her shop. Today, she had a tan, tattooed, and shirtless young man passing out fly-ers for her parasail special: 2 for 1 Sundays. The gim-mick worked because there were already a few teenag-ers looking at the price list. Maybe half an hour flying behind a boat would make my head shrink down to a normal size. Then again, maybe it would explode, and I wasn't willing to risk it. Between Esmeralda's caffeine and Vondya's PB&J, I might achieve human by early evening.

Hank whistled when he came into the office twen-ty minutes later. I was checking the company emails, not technically part of my job description, but hopeful-ly seen as "self-starting" rather than "nosy." He guffawed at my weak attempt at a greeting when he picked up the mail. My hangover couldn't have been more obvious, but his response implied I wouldn't get fired, at least not on the spot.

"You wanna go back out today?" he said, pleased with himself. "The fish might get high off your smell, jump right into the boat. An easy haul."

One mystery solved at least: Speed Stick can't compete when the odor seeps out of your pores. I clicked glumly at the keyboard and waited for Hank to leave me alone. He took his time weighing the options, then finally laughed, one loud bark.

"There's a shower on board," he said, indicating that I should follow him. "The shop can wait thirty minutes."

His nonchalant attitude amazed me. Then again, if anyone could sympathize with a hangover, it was surely Hank. He didn't talk much as we walked over, and I kicked myself over a wasted opportunity to un-cover dirt. All the same, the only conversation topics I could manage related to business operations, and he was cagey. If anyone had given me a gentle nudge off the side of The Blue Lagoon, Hank was the most likely culprit. But what possible motivation did he have for pushing me? Or for then saving me? Sure, I'd asked a few questions, but no more than your average new em-ployee. Dolly's muscle cramp theory made more sense. I wasn't exactly in deep-sea fishing shape, whatever that entailed. The other passengers hadn't thought any-thing odd happened—except for me spouting Revela-tions-worthy fire and brimstone. I was happy that the hallucinations seemed to have subsided.

The men on the boat chuckled when they saw me, Captain Barrera most of all. But then he found me a towel that only smelled faintly of fish before leaving me to the below-deck quarters. The crates were empty but blood-stained, and I covered my mouth. At least the rubber floor mats had been hosed off, and the tiny shower was blessedly clean. The water was warm at first, and I stayed under until it wasn't. I emerged feeling like I might actually survive the day and tugged on a pair of coveralls I'd found. They were a couple sizes too big, but if I rolled up the sleeves, I could pass for a dishwasher repairman. Or an escaped convict.

I emerged into bright sunshine, shielding my eyes and thanking Hank and Captain Barrera.

"We all have those days," said John No Last Name, handing me a bottled water. His long hair was pushed back with a bandana, and I wondered if he'd considered selling it. The locks were thick and inky. He could easily make a few hundred dollars. When John chuckled at my silence, I realized that I'd passed some sort of test. Friendliness hadn't gotten me very far, but a headache brought on by questionable judgement? Access granted.

"Days you get fired," I said, doing my best to grin in a way that didn't look like a grimace.

John waved off my concern. "This is a good place," he said. "Not like the others."

I walked with him as he returned to his breakfast, some sort of fast food sandwich that turned my stomach. He finished it off in a bite, and I let out the breath I had been holding, relieved that I could ask a few questions without fear of vomiting on a potential contact. I needed John No Last Name.

"You're new," he said.

"And temporary. So if you hear of anything…"

John lowered his head. "I hear nothing."

"I understand. Tabor?" I asked, trying to match his reticent tone, but still hoping to gain some information. Whatever suspicions he'd had about me the day before had vanished, and he was downright chatty as he rambled about Tabor. It was a touching eulogy, especially for a man being paid to help, and I said as much.

"He never turned anyone away. He'd find a way. For all my friends. John B. got a gig washing dishes in a pizza shop on Ludlow. And John C. works overnight at a motel nearby."

"You're John A., I assume."

He dropped his voice to a whisper, and I leaned closer. He said his real name was Diego and that in Ecuador he'd worked in a bank.

"Do you miss it?"

Diego started braiding his hair in response, his fingers working with surprising dexterity as they moved down the length of his back. When he was finished, he looped the tail into a bun and tied it in place with the bandana.

"Family. I miss my family," he said.

How many jobs had Tabor lined up for people unable to fill out W-2s? If he'd been taking five percent out of every paycheck, why was he bothering to work as a super at all? The free rent must have been appealing. And then there's the cover story; that was a motivation I understood all too well. Come to think of it, he always had been slow to respond to requests, but I assumed that was because I lived in a run-down building in a neighborhood only recently starting to feel the effects of gentrification. For a few decades, Washington Heights had remained a blend of Irish, Russian, Dominican, and Hasidic communities getting by without a gourmet grocery store or a Starbucks. Those in the know still skipped the flavored macchiatos in favor of cafés con leche at Javier's. But maybe being a martín pescador wasn't a side job. Maybe this was his primary income, skimming off the top, and surely not everyone spoke about him in the friendly tones Diego used.

"Still," I pushed. "It must be a relief, not having to share any money from your next pay day."

Diego looked confused, then angry, and I wasn't sure what part of my question upset him. His eyes sank to slits, and I took a step back from the dark look, ready to retreat if necessary. Diego was young and thin, but he looked like a threat as he scowled at me.

"Somebody's taking a cut from everything you earn? Tabor would never. A one-time fee for an introduction. Tabor was a good guy, I'm telling you."

"May he rest in peace," I said, not making eye contact with Diego even though I knew I should be watching for a reaction. I felt like I was getting somewhere if I could just hold on to the clues, but Diego's intensity shocked me. By comparison, the bay was calm and glinted in the bright sun. I could see a parasail in the distance, glad that Esmeralda had some business. "Ángel helped me out."

Diego spit into the deck of the boat, quickly gain-ing my attention again.

"He's no martín pescador. A kingfisher? A king-fisher takes his time, watches over the water until the fish can be plucked out. Certain of success."

"Should I worry about Ángel?" I said with a worried tone that wasn't all fake.

"I hear nothing," he said, then paused. "But if you're paying every week, Ángel's more shark than bird."

CHAPTER 16

When Salvatore first trapped the man inside of Tesora's tank, there was only panic. The victim flailed purposely, screaming out his oxygen. The shark's demeanor quickly changed; it was clear she didn't appreciate this invasion of her already small space. She rammed into the intruder, using her strong body to push him against the glass. His eyes bulged, and I cried out involuntarily. If anyone noticed my reaction, they ignored it. I glanced around the room, wishing that someone more powerful than me would intervene. Even Zanna could have objected to this crime, but no, she was the last person to find this scene anything other than arousing. When I found her face in the dark room, it was gleeful. She nearly panted with anticipation, waiting for Tesora to attack.

That's when I noticed that the assembled crew wasn't the usual pedigreed lackeys that Salvatore preferred. No, this was the B Team, or maybe more accurately, the D Team. A couple of muscle men, a bookie who liked to inform on his clients, and three dealers. The expendables. At least I knew where I stood. If Zanna realized she wasn't in the same league as her sister, she didn't show signs of being insulted. She moved closer to the tank, claiming a front row seat to carnage.

But the shark didn't take a single bite. No, this was meant to be a death by drowning, and the man's face began to turn purple. If there was ever a time to blow my cover, it was then, but what could I do? I couldn't announce myself as NYPD and expect these men to scatter rather than shoot me. The knife in my boot wouldn't mean much to Glocks. I was outmanned and out-armed, but I took a step forward anyway, just as the doomed man realized there was a gap between the water and the lid. He pushed himself to the top and gulped, half-air and half-water. Salvatore brought out a padlock and attached it the tank, turning to us with a grim expression. While the others might enjoy the entertainment, it meant business for him. A warning, and an effective one at that. An investment, he had called Tesora. Worth every penny of her six thousand-dollar price tag.

I slipped down the stairs to a bathroom, planning to call my precinct at least, see if I could get backup. But there was a woman stationed outside the door, ostensibly to hand out towels, but effectively stopping any fantasies of rescue I might be harboring. I sent a text message on a burner phone, knowing even as I deleted the evidence that nobody would show up. Undercover work was about compromises, sacrificing small fish to catch a big one. I thought I'd understood that philosophy before signing up, thought it would be all logic and no emotion. How many lives would be saved by taking down the Magrelli brothers? Hundreds? Definitely more than one corrupt bookkeeper. The logic provided some comfort, but was more of a band-aid on a bullet wound that needed a surgeon and stat. I flushed the toilet without using it and wobbled back to the spectacle.

The dinner was macabre to say the least. The table sat in view of the tank where every few seconds the man would push himself to the surface and gasp for breath, his noises of struggle inaudible over the roar of the assembled group. They relished the food more than usual, as if one man's pain had made them appreciate their own freedom. But what freedom was that under the watching gaze of Salvatore Magrelli? The rabbit tasted like ash, the potatoes like nothing. I lifted forkful after forkful to my mouth, wondering when I could escape this horror. Thankfully, everyone ignored me, or didn't notice I was there. I watched bread pass in front of me, beer and wine slosh from glasses. A chef brought dessert, too, a sort of tiramisu laced with liquor. I drank and ate to make myself as invisible as possible and made a deal with myself. I could only check on the drowning man if I'd counted to one thousand first. One, two, three, four, again and again.

By ten thousand, he seemed resigned to his fate. He let his exhausted frame sink to the bottom of the tank, entwined his bloated fingers in the kelp. The shark swam above him, returning to her methodic pacing. The spotlight overhead refracted in the clear water, making rainbows. Not a single drop of algae marred the tableau, not a single piece of brine. Someone obviously cleaned the tank daily, and I hoped that responsibility would fall to Zanna. I hated her with as much misdirected anger as I could muster. We wouldn't have been there that night if not for her pointless ambitions. When Salvatore pushed back from the table, I realized that I'd been glaring at Zanna and forced my expression back to blank.

"With excess comes rewards," he said, as if that weren't obvious advice. The group cheered and clinked their glasses, refilling where necessary. He put up a hand, though, because he wasn't finished. "Some would say that I have been lucky, but luck is nothing. Luck is fleeting. Instead, we build our success. You can build it with me."

His grave intonation made the unruly group quiet, but I thought it sounded like he was selling time shares. How'd you like to have your very own beachfront condo? I wasn't buying, no matter how much success he might dangle in front of us. Bait never came without a hook. It wasn't uncommon for police officers to be flipped while working undercover. First, they realized what all the fuss was about in terms of cocaine, the intoxication of feeling invincible, at least for a few hours. Then it's the numb that followed the high, the slow erosion of natural reaction. Someone's legs fractured? At least he wasn't shot in the head. Someone drowning to death nearby? At least he wasn't eaten by a shark. Soon, it was hard to tell why lying was a virtue and making money a crime.

My progress had been backward. I'd been numb when I joined the force, looking for an escape from my parents' early deaths. Indifference had been my best defense, and when feeling started returning to my limbs,

165

I resented the pain. I resented knowing about all the backdoor deals, but not knowing enough to make a trial worthwhile. If Salvatore suspected I was undercover and wanted to flip me, he'd picked the wrong detective. I was wide awake now, every inch of me wanting out—and wanting to take the Magrelli family with me.

Zanna said later that the man lived, that they'd released him before any brain damage. I wanted to believe her, but being a fool never got me very far.

*

I'd come around on sharks since Salvatore used Tesora to make a point. She was a pawn as much as the rest of us, and in the intervening years, I began to feel kindly toward the animal. For starters, sharks used to be known a "sea dogs," a much more appealing moniker. They also healed quickly, didn't get tumors, and could feel vibrations in the water. And who wouldn't want a body without bones? Bones break too easily.

The train ride from Coney Island to my office on the Upper East Side took over an hour, so I had plenty of time to consider their merits and still try to put together the mismatched pieces of Tabor's death. For a job that should have produced a laundry list of enemies, the man seemed well-liked. And New Yorkers aren't exactly known for holding their tongues. "Never speak ill of the dead" isn't really our motto. But surely there was someone who resented the job-finding tax coming out of hard-earned pay. Except Tabor didn't let his greed go too far, Diego had assured me. On the other hand, some people resented the jobs themselves, thought positions—however undesirable—should go to American citizens, full stop. I thought again of the immigration demonstrations that had gotten quite a bit of media attention despite their small crowds. Were the unemployed watching resentfully from their couches? Or perhaps choosing a more active way to deal with their frustration?

The elevator door dinged open on my floor, and I didn't bother saying hello to the new floor secretary, a woman more interested in playing online poker than signing for packages. Her lax attitude didn't bother me much, seeing as how I'd never received so much as a new pair of socks through the mail. I kept my office address as private as possible, preferring to meet clients at neutral spots around the city. Of course, with Meeza dating one of Magrelli's toadies, my efforts now looked pointless. V.P. had been to my office countless times to pick up my assistant. In fact, he'd taken to keeping tabs on where she went after work, noting her grocery shopping trips and mani-pedis. Was some part of her aware that his protective behavior fell short of romantic? Did he know about her dates with a shooting range? With a semi-private address, at least I didn't have to contend with too many crying spouses at the office. A lot of people thought they wanted the truth, but really wanted to be comforted, told they were crazy for smelling perfume they didn't recognize, finding strands of hair that didn't match their own.

When I walked into our shared space, Meeza had her back to me, cooing endearments. I thought for a second she had brought Penny for a visit and looked forward to seeing my rescue. When Meeza faced me, though, I froze, stunned by the sight of several small, brightly-colored birds flitting around an elaborate cage. They chirped excitedly when I entered as if they recognized me. I certainly recognized them.

"Aren't they loves?" Meeza said, sticking her fingers between the bars and waving at the pretty pets. "V.P. sent them. I wonder what they are."

I took a step closer until the birds and I were nose to beaks. Their feathers glowed in the lamplight, emitting a cheerful aura, for a second or two. The shine vanished before I could point the color out to Meeza.

"Parrotlets," I said, straightening. I'm no birder, but I distinctly remembered an awful night at Eva Magrelli's members-only restaurant and club in midtown. I had been trying to dig up some dirt on Salvatore through his new wife; instead, I had watched a young man choke to death. Poisoned. And while Magrelli hadn't been the one to lace his food, he'd been indirectly responsible. The boy's parents hadn't wanted their only son to work for a monster. Mr. and Mrs. Belasco were currently serving thirty to life, but part of me wondered if they believed it had all been worth it, keeping their boy out of Magrelli's clutches. And now I was heading straight for those claws unless I could find a way to offer up some other prey in return. These birds had witnessed Ernesto's death, same as I had. They were another not-so-subtle warning, and I was surprised that Salvatore bothered to play this game with me. Drug trafficking doesn't really have slow days. More likely, Salvatore had assigned V.P. the task of getting me to come on board. A faithful go-between. But was the warning that he knew where to find me or where to find my friends? V.P. wouldn't intentionally harm Meeza, but accidents happened. "Definitely parrotlets," I repeated.

"How clever of you," Meeza said, beaming at me, then back at the birds.

Meeza and I had come to blows over V.P., which made me hesitant. Should I explain the gift's significance? A small, terrible part of my subconscious thought that she might already know, that she was being cajoled into keeping an eye on me. The better parts of me rejected such a notion, though. My friend was the closest living embodiment of a cartoon princess, all giant eyes and goodness. I couldn't leave her in the dark about this particular joke. I mentioned where I had seen the birds last, and Meeza pursed her lips. How an otherwise sensible girl could be so oblivious when it came to her boyfriend was beyond me. A living argument against love, as if I needed a reminder.

"Well then, they deserved a home," she finally said, closing that conversation as far as she was concerned. Hands on her hips, she stared me down until I decided I could wait. At least for a few days longer. I prayed I wouldn't disappear—or be disappeared—before I could help her.

"Was there a message attached?" I asked, and she

handed me a pink card, then plopped down on the futon I sometimes used as a bed.

"I thought your new friend might be getting lonely. XOXO."

"He means Penny," Meeza said before I could object. I raised an eyebrow at her but didn't say anything. I wasn't giving up on brains beating the oxytocin flooding her system, no matter how many hearts V.P. had drawn on the note. Was it petty of me to notice that they were crooked?

"They'll be paling around in no time," I said.

Meeza ignored me and cooed again at the birds. "What shall we name you, little ones?"

"Is everyone furious with me?" I asked to change the subject. I hadn't bothered with any cases since I found Tabor in Fort Washington Park. I hoped clients were too busy enjoying their weekends to worry, but tomorrow morning, I would field some perturbed calls.

"Only Mrs. Brandon, and she was satisfied by the emails I forwarded. No photographic evidence needed."

"You're the best."

"Oh, and I have a new case!"

I was surprised that my former assistant hadn't lead with this news. She'd embraced her role as (almost) licensed private investigator in the State of New York with energy to rival a crowd of New Direction fans. Was there ever a time when I was excited about chasing philanderers? The early days of my PI life were hazy, a charming mix of terror and boredom. I had been relieved when I started making money. My two years undercover had produced a decent amount of savings since expenses were low, but paying rent on an apartment and an office had blown through those dollars. But delight? Giddiness that an ex-husband skipping out on child support payments had been found belly up to a blackjack table? Giddiness eluded me.

Meeza waited patiently for me to show interest in her news, and I made an encouraging noise. She launched into her story about an early morning call from a distraught wife. The woman found incriminating texts on her husband's phone.

"She wants more proof than sexts?"

"Apparently, she's open to other interpretations," Meeza said. Ah, yes. What we all wanted really. A different way to look at the evidence. Meeza asked to use the digital camera we kept handy, and I took it out of storage for her, checking to make sure that the battery was charged. In some ways, I missed the simplicity of these jobs. It felt lurid, of course, zooming into people's windows from across the street, waiting for the money shot. And most nights were spent waiting, too focused to even read a magazine lest you miss your philanderer, well, philandering. Coffee was a luxury that led to peeing in a cup, a move I'd mastered but still resented. Still, there was satisfaction in completing a task, scribbling "Closed" at the top of a file. Maybe after I untangled Tabor's death and formed a plan to get back into Salvatore Magrelli's good graces, I could go back to being Katya Lincoln, private investigator for aggrieved spouses and disgruntled former employees. Only murder and mayhem stood between me and a dull—and more importantly safe—monthly income. Meeza worried when I laughed for no reason, so I adopted an appropriately interested expression and encouraged my assistant with her case. I'd sign the paperwork at the end, and she'd take the payment. Soon, she wouldn't even need me for formalities, and I hoped rather than believed she would stay unchanged by the constant barrage of infidelity and corruption.

"Ballet instructor. I bet you're good with little children," I said.

"How would I ever concentrate with all those little faces running around in tutus, pretending to be butterflies and whatnot? I'd swoon from the cuteness."

Dropping the papers, I sat down at my desk to run background checks on some of the men from The Blue Lagoon. None of the names turned up matching profile photos except for Hank Almy, and his information was pretty minimal. A small business loan, almost paid off, and no credit cards. The lack of credit cards implied the need for a low profile, I knew because of my personal experience. I also preferred cash to plastic, dollar bills never telling on their owners. I checked social media sites as well, but didn't find anything. The birds in the corner chirped when I hit the keyboard too forcefully. Meeza packed up her belongings, and I started to warn her again about V.P., but she could sense my forthcoming attack.

"Home," she said, holding up a hand. "I'm going home so that I can see about some binoculars first thing in the morning."

After a long pause, she hugged me, then asked if she could leave the birds at the office. "They brighten up the place anyway" was her closing argument, willfully ignoring my confession that they reminded me of death—or more likely, not thinking it fair to blame the beauties. And they were beautiful. That was the problem with drugs in this city. At the bottom, lives being ruined with addiction or intent-to-sell charges. Kids being taken from their moms, buddies being shot over a few ounces of weed. Then there were the Wall Street users, doing lines in the bathroom of some bottle service club, hoping to gain enough energy for a model's dance party then still make the trading floor in the morning. And above that, people like the Magrellis with enough money to buy Rembrandts for target practice. The title "kingpin" wasn't just a clever use of a bowling term; these men—always men—might as well have worn crowns. On my most self-pitying days, I couldn't help being frustrated that Salvatore bothered himself with me. I'd gotten his brother locked up, but I'd failed where it mattered. The head of the snake was still flicking its tongue, liking what it tasted on the air.

I could let Ellis know about this new threat, but what could he do besides get himself hurt? My throat tightened at the thought of him in danger because of my shortcomings. While doing nothing definitely had its appeal, I knew I couldn't delay forever and dialed my lone contact at the DEA before I lost my nerve. When a low Texas drawl greeted me, I almost smiled.

Agent Thornfield may not have trusted me at first, but I'd grown fond of him during our brief encounters. We were a bit like ships passing in the night. Well, he was a ship; I was more like a rowboat a little too far out in the Atlantic.

"You got some heat on that armadillo?" he said. Armadillo wasn't some code name in case my phone was bugged; the man had a talent for metaphor.

"Sure 'nuf," I said, trying to match his tone. I was decent with accents, but Southern wasn't my best, and Agent Thornfield chuckled. He grew quiet quickly as I explained my situation, describing the wig and birds as warnings disguised as gifts.

"He wants you to come work for him?"

"That's what V.P. told me. I think he'd just as soon kill me. Salvatore's brother was a leech, but it must look like weakness on his part—that I'm still walking around, arms and legs still attached to my body."

Agent Thornfield considered my reasoning, not rushing into any judgement. He'd once told me about operations he'd run in his twenties, leaving his team behind to plunge into Colombian jungles. But these days, he valued deliberation over recklessness. Which was why I was taken aback when he proposed that I agree to a meeting. He mentioned new recording technology that couldn't be easily detected.

"You want me to wear a wire?" I asked to make sure there wasn't a misunderstanding, that this titan in the cartel-busting community wanted me to play Russian roulette with some new bug that looked like a cockroach or something.

"It embeds in your ear canal. A sweep won't even catch it."

I didn't respond right away, considering what I'd hoped to accomplish by calling a DEA agent, even a highly decorated one. Had I wanted him to second Ellis's recommendation of witness protection? Anyone else on Thornfield's team would have, but for some reason this man believed in me. I knew his pitch speech was coming and wasn't disappointed. I'd come closer to anyone in toppling the Magrelli regime, I'd escaped with only a scar, I'd managed to hide for three years and goshdarnit, three years was enough.

"I'll give it some thought," I said, closing my phone and cutting Thornfield off.

And I did give it some thought. I thought about eyes being gouged out with icepicks and flames being lit under my feet. I thought of caskets if luck was on my side and shallow graves if it wasn't, then I surveyed a row of mannequin heads to decide which one screamed "intrepid young journalist." A nap on my futon sounded like a good idea in my still foggy brain, but I knew I couldn't pass up an opportunity to attend the immigration rallies downtown. And while I'd blend into my surroundings more if I wore a hoodie and a baseball cap, I wanted to ask questions, embrace my busybody side.

The red bob called to me, perhaps because Vondya had suggested that style, and she was rarely wrong about hair. With a few boxes of dye, she could make hues to rival the great Renaissance painters, weaving gold into layers with such a delicate touch, you'd swear the sunlight lived there. I reached out and stroked the soft, human strands, a shiver of anticipation running through my fingers. The ache felt familiar, a need to become someone else, any excuse necessary.

CHAPTER 17

With a tape recorder in my pocket and a fertility mask in my tasteful shoulder bag, I had all the accessories I needed for impromptu interrogations. My green blazer was almost too warm in such a crowd, but I wanted to look professional as I scanned the various faces, wondering if I would recognize anyone. Handmade placards could be seen above the fray, demanding votes or quoting Emma Lazarus. A few street performers took advantage of the captive audience, dressed like Statues of Liberty and charging a mere five dollars for a photo. I shook my head as one woman approached, impressed that her torch seemed to be using real flames, a fire hazard surely, but a touch of ingenuity that made her price tag seem more reasonable.

"Smoke?" she asked, leaning up against the tree I'd claimed as my watchtower and holding out a cigarette. She learned forward, lighting her menthol from the torch, and I knew only practice prevented an eyebrow disaster.

"No, thanks. Working," I said.

"Figured as much. Those shoes get you respect around the office?"

I glanced down at the black heels I'd selected to match my black slacks, wondering if I'd gone a little too Girl Friday. But they would set me apart from the crowd, which was the point.

"Kacey Winters, KXLB-TV." I held out my hand, and Lady Liberty put the cigarette in her mouth before extending her own.

"You early or they late?"

Greasy green paint coated Lady Liberty's skin, sinking into the wrinkles around her mouth. She'd sweated along her hairline, so there was a ring exposed around her temples, making it look like her face floated in front of her body. Her expression gave little away, but it was sharp, calculating. I didn't worry too much about my cover being blown because I could easily start over in a different section of the park, but my pride wouldn't let me give up so easily. It had been months since I'd slipped into a character, and the comfort was intoxicating. No Kathleen Stone in sight with her drug lord and dead super baggage—for the afternoon, I was an information-hungry ball of ambition with the pumps to prove how serious I was about chasing the story.

"I'm early. The cameras can meet me after I've scouted some interviews."

"Ten dollars," Miss Liberty said, crushing the butt under her sneakers, then letting her robes drop to hide the evidence.

"I'm hoping to find someone with a more vested interest," I said, but smiled to avoid insulting the woman.

"Ain't I vested?" She held out her cardboard tablet, spray-painted to match the rest of her. "Tabula ancata." She pronounced the Latin for "tablet" like arugula, swallowing a syllable, but she knew her American history.

"What's it mean?" I said, and was rewarded with a oration about the landmark's key events, from its dedication in 1886 to its closing after September 11th. Her voice took on a crisper cadence, and her posture straightened. From a distance, she could have passed for an amusement park automaton, but as she came to the end of her monologue, her body deflated.

"Re-opened now, though," Lady Liberty finished with a shrug. "I usually hang out in Battery Park City, but this seemed like a prime spot today."

She gestured toward our surroundings, and I glanced away from her. Madison City Park stayed busy year round because of the popular hamburger stand and the dog park. In warmer weather, the grass areas overflowed with sunbathers and folks on quick lunch breaks, but those spots hadn't been re-opened for the season yet. Instead, visitors and protestors competed for space along the wide, brick paths, congregating in patches, even the ones with a common cause. It made the movement seem disjointed, haphazard even, and I couldn't imagine a murder plot being whispered across the benches and around the fences.

I waited to see if Miss Liberty would move away from me now that her smoke break was over, but she seemed comfortable. No boss, no problem was a philosophy near and dear to my heart. Maybe my new green friend would come in handier than I had first expected.

"You've been to a lot of these?" I asked.

"Sure. These sort of things? Don't last long. The young ones lose interest, decide to save moles or some shit instead. See, this group's already smaller than the last."

"Any familiar faces?"

This got a raise of the eyebrows, and I opened my wallet to pull out a five dollar bill, which disappeared into the top of the tabula ancata, her portable piggy-bank.

"You got that councilwoman over there in the windbreaker with the leaflets. Trying to secure her votes, I figure, not much interested in the folks getting tossed out."

"Why do you say that?"

"Oh, you like politicians? The long con, I say. You'll see. And that group of hacky sack hippies, they come. Bored maybe. You want someone camera-ready, the Dominican kid's the one you want."

She gestured toward a handsome young man with a small circle of admirers surrounding him. He shouted something toward them, which was met with cheers of approval. The cop behind him looked less approving. This demonstration had a permit, though, and the officer was there to keep the peace, whether he agreed with the ideologues or not. From my experience, the men and women in blue didn't pay much attention to the causes, couldn't say if it was Greenpeace or Rock the Vote. They worried about a spontaneous riot, not whether there would be free concerts. Nobody liked

these assignments, but everyone worked them. I'd even
been sent out to the Thanksgiving Parade following
my undercover years. I wasn't sure how my presence
helped, jumping at every car horn and spooking the
horses. If the Rockettes could have voted, they probably
would have chosen a different body guard.

"You ever hear of a martín pescador?" I asked,
and Lady Liberty laughed.

"You say your name was Kacey? Kacey, nobody's
heard of a pescador. At least not officially. What station
you work for again? Don't matter. They don't have the
money for that kind of story."

"Thanks for the free tip," I said.

"Anytime, Kacey. I best start working this crowd.
Facebook photos aren't going to take themselves."

Lady Liberty took a step away, and on impulse I
dug out Tabor's mask from my bag and held it up. "Have
you seen this before? Or something like it?"

Lady Liberty paused, squinting at the relic before shaking her. "No, but it looks like bad news to me.
There's a trashcan on the corner of 23rd."

I watched her glide into the masses, being ignored by most, but a few college kids snapped photos
with their phones. If anyone paid her, I didn't see them.
I circled in the opposite direction, introducing myself
to a few people and asking why they were there. The answers varied, but boiled down to the deportations not
being fair, how children were being left behind without
their parents. The phrase "a clear path to citizenship"
was bandied around. The counter-protest—there was

always a counter-protest at this type of march—were more vehement. They were the diehards with signs that would need to be blurred if I really were going to show them on the five o'clock news. One grizzled old man was more vocal than the rest, and I let him rant into my recorder.

"We're not racist," he said, putting his hand over his heart as if to convince me of his sincerity. "But the facts are the facts, and we need to keep ourselves safe."

He had used the word "safe" before, and I parroted it back to him.

"These attacks," he started again. "They could come from anywhere. Anytime. Fuck, right here today."

"Do you know of any threats?" I said.

"If I did, I'd report that. I really would."

He put his hand back to his heart, and I asked him about martín pescadors. When he said he'd never heard that term before, I believed him. He wasn't dodging like Lady Liberty. I looked up to see if I could spot her, but the crowd had grown too dense. I showed my interviewee the mask, but he looked confused that I was changing the subject, so I thanked him for his time.

By the time the groups dispersed, I had talked to a dozen or so people, not learning anything new about the immigration tug-of-war except that the passion seemed genuine. My initial assumption about the movement being disorganized was wrong, a trick of the setting. The college kids might be distracted by a newly endangered animal or a non-union construction site, but I doubted the mothers and fathers in attendance would give up. If anything, the situation would grow more and more volatile, threats turning into attacks. Have we already reached that point? Are we here? I wondered.

With more resources, I had no doubt that there would be a primary suspect in Tabor's murder. It wouldn't be little ol' me canvassing this gathering of a thousand gung-ho activists, but a team of foot soldiers, rounding up information then checking the tip line. Hank and Leesa Almy could be interrogated rather than deceived, and Tabor's friends could identify enemies and shuffle the blame around. But no, I was always the sneak, never the above-board detective. It was fitting that I had twin offers from drug lord Salvatore Magrelli and DEA leader Agent Thornfield, both asking me to pretend for a little while longer. No boss, no problem. Wishful thinking on my part. I seemed to find plenty of trouble even if I did sign my own paychecks.

"Kacey Winters, KXLB-TV," I said in my best Midwestern accent, smiling at a woman with an American flag t-shirt and resisting the urge to smooth my wig. "Could I ask you a few questions?"

Chapter 18

The smell of mothballs competed with cologne to make the church seem like a TB ward on visitor's day. I cringed every time mourners coughed or blew their noses. From my seat near the back, I could observe the crowd, though "crowd" was a generous word for the smattering of Tabor's acquaintances paying their respects. For such a well-liked man, he didn't know many people willing to leave their jobs early for services. The timing worked out well for me since The Blue Lagoon didn't operate on Mondays or Tuesdays.

My head itched from the tape I'd used to hold Kacey's wig in place the day before. Clawing at my neck would draw undue attention, so I poured my concentration into the pastor's generic words. His "better place" rhetoric made everyone uncomfortable because the speech highlighted the fact that no family members could afford to fly in for the ceremony. How could we forget that nobody had volunteered to give a eulogy? Señora Amador had taken on the responsibility of making arrangements at least. I'd caught her earlier berating the director about flowers. My neighbor had some pretty strong opinions about the tackiness of red roses.

Her grandson tried to make himself as small as possible in a corner, playing with a handheld game on silent. He was the only child in attendance, and I wondered if Señora Amador ever let him out of her sight. It didn't seem fair to make a young boy attend a funeral, especially one with an open casket. Whoever made that decision couldn't have guessed what foundation would do to Tabor's once handsome face. I wasn't sure what magic they'd used to fill in his skull where it had been smashed, but the head shape was normal enough. The cheeks, though, were a sickly pink, two splotches of Pepto-Bismol threatening to drip onto the white sateen. It looked like baby powder had been rubbed into every wrinkle. The corpse's eyes were closed, of course. I tried to focus on their almond shape and remember their warm caramel color rather than the spider-like mascara someone had deemed appropriate. The ghastly makeover had made me gasp when I walked by, and I wondered how Ángel and Dante were handling the sight from the front pew.

Dante's wife Luna covered her mouth with a handkerchief and rubbed her protruding belly protectively. She shifted in her seat every time the preacher said amen, using the word as an excuse to try a different position. Without any personalization, the service would be quick, and I was glad for her sake at least. My gaze was still directed toward her dark brown hair when I felt someone slide next to me. The familiar soap calmed me, and I took a deep breath before glancing at Ellis. His crisp, dark suit was the same color as everyone else's clothes but that was where the similarities ended. His tailoring alone cost more than my nicest dress.

When I tried to ask why he was there, he shushed me.

Tabor's death still wasn't officially considered a murder, and even if a change in status occurred, the case was unlikely to fall into his lap. Detective Dekker already had an open homicide in addition to acting as a vice liaison. He worked harder than his fellow officers, hell-bent on proving that his silver-spoon childhood didn't create bias. A few months ago, I would have sworn his loyalty resided with the city, not his family, but he hadn't done much to bust his brother, and Lars Dekker had admitted he was on his way up the food chain of Magrelli's cartel. Had Ellis changed while I was gone and I had simply failed to notice? Or hadn't wanted to notice? A little cynicism was inevitable—show me an officer with a pension and I'll show you where he kept his will. But thinking of Ellis making compromises made me nauseous.

As if the silence revealed my suspicions, Ellis squeezed my hand, and for a split second, I thought he'd come for me, in concern for a friend or maybe even something more. We'd danced around our attraction to each other for years, and my more sensible side knew that was for the best. Still, his warm fingers felt nice entwined with mine, and I left them there. If anyone was wary of a well-dressed stranger, they would assume he'd come with me. Everyone knew I was running a prostitution ring out of apartment 3B anyway. Maybe funerals were the new fetish, one legal step away from necrophilia. I recognized a few neighbors—the woman around my age who admitted to finding Tabor attractive. Two of the young men he'd helped find work. Mr. 3F was nowhere to be seen.

Another hymn, another psalm, and everyone made their way to the gravesite. I held back, believing this particular ceremony was private, and watched from a distance, trying not to envision my name on a tombstone sooner rather than later. Ellis huddled next to me under a gnarled oak tree, its roots pushing up the oldest markers. The small, square blocks looked more like housing cement blocks than memorials, and I couldn't make out any of the engravings. A somber little angel perched crookedly next to a plastic vase, and the pair looked ready to collapse.

"Cremated," Ellis said, his voice low even though we were a good hundred yards from the others. "Ash to ash and all that."

"Where should we sprinkle you?" I asked, then cringed, thinking the possibility of me surviving him wasn't great.

"Who cares at that point? If you haven't make some sort of impact by then, it's game over anyway."

"Not really an argument for witness protection."

"You've done enough," Ellis said, glancing at me, then away. There was something he'd come to say, something that couldn't be said over the phone, but now it seemed like he might lose his nerve. The pause that followed was too awkward for me to stand, and I made a joke about his family surely having a crypt, even though the Dekkers were new money. I'd never bothered to ask when they had arrived in the United States. I'd never cared before, and now I wished I'd asked my own parents for more information. It was the latest trend; between ancestry.com and 23andme, Americans were eager to know if they could register for Daughters of the American Revolution or how much Cherokee ran through their veins. There was even a television show where ordinary folks could watch famous ones learn about their histories. If there was a better metaphor for haves versus have nots, I couldn't think of one.

Ellis cleared his throat, a signal to change the subject. He didn't like to talk about his family's wealth, not even to joke about gold-plaited urns. When he started talking about an artist, I wasn't sure what had prompted the digression. I would have bet my rent money that there was something else he wanted to say, but I tried to concentrate on the catalogue raisonné he recited.

"You ever heard of him? Timothy Borowitz?"

I shook my head, but I didn't keep up with the contemporary art world. Little scared me as much as a SoHo gallerista in six-inch heels wielding a guest list. There's no getting past that kind of security, not even in my knockoff Jimmy Choos. I glanced down to see how they had fared the afternoon. Mud stuck to the toes, ruining the effect or helping me relate to my neighbors. I'd put on a cheap windbreaker, the one I'd been wearing when I found Tabor, as a matter of fact. The pen I'd used to sign my statement was still in the pocket. Never again could I say that the NYPD hadn't given me anything.

"They call him Tin Man," Ellis continued, and I

looked at him, silently questioning the relevance and proud of myself for not making a sarcastic remark.

"Not exactly a dignified nickname."

"Easy to remember, though. His masks scll for thousands of dollars."

Now he had my attention, and he smiled for the first time that afternoon. I found myself grinning back for no sensible reason and tried to shake myself back into being serious. The opening phrases of "Amazing Grace" brought me back from a brief fantasy, and I looked again at the small group surrounding Tabor's casket. Ellis nodded in their direction and continued.

"Tabor was arrested for assaulting Tin Man a few months ago."

"That didn't come up in the background check."

"It was expunged. Tin Man dropped the charges. I think it might have been more of a mutual fight, but Tabor definitely won."

Somehow that didn't shock me. If all of the stories were to be believed, Tabor cooked like a five-star chef, spoke three languages, collected masterpieces, and travelled the world. A small part of me was even jealous, and the man was about to be lowered into the earth. At least he'd never hidden from life.

"Oh, and this may be nothing, but Hank Almy changed his name from Almiletta."

Ellis shoved his hands in his pockets and hunched against a brisk wind that picked up. He could have called with the information, but I was glad he didn't. When I tried to thank him, he grew restless, brushing off my gratitude. But we were in the middle of the Bronx, a long way from his West Village apartment—a long way from his uptown precinct, too—and he'd travelled to assist me with a case that wasn't really a case. I let myself be flattered, ignoring the hunch that said he wasn't telling me everything.

When I mentioned that I'd attended one of the immigration rallies, he didn't tell me the trip had been a waste of time, but instead asked if I'd learned anything useful. It was the right question, but I didn't know the right answer. I knew that politics was the powder keg where immigration and race went to meet, but watching Señora Amador wrap a scarf around her grandson's ears, I couldn't help but be reminded that my victim was a person not a talking point. The most vehement anti-outsider voices hadn't seemed to know that there was a career path devoted to finding jobs for people in the country illegally.

"Part of me hoped you wouldn't be at the church," Ellis said. "That you'd be on a bus to Albuquerque." I looked up at him, but he was studying the horizon.

"I could sell jewelry out of my basement."

"You'd make a fine tour guide."

"Or a swim instructor."

"You swim?"

Apparently, I thought, but didn't answer since I hadn't told him about my unseasonable dip. Instead, I rocked back and forth, knowing that the air wasn't the only thing making me cold. It was frustrating, not being able to remember if I'd slipped or been pushed out into the Atlantic, not knowing real from fake, suicide from murder.

"Another part of me was glad to see you today," Ellis said quietly, and I froze.

Before I could respond, a figure approached us from the direction of the ceremony, her black dress dragging the ground until she gathered it in her hands. Her pace was slow, and I soon recognized Luna, a pained expression on her face. My first thought was labor, and I rushed to her side, asking if I could call an ambulance. She waved off my concern, her thin hands fluttering like paper planes.

"Not yet. Too bad, too. This monster is taking her time." I'd never heard the word "monster" more lovingly uttered. Luna's face was bright for a moment, and she straightened up while she considered being a mother. Then her shoulders hunched again, and she rubbed her belly.

"Any day now, surely," I said.

"Surely."

She let me walk her toward the nearest street, leaning some of her weight onto my arm. Pretending the weight didn't bother me or my ridiculous shoes, I squeezed her arm. I regretted leaving Ellis with so much unsaid, but I thought perhaps Luna might open up to me if I got her alone. I wanted to hear her story, at least for a different perspective of my super. Maybe she would be the one to finally admit that Tabor had flaws like everyone else.

"I need a bathroom," she explained sheepishly,

perhaps thinking I was judging her for leaving early.

"There's a McDonald's nearby. We passed it on the way," I said. I glanced at Ellis to see if he knew we were leaving. He watched us, his expression unreadable from a distance, but still intense, I assumed. Always intense, and I wondered again why he had come. When I waved goodbye, he didn't move.

What would have been a five-minute walk took ten with Luna stopping every block to catch her breath. It gave me a chance to check out the neighborhood, a peculiar combination of abandoned buildings and renovated brownstones. As we got closer to the subway, businesses crammed on top of each other, check cashing joints next to takeout counters. There was a dollar store and a florist, which I assumed supplied all the arrangements for the Carson & Carson Funeral Home. Señora Amador could blame them for the inappropriate roses.

"I'm so much trouble," Luna said as we paused beside a bus stop. When the Bx40 arrived, the driver hopped down to help Luna, offering to drop us anywhere along his route, but Luna declined his offer, joking that the walk might finally make her daughter arrive.

"I've tried hot sauce, too," she told me after we started walking again. "And dancing and stretching. If I could cartwheel, I would cartwheel." She brushed her hair back from her eyes, and I patted her back in what I hoped was an approximation of "there, there." How did women do this? Did getting pregnant give you superpowers? I didn't think I wanted to find out even if super strength or X-ray vision were part of the package. Shuddering might be considered rude, so I forced myself to keep still.

When we finally arrived, I bought Luna some fries as I waited for her to use the facilities. At a corner table, I could watch pedestrians hurry by, eager to get out of the congested area. It was in sharp contrast to the cemetery where only Tabor's mourners disturbed the quiet. Who had paid for the plot? In New York City, a six-foot hole couldn't be cheap. That was prime real estate. I made a mental note to check with Carson & Carson later, see if they would cough up a name without a warrant.

Luna slid into the booth across from me, sighing in relief. She opened three packets of ketchup and dunked her fries, looking content for a moment. Then her eyes filled with tears, and I found myself reaching for her hand.

"Did you know Tabor well?" I asked, keeping my voice soft.

"Oh yes, he stopped by a lot. Wanting to talk about the Mets with Dante. Or grab a beer sometimes."

I gave a sympathetic nod, and she talked about how kind he was, helping so many of their friends. A living saint, I thought, starting to get frustrated that nobody had a bad word to say about him. Even Ángel reluctantly admitted his admiration. How was I supposed to find a killer without a motive? And with all the compliments, why wasn't anyone willing to stand up at the service and laud him in public? Maybe Ellis had given me a gift, telling me about the fight. Despite the fact that I'd spent the last three days smelling like fish, his tip might be my first concrete lead. It wasn't exactly a happy thought—that my immersion tactics had failed where a little precinct gossip had succeeded—but I still wasn't signing back up for the force anytime soon. Freelance had its perks, and I would find them some day.

"I can't believe he'd kill himself," Luna whispered, a few tears slipping down her face. She apologized, saying that the hormones made her emotional, and I stood up to order more food. She brightened at that news, and I decided that the day had revealed at least one truth: pregnancy was the rollercoaster of human experience. "I'll let Dante know we're here," she said.

Had her husband already missed her? I remembered his friends teasing him that he didn't like to leave Luna out of his sight in her current condition. In fact, I wouldn't be surprised to see him barreling through the door. But Luna didn't seem worried as she texted him, and I could even hear her humming softly to the Shakira song playing above our heads. She wiped her face again with a napkin, her expression clouding then clearing, clouding them clearing. It was exhausting to watch, and I ordered myself fries, too. Even us non-breeders need a treat from time to time.

"Is everything ready at home?" I asked, knowing better than to ask about a nursery. Most families couldn't afford such a luxury in the city. Luna nodded, telling me about the bassinet in her bedroom and the blanket crocheted by her mother.

"Dante painted the living room pink. That's where she'll sleep when she's old enough. The color looks awful with our furniture, but he wants to help."

"Are you tired of his hovering?"

"Oh, no, it's sweet. This will probably be our only child. We had—the first pregnancy took a while."

We ate our fries silently as I thought of how to respond. I'd never had any girlfriends to confide in me, at least not since high school, and none of those girls had been trying to get pregnant. Finally, I mentioned that I was an only child. I didn't add "and look how I turned out" because I didn't want Luna to cry again.

"Maybe you can paint over the pink when she turns one," I offered instead.

"Purple?"

"The color of royalty."

Luna beamed, then turned to stare out the window. She started humming again, but it wasn't a song I knew. Some sort of lullaby maybe to lure her daughter into the world.

CHAPTER 19

Gallery Darling Tin Man Borowitz
Debuts New Work

It was the sort of headline I would usually skip, but I settled down on my office futon to read the *Village Voice* profile. The recent two-page piece showed a picture of the artist, a man in his forties, wearing giant gold sunglasses and leaning against one of those concrete chess tables in Washington Square Park. The article indicated that he spent his afternoons there, relaxing after his morning studio time. I could think of a few activities more relaxing than chess, like sky diving or alligator wrestling, but to each his own. Tin Man was a high school chess champion and liked to keep his skills sharp, the writer explained. It was a smart angle, making the hip artist seem more relatable, a former nerd like everyone else. But the price of his wares was included as well, and all "just another neighbor" illusions were shattered. His large sculptures went for hundreds of thousands of dollars. Where did people even keep a life-sized tiger with skates for paws and gems for eyes?

I took out Tabor's Tin Man special, wondering how he could possibly afford to have half a dozen of these masks in his apartment. And where were they all now? Without any family to claim his possessions, I feared that they had been tossed in a dumpster. Or worse, perhaps Ángel had snatched them up for his store. He might have returned from the funeral to hang up his new, expensive merchandise. Of course, most of his customers probably couldn't afford such pricey items. He'd have to take them to a gallery, and there would undoubtably be questions about provenance.

I imagined that other single ladies in the city spent their days off binging on Netflix or meeting friends for frisbee, but I couldn't pass up an opportunity to meet a real, live artist. Why live in New York if not to rub elbows with celebrities? Me, I'm partial to the one-dollar slices of pizza, but it was only a half hour on the train to Washington Square Park. I was standing under the arch, admiring daffodils before I could second-guess my instincts. Ellis wouldn't have told me about Tin Man if he didn't think I should check him out. And in broad daylight, the risk-to-reward ratio worked in my favor.

The gray skies from the morning had been painted bright blue—cerulean, a painter might say. One of those spring days that made the whole town seem twitterpated, hearts bubbling from eyes and floating like hot air balloons. NYU students had given up on their textbooks in favor of socializing, making daisy chains in pleather skirts and thigh-high boots. Toddlers splashed their fat feet in the fountain, and musicians competed for attention and dollars. A group of breakdancers tried to gather a crowd before their performance, but I dodged their invitations. The dog park was busy as well, mutts and purebreds romping around the enclosed space, delighted with their taste of freedom. This used to be the place to score pot or ecstasy, but I didn't spy any dealers among the magazine-ready crowd. I'd have been less surprised by a spontaneous musical number than a man whispering, "You like to party?" in my ear.

The chess corner was more sedate, and I watched at the edges before approaching my target. Tin Man sat across from a teenager, teaching rather than playing I surmised after a few minutes. Sometimes he would back up the pieces and demonstrate different scenarios. Once, he made a flurry of movement and uttered, "Checkmate, see?" before righting all of the pawns and knights. The boy nodded intently, his concentration making beads of sweat pop out on his forehead. Neither player noticed me, and I appreciated the anonymity for a moment. I couldn't remember the last time I'd gone by Kathleen Stone so often. In college, I suppose, when I paid more attention to Friday night parties than forensic science. Then I'd been Khalida during my two years undercover. After, Kathy or Katya or Kennedy or Keith. Kacey had been new, but I liked her pluck. I ran my hand over my short hair, surprised to find that the strands reached my ears, curling at the ends.

Tin Man and the teenager shook hands, signaling that the lesson was over, and I approached before anyone could cut in front. The chess etiquette was foreign to me, but it seemed to follow a speed dating pattern, some players moving from table to table while others remained seated. Tin Man was a sitter, letting others come pay their respects, and I suspected his dance card was full.

"Mr. Borowitz," I said, sliding into the seat across from him.

He lowered his sunglasses to look at me, revealing eyes so dark they could be mistaken for black pools. Drugged maybe, but Tin Man was alert, scanning my face and clothes before responding.

"Which tabloid wants to know?"

"Private investigator," I said, sliding one of my real business cards toward him. I didn't hand them out very often, preferring word of mouth advertising. For a moment, I wished I'd put a little more effort into their appearance. The white background and black lettering must have looked bland to a man who made seven-foot, bedazzled wooden scissors.

"Reporters get ten minutes. PIs five." He pushed the frames back up his face, hiding his eyes from me. Not for the first time, I wished I had the authority to request he look at me directly. It's easy to dissemble behind tinted glass. I could see myself in the reflection, a shiny version who exuded tough-guy attitude. I wasn't fooled.

"You field a lot of questions about murder, Mr. Borowitz?"

If he was disconcerted by my question, it was hard to tell. He gestured toward the board, and I stared down at the pieces. They were clearly hand-carved, his own most likely. Animals rather than the traditional shapes. A glitter-tailed fox for a queen. Purple turtles for pawns. They should have been whimsical, but their jeweled eyes made them all look dead. There was something about their expressions that seemed familiar, their mouths almost too-human. I put my hands on a turtle and moved it forward. I doubted the game would take more than five minutes seeing as I couldn't quite remember if the knights went up two spaces or three before sliding over. Perhaps Mr. Borowitz would be so kind as to remind me.

"Murder," he said, moving a turtle to match my sentry. "You think Tabor Campion has been killed."

It wasn't a question, which I appreciated. Most people, even the innocent ones, pretend they don't know why a police officer or pesky PI is bothering them. As if the unexpected death of someone they knew—and recently punched in the face—couldn't possibly be relevant. I pushed another turtle forward, trying to remember if I knew of any strategy, even a basic one. My mind was a blank, so I focused on what mattered instead. The sting of losing wasn't so bad once you got used to it.

"You don't seem surprised. Did you know him well?"

Tin Man picked up my business card and folded down opposing corners. In a cascade of gestures too quick to follow, he made a box then a pyramid then a cloud. When he blew on his creation, it hovered above his palms. He let the paper fall back to the table, an unimpressive card once more.

"Do you think there are more lady cab drivers or private eyes? It's risky, no? Alone with strangers," he said.

He made "strangers" sound sinister, but I knew better than him the kind of mayhem an anonymous source might cause. I didn't need Bob Ross to remind me that my profession was dicey. Unfortunately, I wasn't cut out for retail work, and a criminology degree didn't open doors to advertising agencies. I stared at Tin Man without responding and eventually he sighed, squeezing one of the many pieces he'd won from me.

"Ms. Stone, let me see if I can hurry this along. You've been hired by God knows who to investigate a man's suicide, and in your Google search—excuse me, extensive research—you've alit on a story about fisticuffs between my friend and myself. That about right?"

He moved a one-footed rabbit forward, and I glanced at the board, then back at him. His tone was nonchalant, but if I were looking for the lie in his response, I'd bet on "friend." A recently deceased friend, jumped or killed, should produce some sort of emotion. It also seemed odd for him to think that this fight would show up on a Google search. I'd spent an hour looking for information on Tabor and found next to nothing. His name was listed on some legal documents for my apartment building, but he wasn't on any social media sites and had never been a news item. I would never have known about the fight without some help from the NYPD. Then again, I supposed famous people assumed their indigestion warranted news coverage. Thankfully, my chances of becoming famous were slim. Infamous was more likely. Former NYPD Detective

Gets Her Throat Slit Trying to Play Games with a Drug Lord. How much longer did I have left before Salvatore noticed I hadn't responded to his summons? A couple of days tops, I thought, and tried not to let my desperation show. If Tin Man couldn't help me with this case, I wanted to know as quickly as possible.

I put my fingers on a horse, bringing it up to eye level for a better look. I wasn't nuts—there was definitely something about the slack-jawed mouths that I'd seen before. I assumed this piece was functioning as a knight and hoped I guessed right on the number of allowed spaces. Then I dug in my bag for the mask I'd found in Tabor's place, removing the bubble wrap and placing it on the table. Borowitz didn't react. He didn't think about his move either, and my knight quickly disappeared.

"I found several of these in Tabor's apartment, and I assume he didn't buy them from you."

"Your turn, Ms. Stone."

I pushed another turtle forward and waited for a response to my question.

"They were gifts. As I said, Tabor was a friend."

"Funny, I didn't notice you paying your respects yesterday."

"Not all of us like to perform for crowds. You understand. Check."

Four moves, but I wasn't surprised. I moved my badger king, guessing I had thirty seconds or so left in the game.

"I was one of Tabor's first acquaintances when

he arrived from Paris," he continued when I didn't say anything. "Exactly what my circle was missing. A bona fide Renaissance man, self-taught to boot, with a taste for full-bodied Bordeaux. He could recite Rimbaud and was handsome as a movie star. A hit at my salons, you understand. Check."

I moved my badger again and didn't interrupt my partner's inflectionless recitation.

"Half the men fell in love with him and all the women. Never mind that his talents lie in dry wall and schemes."

"What sort of schemes?"

"He called them charity works. The masks were gifts, and gifts should be treated with respect. Checkmate, Ms. Stone. Our time is up."

Tin Man rummaged around in his own bag, and for a second, I thought he might pull a gun. There was something about his flat delivery of personal history that smacked of psychopathy. Instead, he removed a tiny version of Tabor's mask, two-inches tall at most, and handed it over.

"A gift," he said, and I ran a finger over the small but protruding lips on the face. "Love eludes even the most gifted sorcerers, but desire? Desire is fluid, limitless. Desire can always be found if you look hard enough."

"What if I'm not looking?" I asked.

"Everyone's looking," he replied, dismissing me.

As soon as I rose, a man wearing a bowtie took my spot impatiently. Amateur hour—amateur five minutes—was over. I watched from the outskirts for a little while longer, wanting to get another glimpse of Tin Man's eyes. But he never took his gaze off the board, more impressed with his new opponent. A man who liked winning. Was there ever a more dangerous breed?

CHAPTER 20

Showing off my chess ignorance had been a snap, so I decided to make incompetence a theme and headed toward a nearby gallery in Chelsea. I knew that Borowitz's dealer placed works in a handful of elite showrooms, including The Fire Tree. I wanted to know if the masks were part of his regular lineup or, as he implied, baubles he swapped between friends. Friends. The word made a "Game Over" sound effect in my head. The crew at Madigan's? I believed they would hang out with a maintenance man, take turns buying rounds of Bud Lite. But did Tabor really circulate with sculptors and models? Did they really treat him like an equal even after they found out he was a super in a Washington Heights apartment building? It was hard to imagine the art crowd overcoming their snobbery, even for a man fluent in poetry. Nary a one had bothered showing up at his funeral.

As I walked down Sixth Avenue, wishing that I had changed my dirty heels, I passed an apothecary and a card shop both advertising an upcoming Easter parade in the Village. I wondered what sort of floats could possibly compete with the 5th Avenue extravaganza immortalized by Judy Garland and Fred Astaire, but there's room for more than one party in Manhattan. And was that the problem? The endless options, the rotating cast of confidants. If Tin Man could be trusted, Tabor hadn't treated his masks with the level of respect the artist thought they deserved, so they'd fought, cut ties. But was that motivation enough for murder? It depended on what the art was worth, I decided, and braced myself before ringing the gallery's doorbell. This wasn't the sort of place where riffraff wandered in from the streets, and I hoped my deodorant concealed my eau de hoi polloi. Furtively, I tried to rub mud off the toes of my shoes.

The gallery assistant cracked the door before opening it fully, enquiring about my purpose. Her perfume danced through the air between us, an orange-based fragrance that managed to convey ambition rather than suntan lotion.

"Do you have an appointment?"

I hedged, wishing I had donned my Kennedy S. Vanders disguise and could peer down my nose at the barely adult barring my way in her green stilettos and matching green belt. If I live to a hundred, I will never know the secret of hair that looks dipped in unicorn blood and shines from every angle.

"I'm sorting the affairs of the Starkweather estate," I said, pushing past this well-dressed Cerberus and deciding if I didn't scream "Money," I could at least pull off "Works for Money." Anyone can manage that trick with enough chutzpah and lies. I strode leisurely into the space, studying the paintings of daisies that hung on every wall. They looked like the sort of souvenir one might pick up on the way back from Daytona Beach, but their placards suggested I was missing the craftsmanship—or the joke.

"Dan Rickleson, of course."

The young woman gestured, and I tilted my head. "Pretty," I said, eliciting the sort of sneer you might find on a junkyard dog. Somehow the expression worked with her pristine ensemble, and I almost clapped at how well she played her character. The owner of this establishment was, in all likelihood, doing alright. But the employee who sat behind the counter all day? She was either barely making rent or waiting tables at night. We were well-matched.

"Who may I say is calling?"

"Kacey Winters on behalf of the Starkweather estate."

I hadn't changed after the funeral, and my pants and turtleneck got another once-over before Miss Prim deigned to leave me alone with priceless depictions of field flowers. I took a step closer to one, hoping to notice something special about the brush strokes. I had used the word "pretty" to be annoying, but the petals earned that moniker. They were lined faintly in red, as if shot through with veins. The high gloss topcoat caught the light, reflecting my face into the background. It would look nice in my bathroom.

"Perhaps the Starkweathers would like to expand their collection?"

I turned toward the immaculate woman who had

appeared to deal with me. Her heather gray suit shimmered slightly when she held out her hand.

"Ariana Blanckwell. Welcome." Her smile was shy of warm, and I surmised she kept a gatekeeper so that she didn't have to put on airs anymore. Instead, she was airs incarnate, elegant and knowledgeable. It wasn't easy to keep a gallery open even in a sellers' market, and according to the website, The Fire Tree had opened its door in 2007, right before the recession. "I pray your appearance doesn't mean that Carl has left us?"

"Oh, no, nothing like that. Between you and me, Ms. Starkweather—Kennedy—is thinking of giving up the townhouse. She'd love a general estimate on a couple of recent acquisitions."

I'd only done a cursory search on the Starkweather families in Manhattan when I decided to adopt the name. People rarely question the name you offer, but I should have counted on a well-known art dealer being on first-name basis with a family's patriarch. If she questioned my story, her expression didn't show her skepticism. All the same, I hoped she wouldn't call anyone after this tête-à-tête, forcing me to retire Kennedy from rotation.

"We're losing all our best clients to Fort Lauderdale," she said after a pause long enough to make me panic. "Your pieces must be quite small."

She walked around to stand behind the glass counter, opening a drawer and removing a magnifying glass. I removed Tabor's mask from my bag, untaped the bubble wrap, and carefully laid it in front of Ariana, confident that Ángel had been trying to con me when he said the piece was worth forty-five dollars. Turns out, he was being generous.

"I'll never understand why Timothy insists on flooding the market with these. He must find them relaxing to make between commissioned works. I do hope Ms. Starkweather hasn't been collecting them."

"I'm afraid she has quite a few," I said, and Ariana sighed, looking genuinely disappointed in Kennedy. I tried not to be offended since Ms. S. only existed in my head. Still, I'd grown fond of her over the years and considered her savvy in all the ways of art and culture.

"There's apparently a small market for them among people interested in the occult. They're supposedly imbued with supernatural powers, good fortune and other nonsense. I wouldn't be surprised if Timothy didn't start the rumors himself."

"It sounds like at least some people find them valuable."

"On eBay, they can fetch a few hundred dollars, but only in mint condition, and this one, I'm afraid, is a lemon."

I scrutinized the mask, looking for the flaw that Ariana had spotted with only a cursory glance through her magnifying glass. The owner put me out of my misery by flipping the face over and pointing to a small crack with her manicured pinkie finger. I pulled out the smaller mask Tin Man had just given me and handed that one over, not caring if my cover story was blown. Ariana wasn't a suspect, and I needed to find out the extent of Tabor's so-called friendship with this renowned artist.

"No bubble wrap?" she asked, letting me know that she wasn't buying my act anymore.

"Why bother if it's a lemon?"

She quickly flipped over the face again, then pointed out a crack in the exact same place as the previous one.

Intentionally damaged. Some gift. Not that I'd been expecting to make my fortune from a knickknack, but it seemed rude of Tin Man to give Tabor worthless items. And why did Tabor bother hanging them on his walls? If his display implied a genuine affection for the artist, then why had they fought? More questions than answers from my dip into the gallery scene. That sounded about right.

Ariana interrupted my silent musings to direct me toward the exit. Her polite veneer never wavered, but I doubted her assistant was going to enjoy the rest of her day. In the end, I'd proven myself exactly what'd she thought at first glance: riffraff.

*

The next morning, Meeza held one knee in front of her, balancing like a flamingo as she waited on hold. I'd offered to take over, but she'd waved me away. We had an unspoken agreement that she was better at obtaining information over the phone. While I'd try to weasel my way into details, she would use honesty, succeeding nine times out of ten as if her sincerity were a secret password. I'd considered asking her directly whether she was spying on me for her boyfriend, but I knew she wouldn't lie, and I couldn't bear either response: her confession or her hurt feelings.

I threw myself into some easy assignments, running background checks for skeptical fiancées and worried parents. I faxed those off with bills attached, then ran a few more searches, finding Tabor's information had been updated to include his date of death. Timothy Borowitz had a citation for public urination in the '90s, but Hank Almy née Almiletta was perhaps the most interesting. In his early twenties, he'd served five years at Fishkill Correctional Facility for smuggling.

Meeza shifted her position, letting her head roll from side to side. She had her eyes closed, concentrating on the movement rather than the tinny music crackling through the speaker.

"Must be a busy funeral home," I said, grateful that she had volunteered to call Carson & Carson and ask about who had paid for Tabor's plot.

"Death is good business. And don't start with suggesting I become an undertaker," she wagged a finger at me, but the corners of her mouth turned up.

"Maybe a makeup artist," I said, knowing she would reject this suggestion as she had rejected all of my others. She didn't even wear any makeup as far as I could tell. Meeza was smart with good instincts, and if she hadn't met me, she could be using those skills in a more glamorous position. Did I mention that the

211

birds made me feel guilty, their sweet sounds like pin-pricks under my nails? Today, I'd decided to press my luck some more and ignore all of my current options in dealing with a dangerous drug cartel leader. I'd ignore Magrelli's summons, Ellis's suggestion to join witness protection, and Agent Thornfield's plan to wear a wire. If I said I was actively working on a Plan D, that would be dishonest, but there was something back there in the dustier recesses of my brain. If I could just pull it into the light.

"Another one?" Meeza asked, and I glanced up to see that she was examining my gift from Tin Man. "Sundar. This little one is rather beautiful."

I'd noticed that as well. While the life-sized one made me uncomfortable, its rapture almost too personal, the gaping mouth didn't look so salacious in miniature. It could as easily be an O of surprise as an O of orgasm. Plus, slip-thin eyelashes lined the eyes, softening the whole effect.

"Yes, but worthless," I said, standing up to look at the face again, wondering why Tin Man had given it to me. I couldn't sell it on the black market, but it was hand-painted. Even working with blistering speed, it must have taken an hour. I supposed if you sold a sculpture for three hundred thousand dollars every month, your mood turned to generous. I flipped over the mask to show Meeza the crack, rubbing my finger along the flaw. I never would have noticed it by staring, but I could feel the ridge.

"Our flaws give us character," Meeza pronounced,

and I resisted the urge to tease her. That was an easy philosophy when your unmarred skin glowed year round. I knew that she hadn't left the city this winter, but a stranger would swear she'd recently returned from the white sand beaches of Saint Martin.

"Hello," she said in a bright voice, giving me a thumbs-up. "Is this Mr. Carson?"

I could hear the muffled sounds of another voice, and Meeza slipped into soothing tones as she told the man she understood that they were busy and that there was no need to apologize for the wait and could he do her a small favor?

Distracted, I had started picking at the crack on the mask with a fingernail, and I felt the wood pop up. Despite its size, the piece didn't seem fragile, but the frame had splintered quickly enough. On closer examination, though, the hole looked planned, a secret compartment of some sort. A fun discovery, but not large enough to store anything useful. A sunflower seed perhaps. I dug in my bag until I unearthed the larger version, noticing that Meeza blushed and averted her eyes, focusing instead on her phone call. Mr. Carson was checking his records and looking for a receipt.

This time, I used a pencil to jab at the wooden crack, not surprised when it also popped up, revealing a space below. There was something inside, and I felt that familiar thrill of finding an honest-to-God clue.

I shook the small white wrapper into my hand, then peeked inside at a single blue pill. For a moment, I imagined myself in Wonderland, but there was no

"Eat Me" sign, and I figured using myself as a guinea pig wasn't the wisest decision. Especially when I had a detective at the NYPD who'd taken a sudden interest in my case. Was I making excuses to visit Ellis? You know what they say: our flaws give us character.

CHAPTER 21

If I were Alice in this scenario, he was definitely the Cheshire Cat, canary-eating grin and all. Ellis held the blue pill up to the hard fluorescents. For a moment, I had the wild idea that he might make it disappear.

"What's the joke?" I said, and Ellis walked behind me to close his office door. I couldn't imagine what would elicit his need for privacy or understand why he'd started to chuckle. Ellis wasn't really the go-to guy for comedy, but I found myself smiling rather than being irritated at him. His expression made him look younger, the determined but fun college boy I'd met almost a decade ago.

"A substance test? I don't think that's going to be necessary," he said, squeezing my arm as he returned to his desk. My stomach fluttered, and I tried to ignore the sensation. Was Ellis's interest in Tabor's case more for my benefit than his usual quest for truth? Did I dare to entertain those kinds of fantasies? I could feel myself flushing and focused my attention on the drug he handed back to me.

"Care to elaborate?"

"A small, diamond-shaped blue pill? Not that I have personal experience, but I'd say you're looking at a single dose of Viagra. More of a prank than a drug-smuggling conspiracy."

I sank down in the chair opposite of Ellis, staring at the pill and wishing it would be more forthcoming. A little note might be helpful. At least a punchline, so that I could be sure this wasn't a clue after all. Now that he'd pointed out its telltale signs, yes, it was clear. This was an easily obtained cure for impotence. Could the masks be used to transport other substances, though?

"In such small quantities, why bother?" Ellis voiced the question I had been asking myself. "You could get five, maybe six pills in one of those packages."

"Maybe a gram of cocaine," I said, but knew a dealer wouldn't bother with such an elaborate setup for seventy bucks. "The pawnshop owner sells them for two hundred dollars. They're used in some sort of fertility ritual."

"Men will go to great lengths to avoid embarrassments related to their reproductive health." I cringed at "reproductive health," but Ellis cleared his throat and kept going, undeterred. "Or if you don't have health insurance, black market Viagra might be the only option."

"Tin Man told me that he'd been giving Tabor the masks for free. He wouldn't necessarily have to mark them up to make a profit."

"And maybe the artist found out?"

I paused to consider whether Tin Man's hurt had been genuine when he suggested that his friend had been disrespectful of his gifts. Selling penis pills out of his art was, if not disrespectful, at least a little bit tacky.

No voodoo here, only science and profit. Was this the scheme Tin Man mentioned? Would Tabor consider helping men with ED a kind of charity? I felt like the target of an elaborate hoax, slightly embarrassed but mostly confused.

"You don't need my advice, but I'd find someone who's purchased one recently. See what he knows."

I stared at Ellis, running through the reasons again for why he was suddenly eager to help me. He hadn't acted that interested when I told him about Tabor's body. Did he feel bad about not getting an autopsy? It was too late now, the process for disinterment a bureaucratic nightmare even if I had more than pharmaceuticals. I tried not to think about other scenarios, but my mouth felt dry.

"Tabor paid for his own cemetery plot, headstone and all. His will specified which account to use," I said. Ellis nodded, but didn't seem particularly riveted by the news. So I continued, making speculations along the way. "One-way ticket to Paris and recent funeral arrangements? I'd say he knew that he'd pissed someone off."

Ellis agreed with me, but didn't elaborate. I stood to go, shifting my focus to approaching Tabor's macho friends about their possible, ahem, difficulties. I didn't relish the thought, but figured I'd start with a man I knew had been having sex recently, assisted or not. I thanked Ellis for his time, and he watched me with an intensity that made me uneasy. Again, it seemed as if he were on the verge of saying something, picking up our conversation from the cemetery. I waited, hoping that my silence would draw him out.

"Anytime," he said, crossing to open the door again and show me out. My stomach sank, and I let him know that I could find my own way to the street.

The train ride to Washington Heights gave me time to consider a few possible motives. Mid-day, the 1 wasn't as crowded as usual, and I had a bench to myself. The ads for healthcare implied that sunshine and bunnies would follow us around if we enrolled, but the chipper colors didn't fool whoever had drawn cartoonish genitalia over the phone number. Could Tabor have threatened to rat out his friends needing Viagra? That seemed more like a bar anecdote—a good ribbing— than a reason to kill. Of the characters I'd met, Tin Man and Hank presented the most obvious signs of men who could turn violent given the right nudge. Hank's drug smuggling past meant he wasn't afraid to get his hands dirty either.

Luna answered the door rather than Dante, and I wasn't about to complain about the brief reprieve from confronting a soon-to-be father over his virility. I'd prepared a pathetic speech that included such gems as, "Five percent of men your age experience problems. It's nothing to be ashamed of," even as I was ashamed of my PSA voiceover speech patterns. Preoccupied, it didn't strike me as odd at first that Luna wasn't surprised to see me. The address had been easy enough to find online, but what kind of nut job randomly showed up at someone's house? We hadn't bonded for life over fries.

"The front door was unlatched," I said instead of hello, and Luna nodded.

"That's always the way of it. Cheap rent, cheaper locks."

She led me into her kitchen, where a kettle shrieked, then calmly poured us both tea without even asking why I was there, almost as if expecting me. I shivered, staring at Luna with new appreciation, but no—there was no such thing as telepathy.

"Dante said you came to the bar," Luna said by way of explanation as she sank into a chair and propped her feet onto a small stool. She was barefoot, and I could see that her ankles were painfully swollen, probably from walking so far from the gravesite yesterday. Dark circles had emerged around her eyes. I'd heard expectant mothers didn't sleep much during the last trimester.

"Yes," I said, wondering how much Luna had figured out and not willing to give anything away. I blew on my tea, stalling.

"Were you in love with Tabor?" she asked. "You wouldn't be the first one."

When she looked at me kindly, I considered letting her believe that I was a distraught ex-girlfriend. It would explain a lot of my irrational behavior. But perhaps the time had come to be more honest. I didn't believe that Tin Man and his crowd were Tabor's real friends. These were the man's real friends. Wouldn't they welcome someone looking into his death? I pulled out the mask from my bag and placed it on the table.

That was fast becoming my favorite parlor trick, and it definitely got a reaction. Luna's eyes filled with tears, and she tried to blink them away.

"Tabor was my super," I said. "But I'm also a private investigator."

"Someone hired you?" she asked. "His family?"

Her voice slipped into hopeful, and I hated to disappoint her. "No, I haven't heard from his family. I don't think he jumped, though. Do you?"

Luna shook her head, letting the tears flow this time. I waited for her to compose herself, blowing on my tea again for something to do. Their kitchen was what a realtor might call retro—the linoleum floors blue and cracked, wallpaper stained in places. But there was a big window over the sink that flooded the room with light. Someone had already set up a highchair, a hand-me-down from the looks of it, but clean and bright. There was even a rattle tied with a ribbon on the tray.

"I like your pink living room," I said as Luna wiped her face with her sleeve. This made her laugh, however forced. When she first pushed herself up from the table, I thought she was avoiding my questions and ready for me to leave. Instead, she motioned for me to follow her down a hallway and into a bedroom. I noticed the bassinet right away, white wicker and filled with stuffed animals. This was a couple excited to welcome their baby.

"Tabor was going to be Fleur's godfather, but Dante hadn't told him yet."

I looked at Luna, who was gesturing toward a familiar face—a mask hung above the bed, its mouth grimacing. Luna grimaced, too, as she pulled it from the wall and handed it to me.

"It's a sin, but we wanted a child so badly, you understand?"

The face did look evil next to the toys and blankets, but I wasn't superstitious. I also knew that it wasn't the ritual that helped, but the medical supplies inside. Did Luna even know that her husband had ED? I imagined that discretion was part of Tabor's business model.

"Take it," Luna said, and I paused, worried that Dante would be confused to find it missing. "Please, I don't want it in the house anymore. We should have trusted in prayer not an old wives' tale."

I tucked the object away, and Luna relaxed. She hummed softly as she walked me back to her front door.

"Do you think—" I tried again, but Luna cut me off.

"I keep asking myself, what drives a person out there, to those heights? How do you step out into nothing? That's not flying. That's losing faith." She let her hand come to rest on her belly and paused. "I'm saying no, I don't think he jumped. Why would he jump? He had a good life. I'm saying—I'm not sure really. I guess I'm saying, you should get rid of those masks."

CHAPTER 22

And then there were three. I tried not to get a contact high from Luna's superstitions, but I'd admit that I didn't like carrying the masks around with me, voodoo believer or skeptic. Their expressions might have represented the throws of sex, but tilt them into the light, and they might as well have been screaming for help. I shoved the faces in my bag, not bothering with bubble wrap. Maybe a little damage would break whatever spell they cast. This investigation had become a process of reconstructing a personality rather than a murder. I thought, if I could learn enough about this man I'd seen every week but never really knew, I could find the killer. And there was a killer, wasn't there? I wasn't chasing a ghost? Why would he jump? Luna asked. I couldn't find an answer, but that didn't mean one didn't exist.

I tried to put myself in Tabor's shoes, imagine his life as the consummate hustler. In addition to being a super, he had quite a few side operations. Talents, I might call them in a better mood, but I was too close to my apartment to forget the kind of danger I had been courting by ignoring more personal risks to look into Tabor's death. When I got to 181st Street, I paused to glance down the tree-lined street beginning to look more and more Parisian. My favorite Russian store was still there, hanging on by its fingernails, but it was abutted by a faux-Irish pub and a swanky Italian restaurant. In the distance, the George Washington Bridge loomed, impervious to the changes. For a hundred years it had towered over this little stretch, watching its denizens' skirts get higher, their accents less noticeable. It was a familiar story for the city, even down to the twenty-seven-year-old woman figuring out what to do next. With her investigation, with her life. Soon, I'd start smoking and complaining about ennui. No wonder Tabor felt at home here.

Another day in funeral clothes sounded like a recipe for the blues, so I risked a visit to my apartment to change and gather supplies. The trip made me wistful. I'd worked hard to have a space of my own, never mind that the refrigerator was empty and silverfish used the bathtub as a personal spa. On bright days, the sunlight made geometric shapes on the wall, and I could forget about the smell of grease that wafted through the windows. A shower seemed too risky, but I changed and threw my dirty clothes into the hamper. I unearthed a duffle bag and filled it with pants and underwear, not sure how long I'd be gone. Visions of laundromats danced in my head.

When I locked the door behind me, Mr. 3F came out with a bag of trash, wearing his signature sweatpants and stained undershirt. I glanced at my watch, considering for the first time why a middle-aged man might be home in the middle of the day. He could work a nightshift, but I'd never heard him come home in the wee hours of the morning. Unemployed was a better guess, and that almost excused his defensive attitude. Even with a rent-stabilized apartment, the city was too expensive to last long without a steady income. My sympathy quickly dissipated when he asked about getting an invitation into my jeans.

"Or what, you still jonesing for a dead guy?"

When he laughed, I wanted to cover my ears and block out the wheezy sound. Instead, I headed for the stairs, not wanting to get caught in the elevator with him.

"Not your favorite person?" I said when he started to follow me down.

"I could do his job is all I'm sayin'. Leaky toilets? Who gets a free place for fixin' leaky toilets?"

"He did more than that for me," I said, defensive. And it was true. Tabor had replaced my broken door with reinforced steel, never asking for an explanation for why the first one was busted. Come to think of it, his nonchalant attitude had been odd. He decided it was normal for a woman to be in danger, or at least not strange enough for comment. Or was respecting tenants' privacy part of the deal? Who knew what shenanigans went on behind closed doors. There could be illegal tattoo parlors, hidden beauty shops, and amateur UFC tournaments. Whatever the reasons for Tabor's secrecy on my behalf, I was grateful. It had saved me some grief.

"Oh, I'm sure he did a lot for you." Mr. 3F wheezed again, and I picked up my pace. My curiosity hit a wall when it came to this neighbor. He could do whatever he pleased so long as he left me alone. When he stopped to wait for the elevator, I clomped down two stories to our large but empty lobby. There was nothing in my mailbox except a few bills for previous tenants, and I nodded politely at Señora Amador. She was leaning on a wooden cane I hadn't seen before, but I didn't dare ask if something had happened. Instead, I complimented her funeral efforts.

"Touching ceremony," I said. "That must have taken a lot of effort to organize."

Señora Amador pretended not to know what I was talking about, but when I mentioned the roses, her face flushed.

"Blasfemia. Roses are for romance, not eternal rest."

"Amen," I said, and Señora Amador's eyes narrowed, sensing my insincerity. She mumbled something I couldn't hear and turned away, slowing creeping toward the elevator. Well, I supposed friendliness wasn't a selling point of my apartment building, but that had never bothered me before. What would happen to her grandson when she passed? I hoped there was a parent in the mix, someone ready to step in and step up.

I pulled my duffel bag across my stomach and headed toward the exit, but the methodical whine of a circular saw drew my attention. All tools sounded ominous coming from a basement, but I steeled myself and slipped down the last stairs. The temperature dropped a few degrees, and I ran my hand along the stones, pulling away when my palms got damp. Orange sparks flew from the door of Tabor's old apartment, inviting comparisons to hell.

"Laundry," said a voice at my ear, and I jumped, swiveling to find myself face-to-face with Mr. 3F again. He smirked, gesturing toward my bag, which had pulled my t-shirt down in the front. I yanked it back up and ignored how close the man stood to me.

"Not with this racket," I replied, repeating myself when he couldn't hear. I took a few steps backward to give myself more space, but Mr. 3F closed in.

"They'd better bleach the place," he said, and I glanced into Tabor's old apartment. The kitchen appliances had been removed, and someone with safety goggles cut wood for a new counter. I recognized the young men laying down tiles, and I waved, but they didn't recognize me or pretended not to. Which one had watched me through the peephole when I tried to talk to them? They hadn't been at Tabor's graveside either, slipping out after the service. It meant something that they had come, though, paid their respects.

"Cheap labor," Mr. 3F continued, spitting onto the concrete floor. The saw abruptly cut off, and one of the men glanced up, his face worried then going blank again as he wiped away grout from where it had splattered on the wall.

"Your application was lost in the mail?" I said, setting down my bag so that my hands were free if I needed them.

"I'd check that smart mouth if I were you," Mr. 3F

said, and I decided he didn't deserve the "Mr." part of his nickname.

I watched the renovations for another minute, speculating on how much money our landlord could charge for rent. It was a basement apartment, but had its own private entrance. And with the changes in our neighborhood, the new restaurants and bars—a lot of money, I finally decided, leaving my speculations there. When a tenant moved out for any reason, death included, the place lost its rent-controlled or stabilized status. A landlord could charge whatever he wanted. It was fortunate the rest of us hadn't been encouraged to mosey on down the road.

I turned to head back upstairs, but 3F blocked my way with his large frame. When I tried to pass, he stepped in front of me, and I felt my pulse quicken.

"You don't want to dance with me," I said, happy that my voice didn't shake. His meaty hands could turn into fists, and then where would I be? I knew self-defense, but I'd be lying if I said I wasn't afraid of a man twice my size. Training could only get you so far. After a second, 3F backed away, and I figured my bravado had worked. A quick glance behind me told me not to get too proud of myself. My young neighbors had emerged from Tabor's apartment and stared daggers at 3F. I slipped past him before trouble started in earnest and darted upstairs. Once outside, I let my breath return to its normal speed, and congratulated myself on the boatload of trouble I'd managed to find in such a short period of time. I'd gotten used to prioritizing threats, though, and knew at least one enemy deserved most of my attention.

To say my scheme was fully formed would be overstating matters, but I sat on a park bench and removed the mask Luna had foisted on me. Its secret compartment held two blue pills, and I slipped those into my pocket, keeping my fingers crossed that Dante didn't overreact to no longer having a supply. He probably wouldn't notice for a few months at least, with the baby's arrival imminent.

My note couldn't be large, say the size of a gum wrapper, so I thought carefully about what message I needed for Salvatore Magrelli, a man I'd hoped to see behind bars or never again. In the end, I rushed, so that I didn't lose my nerve, then texted my least favorite Magrelli lackey for a car. To his credit, V.P. responded quickly, and I was walking toward a questionable rental within half an hour. It was usually pretty easy to spot the vehicles, even if the make and models weren't identified—look for the rust bucket with tinted windows. Since I'd been upgraded, or Meeza had at least, reservations came with a grainy photo, low-res enough for burner phones to display. There was a 2012 BMW X5 waiting for me on Amsterdam and 176th. I reached underneath the passenger side door and found the duct-taped key, all classy like.

The traffic didn't bother me as I made my way slowly into Queens, trying to give myself a pep talk. When I'd lived in a safe house waiting for the Magrelli brothers to be put on trial, I'd been resigned, too glad to be released from my civic duty to fully consider the consequences. Even when a judge dismissed the charges against Salvatore and focused on Frank instead, part of me thought that was good enough, a partial win. It wasn't until later that I realized how badly I'd botched the job, that getting a minion out of the way only meant the devil could give you personal attention. Most of the time, nobody paid much attention to me while I was undercover. A female narc might as well have been a sasquatch. Plus, I was Zanna's friend, and Zanna was crazy—burn you with a cigarette for not laughing at her jokes quick enough crazy. But Salvatore always saw me when I was in the room. His eyes lidded and impossible to read, but I got the sense that he evaluated me, seeing how I fit or disrupted his plans.

When I'd asked to be extracted after Tesora, my sergeant asked for proof of the drowned man. I didn't even know the victim's name. I had nothing to offer, so the NYPD had nothing to offer me. And that's how it had always been; the precinct's attitude toward my job a charming mixture of dismissive and oblivious. I got the standard promotion to detective, but it was a title in name only. Any hope I'd nursed of being pulled out had been squashed by the two words I came to hate most in life: more evidence. If I lived long enough to write my memoirs, they were going to be called *Caught Between the Devil and the Boys in Blue Sea.*

A Kia Sorrento pulled in front of me, and I slammed on the brakes, bringing myself back to reality. My attempt at steeling my nerves had made me angry at least, which was a step in the right direction. I'd been fueled by worse emotions. Anger could get me through the afternoon, then I'd focus on calculating in the morning.

The congestion eased once I exited, pulling into a family-friendly neighborhood, then farther into an industrial one. Chain link fences surrounded all the warehouses, and I squinted at the signs, looking for the unmarked entrance I needed. When V.P.'s stretch of derelict came into view, I flipped off the security camera, then waited until the gate creaked open, noting the new razor wire at the top. "Spare no expense" must have been V.P.'s new business model. And, in fact, there was less broken glass than usual, fewer ways to damage merchandise before it even left the lot. Hired muscle approached, holding his hand up for me to stop. I complied, noting the handgun he hadn't bothered to hide. It wasn't pointed at me, but that didn't make it any less intimidating. It had been a while since I'd visited V.P.'s lot, and he'd definitely made some changes. I wondered if they were his own ideas, or if Salvatore had his hand in the operations now.

"Mr. Patel requests a search, ma'am," the security guard said when I rolled down the window.

I cut the engine and climbed out, holding up my hands for a pat down and feeling relieved when it was professional. Satisfied, the man slid into the driver's seat and pulled the car around to a private hanger where the nicer vehicles were kept. In front of me, the offerings looked more like a junkyard than a car lot, but this wasn't Enterprise. And I'd always known that, hadn't I? Wasn't I to blame for taking Meeza here in the first place?

I made my way toward the doublewide trailer V.P. used as his office, noting that the bullet holes I'd noticed last time had been patched over. There were also flower pots outside, and though they were empty, I cringed, imaging Meeza's touch trying to brighten up the place. I thought even her powers would fail in the face of such ugliness, but I'd underestimated my friend before.

V.P. didn't bother to greet me when I walked in, placing his hands behind his head instead to show me that he had not a care in the world. His black hair drooped in curls on his forehead, and he looked more like an Indian soccer star than a criminal. But there was tension in his jaw, and I knew that I made him nervous. His job was to deliver me, and what would happen if he failed Salvatore? He liked power, but he loved Meeza, and I could see the scales he tried to hide beneath suits and cowboy boots. He had those boots propped on his desk, an obvious pose, since you couldn't get much work done in that position. A meow from the corner pulled my attention, and I turned to see Penny stretch and come toward me, rubbing her sleek body against the desk before deigning to acknowledge me.

"Thanks for the birds," I said, bending down to scratch the cat's ears. She purred in appreciation, smashing her face against my palm. Her sweetness didn't alleviate the knot of anxiety that grew boulder-sized in my stomach.

"A gift," V.P. said, throwing open his arms in a grand gesture that startled Penny, who darted under a chair. I made kissing noises at her until she reemerged, then continued my petting.

"I thought I'd stop by and return the favor." I held the mask out to him, but he didn't take it immediately, wondering what poisons I could have left on the surface perhaps. After a moment, he grinned, a boyish expression that had gotten him out of more trouble than he deserved to escape. "You know who it's for," I said.

"Mr. Magrelli would prefer a more personal performance."

"Salvatore would prefer my head on a plate, but he's getting a one-of-a-kind, hand-painted knickknack worth between zero and two hundred dollars. I'm no appraiser."

My heart sped up, and I felt like a palm tree in a hurricane, bending to survive. I wasn't pretending to be Kacey Winters or Kay Moroz or even Khalida Sanchez. I was Kathleen Stone, and I knew my own mind for once. Penny curled up at my feet, and I took that as a sign. Scooping her up into my arms, I marched out of the place, kittens blazing, as it were.

CHAPTER 23

A grimacing face swam toward me, the O of its mouth stretching to reveal a row of teeth then gums then the whole skull. "Yours," it said before turning to ash. I jerked awake, batting away the image. It took a moment before I recognized Dolly's cashmere throw that I was clutching to my chest. The scent reminded me of rose gardens and high tea, though I'd never experienced either. Once my breathing returned to normal, I wanted to stay ensconced forever. Nobody could find me here, right, if I pulled the blanket over my head? A part of me missed waking up in my clean, bright studio in Washington Heights, but another part knew that if I stumbled to The Pink Parrot's public space, I would find coffee already made. And if a few of the early-shift performers wandered in, they would recognize me. I'd helped them find the culprit when their float had been sabotaged during a parade. And if my suspicions had fallen on a few of them? Well, I would understand the shade thrown in my direction at least.

I made my way toward the bar, and Dolly pushed a mug toward me before I even sat down. He took it back, though, before I could take a drink, and I whimpered pitifully. Unimpressed, he added a healthy splash of milk then dumped in two spoonfuls of sugar.

"Uh-huh, if this is your breakfast, it should at least taste like something."

I wrinkled by nose at the sweetness, but obeyed. Dolly's dressing room was a refuge. In addition to bouncers around the clock, there was a state-of-the-art security system. The club had received death threats from a deranged hate group, and the owner was careful. Now if I could learn to live off coffee and strawberry daiquiris, I'd be all set.

"What do you know about fish?" I asked.

"I know fish and guests stink after three days." Dolly patted my hand to lessen the sting, but I knew that soon, I had to take care of my own business. As if to prove the point, Penny scurried into the room, batting around what looked like a cockroach but turned out to be a set of false eyelashes. She sprinted the length of the bar then took off back toward the dressing rooms, making herself at home. Dolly raised a perfectly sculpted eyebrow at me. I'd have to drop the cat off at Meeza's before heading back to The Blue Lagoon. If my meeting with Salvatore went well, maybe Meeza and I could share custody. I'd grown fond of Penny's furry face.

"How did Mamma Burstyn get the mob to leave her alone?" I said, glad that my friend never minded when the conversation dipped into strange.

He sat down beside me before answering, wondering perhaps what information he could share without betraying confidences. When Lacey Burstyn set up shop, resentment rose like steam off summer asphalt. The graffitied slurs would have been bad enough, but there were also a couple of Italian henchman talking to her about security payments. Bricks tossed through the front window, fires started in the back.

"She told me that her family was in Georgia. They were untouchable, which made her brave. Braver than usual, I suspect."

I understood that much at least. It was the main reason I had avoided making friends for so long, and now, if anything happened to them, I wasn't sure I would survive the guilt.

"She kept declining protection. Phone lines would be cut and she'd say, 'No thank you, sir, I'm fine on my own.' Then the broken doors. The threats. The nights sleeping with a baseball bat." Here, Dolly paused, and I worried that he regretted telling me secrets that weren't his own. But when he continued, I could tell that he was simply proud of her. "Eventually, they stopped asking. I've never hear her call anybody sir."

It was an exit line, and he knew his cue. Dolly left me at the bar, watching the shop owners across the street raise their metal shutters and set out their signs. The Pink Parrot hadn't always been on this manicured stretch of SoHo, hadn't always been able to pay lease prices that would make your heart stop. It had started in an unassuming building in Hell's Kitchen, far enough away from the Times Square strip clubs in order to draw a different clientele. The theatre crowd that didn't want to lose the high they'd gotten from seeing *A Chorus Line* or *A Little Night Music*. They'd stumble into The Pink Parrot wanting to drink martinis and laugh at men dressed like women and instead found themselves enchanted. Even before Dolly and his co-stars, Ms. Burstyn had insisted on the highest quality. Men auditioned, but some were lured from more volatile clubs in the West Village. She'd snatched them away with one word: respect. At her place, their art would be respected.

When my cell phone rang, I jumped, not sure how my message to Salvatore would be taken or how I would receive a response. I recognized the precinct number, though, and my stomach dropped. It was muscle memory, always expecting bad news. But hearing Ellis's voice made me feel better, made me blush, in fact, and I wondered again if his interest in the Tabor case had more to do with me than an unsolved murder.

"What time does your shift start?" he asked, and I envisioned waffles and more coffee at our old favorite diner. Maybe I wouldn't have to steal peanuts after all.

"I've got some time," I said, heading back toward Dolly's dressing room to find some clothes. In my anxious state, I'd left my duffel bag in my building's basement, and I doubted I would see my favorite Yankees t-shirt again. I would have to pay Dolly's dry cleaning bill for him if I kept acting like a sorority sister with a "what's yours is mine" policy.

"Good, I'd hate for you to be late," Ellis said as I squeezed the phone between my shoulder and head.

"Those fish won't catch themselves."

If a closet could have Feng Shui, Dolly's dripped with harmony. Organized by color, style, and even warmth, it was easy to see at a glance that nothing was exactly appropriate for receptionist work. I pulled out a pink mini skirt, then returned it, thinking that Ellis had never been partial to pink. Would the green rhinestones make me look too much like a mermaid? It was a risk I had to take. While Ellis waited, I wiggled into the dress and looked for something to lessen the "walk of shame" appearance of the whole ensemble. Of course, the crew of The Blue Lagoon had warmed to me only after I'd shown up hangover. Maybe they'd take one look at my sparkles and finally spill their guts.

"I wouldn't want you to be late," Ellis said again when I returned the phone to my ear. The repetition made me pause, antennas finally rising. This wasn't Ellis calling; it was Detective Dekker, and he wanted something.

"This isn't about scrambled eggs and hash, is it?" I asked.

The silence on the other end of the line was revealing. I waited for whatever impossible task the city's Batman wanted me to perform. In this scenario, I wasn't even Cat Woman. Robin at best. Finally, Ellis—excuse me, Detective Dekker—mentioned the distinct possibility that The Blue Lagoon was a cover operation. His vice contacts suspected that the boats were drug runners, dropping paying customers, then returning a hundred nautical miles into the Atlantic at night to meet their liaisons. I pictured Captain Barrera's worried face helping me when I'd fallen into the water. His concern for more than a lawsuit. And there was Hank, a man who morphed into a Grade A jerk given enough booze, but he was also a soon-to-be-father who acted genuinely happy about that prospect. Not to mention Diego, with his long, valuable hair and even more valuable family devotion. Of course, I'd suspected as much as soon as I saw Hank Almiletta's smuggling arrest, but I hadn't drawn a line between Ellis's interest in my case and the possibility of a vice connection. I guessed there was a reason I was no longer one of New York's Finest. I'd made a newbie mistake, letting my affection for my old friend obscure his real motives. The dawning understanding hurt.

"You're only telling me now," I said when I thought that my voice wouldn't shake.

"I tried at Tabor's funeral, but you went off with the wife." His tone was impressively dry, void of defensiveness. But I'd always known he was good at his job. He had more loyalty to the force than to any person. Still, it bothered me, being lumped in with the rest of humanity, and I hung up before I confessed as much, some sliver of dignity asserting itself while I slipped into mud-covered heels.

I showed up early for my shift, now with bigger worries than being mistaken for a mermaid in my rhinestoned dress. When I'd been hired by The Blue Lagoon, Ellis had seen an opportunity and taken it. If I was angry, it felt a lot like disappointment. I closed my eyes, letting myself enjoy self-pity for a minute before marching back into my life. He'd tried to tell me: "Another part of me was glad to see you today." We'd been interrupted before he got a chance to explain that I'd stumbled into an opening for him, that he could use the undercover identity I'd formed without having to expend any department resources. It made sense why he'd introduced Hank's real last name so casually into our conversation now. Logical or not, the revelation felt like a gut punch, and an embarrassing one at that. But if I could manage to stop feeling wounded, I knew I could use this turn of events to my advantage. The idea that The Blue Lagoon was a front had been simmering in the back of my mind for a while anyway. The low customer count. Leesa's insistence that the tours sold themselves. To be honest, the news would have been welcome coming from anyone but Ellis. And while I didn't want to lie to him, I knew that I could if the chips were down. If that peek into my soul made me cringe, so be it. Ellis didn't seem troubled by using me, so why should I give more than I get?

Esmeralda waved at me as I unlocked the door, heading my way and giving my outfit her approval. "Lose the sweatshirt. Around here, if you don't have your boobs out, nobody's giving you a second glance. Without a scoop of glitter? You might as well be invisible."

She winked at me, her false eyelashes making the gesture look more lascivious than friendly, but I tried to smile. She was right, of course. It was 9:30 in the morning, and looking around, I saw a man with dumbbells hanging from his nipples and a woman dressed like a butterfly. New York City was full of freaks, but the kind who disguised themselves under suits and reputable careers. Most pretended to be normal with Oscar-worthy intensity, but here? On Coney Island? Here's where the weird congregated and worshiped, shocking nobody with their real selves, however serpentine.

"Coffee?" I suggested, turning on the pot and planning to lure Esmeralda into a little more gossip. I'd been so focused on Tabor the last time we'd spoken that I hadn't asked about my work buddies. I started with whether she knew if Leesa had gone into a labor. A safe subject, I thought, and Esmeralda latched onto it.

"No, and a week late already. Stubborn little sweet pea. She'll fit right in." Esmeralda misinterpreted my question as fear of losing my job, and she told me she'd asked around for me. "You're a good egg. I can tell."

I tried not to wince at the words, knowing that I might inadvertently be part of a sting operation to take this family business out of commission. It was unlike me to sympathize with drug dealers, but Hank's daughter wasn't to blame. And runners weren't the ones chopping off hands and gouging out eyeballs. It was poor logic, and even I recognized it as such. Without the runners, the drugs couldn't get into the country, and monsters like Salvatore Magrelli wouldn't profit.

"You want a free pass?" Esmeralda asked, and for a second, I thought she'd read my mind and was reprimanding me for being soft on crime. Then she held a parasail flyer in my direction. "People on the beach see someone in the air and get ideas. I don't mind."

I demurred, not crazy about the idea of a small harness standing between me and a hundred-foot drop. Death-defying feats liked me a little too much to tempt fate. I wasn't really dressed for dare-deviling in any case.

"Suit yourself." She poured her coffee into a Styrofoam cup and finger-waved her goodbye. I flipped on the "Open" sign and logged in to the company's email account. It had accumulated over my days off, but there was nothing that needed a reply. A few ads for boating accessories, a complaint about a missed reservation. Nobody enquired about buying tickets, but I was pretty sure I knew how The Blue Lagoon managed to stay in business during the off-season.

The bell above the door chimed, and I closed the browser windows, worried that my snooping would be discovered. Captain Barrera's somber face didn't ease my concerns, and I stood to greet him. He poured himself a cup of coffee before speaking, and I worried more when he shook his head.

"She is curiosa, that one. Too nosy."

"Esmeralda?"

"Sí. Dangerous."

I tried to imagine how the owner of a parasailing company could be dangerous, and I knew there was only one likely answer. A fishing company would object to a gossip-hungry neighbor only if they were doing something questionable, possibly even illegal. Had Tabor known all along? Or had he discovered the secret and suffered the consequences? To be honest, I'd started to guess that The Blue Lagoon had nothing to do with

Tabor's death, but I needed the place all the same if I hoped to escape Magrelli's clutches. My past experience with games included a few nights of poker and a memory of beating Mom at Monopoly once, so my confidence couldn't exactly be called winning. But bravado could be faked, especially with a little prep work.

"A busybody," I said, and Captain Barrera agreed with my insult.

"Yes, yes. A busybody. You'll stay away from her."

He dumped some sugar into his cup, then shook my hand before departing. Captain Barrera looked tired, and no wonder. I now suspected that his responsibility exceeded two daily fishing jaunts. There were the morning and afternoon trips, but also the clandestine ones at night. How often? I wondered. Then dialed Agent Thornfield before I could second-guess my actions. I needed an ally if I hoped to pull my little con off.

"It's unusual for coke to come around that way," he said when I told him Ellis's suspicions. The open waters of the Atlantic Ocean were harder to navigate, especially after dark. Most drugs came in through tractor trailers up Highway 95 or through shipping containers on the Hudson. Runners were a Miami-style method, perfect for short trips from Mexico or Cuba or Belize. If The Blue Lagoon was involved, it was inventive, a way to compete with more established cartels perhaps. Taking the long way home.

"The company was founded in 2010," I said, flipping over a brochure to see if anything else might be useful. I felt some hesitation about going behind Ellis's back, knowing that the NYPD didn't like interference from outside groups. It was mostly machismo, but there was some truth to the argument that New York detectives knew their city better. With eight million people, it operated like its own country, especially where crime was concerned. The more cynical part of me believed that the department didn't want anybody looking at their reports, seeing where numbers were fudged, eyes turned the other way. My guilt lessened when I focused on how Ellis had played me, insinuating himself into my Tabor case for his own benefit. And that small voice reminded me that Ellis wanted me to join witness protection, to get myself as far away from danger, as possible. I told it to hush up and let me wallow. Plus, the rational side of my brain assured me that the DEA wouldn't get involved with something so small potatoes.

I could hear a woman's voice calling Agent Thornfield to dinner, and I apologized for using his home number.

"You can't get lard unless you boil the hog."

He hung up before I could ask for a translation, and I vowed never to work in Texas. I could pass for a socialite, but a debutante? I'd be chased out of a cotillion faster than a rattlesnake at a pool party. Or something.

Acting normal when your insides were soupy required a healthy dose of make-believe with a side of can-do spirit. I kept my suspicions in my stomach where they belonged and tried to lure in paying customers with laminated photographs of swordfish. I wondered if anyone had ever caught such a prize, but did my best to sell the sunset tour. Around three, I locked up and headed toward the boat to say goodbye. There were four ticketed passengers lined up, and the evidence spoke to me sotto voce, singing about how no company could pay rent and employees, not to mention buy gas and supplies, with two hundred dollars a day. I was worried about hearing voices so often, but decided that living with delusions was easier than fighting them.

CHAPTER 24

I was no psychic, but the next morning, I knew something was wrong as soon as I exited the subway station. The rubberneckers were my first clue, a small group of spectators at the boat docks. I spotted Esmeralda quickly enough, her towering hairdo obstructing the view of a young couple standing on their tiptoes to see. I walked briskly toward them, sick with fear that there would be another body. Then I noticed the row of unmarked cars, men in blue parkas swarming like bees around their hive. The DEA had arrived, and I marveled at how quickly Agent Thornfield turned a hunch into action. There must have been a Texas saying about storming the corrals.

I was shocked, to put it mildly. I'd called Thornfield for a friendly ear, moving my bishop into striking position, but this raid wrecked the whole board. Some days, you're the pawn, I guessed. Most days, it seemed like, for me. My hands shook as I looked over the scene. Agent Thornfield wasn't there himself, of course, though I suspected he was on the other end of those headsets. I walked toward The Blue Lagoon boat, but Captain Barrera caught my eye and quickly jerked his head. He was warning me, and I could either comply or blow my cover. It was hard to see everyone lined up and waiting for bad news. Barrera was right, though, and I turned away and headed toward the doughnut shop on the corner. It's neon pirate sign had never looked so menacing, but I ducked inside before I did something stupid.

The sprinkles did little to calm my nerves, but I ate them anyway, picking each one off as the minutes ticked by. At the end of an hour, my fingers were a ghastly rainbow, colors bleeding into a tiny swamp. Normally, the site of dogs in vests would make me happy, but these furry officers were all business, their snouts moving around vehicles and onto our boat. Not our boat, I reminded myself, surprised at how quickly I'd grown attached to Captain Barrera. They said surviving danger could do that to acquaintances, but I'd survived plenty of danger with the Costas and never wanted to put my neck on the line for any of them. That day, though, I had an itch to interfere, knowing this was my fault, that I'd set wheels in motion that I couldn't stop. Never mind that it was the right course of action. Right and wrong bled into each other sometimes, turned rainbow sprinkles into a gray mess.

After the unmarked cruisers zoomed past me, I crept back toward the docks, wondering if I'd find a ghost ship. Gawkers continued onto the boardwalk with a story to share over hotdogs and beer. I was surprised to see Hank checking nets for holes, his daily routine uninterrupted by the fuss. For a few minutes, I watched him work his hands through the threads, moving in a pattern I didn't recognize but knew was consistent. This was a man with method in his madness.

"Can I help?" I asked, and Hank looked up at me, his eyes shining.

"Aw thanks, but no. Best to get on home."

I shoved my hands in the sweatshirt I'd picked up from a tourist shop near The Pink Parrot. It proclaimed "I ♥ NY.".

"Maybe I could go out with you all again this afternoon?" It was more instinct than strategy, but I was trying to work out why Hank wasn't in handcuffs in the back of cruiser. Had Ellis's intel been wrong? There was only one other man on board, somebody I hadn't seen before, hosing off crates and wiping off seats. I knew those actions for what they were: tranquilizers. We could lose our nerves in work sometimes.

"No tour today," Hank said. He paused, standing up and shading his eyes as he looked out over the horizon. "No captain, no tour."

"What's wrong with Mr. Barrera?" I asked, even though I didn't really want to know the answer. Hank looked at me, and I stared back, worried he'd know that I had called the DEA if my gaze shifted down to the planks beneath my shoes. I could sense the wood as if it pulsed.

"He may as well be family. As close to blood as a man can get," Hank said, not seeming to see me. Then his gaze sharpened, his anger crystallizing. "He's being deported."

*   *   *

If guilt could be masked with trail mix and olives, I was trying. While we were chatting, Hank had been called away for what should have been happy news. His wife was in labor and on her way to the hospital. But he'd looked at me sadly when he'd delivered that message. Of all The Blue Lagoon crew members, I wouldn't have guessed that Barrera was in the country without papers. His story was complicated because he once had a work visa, but when the document expired, he'd struggled to get it renewed. By that time, he'd built a life in America, married and made friends.

Dolly was headlining, so The Pink Parrot was packed, every table reserved, every bar seat taken. I was savoring my snack by the exit, leaning against the wall and hoping nobody would notice me. The patrons mingled in their weekends-start-on-Thursdays best, dresses and high heels, suits and boots. I'd zipped my sweatshirt and pulled the hood up over my now definitely, I'd decided, too-long hair.

The message Ellis had left for me dripped with ice, and I didn't blame him. If the bust had gone through, he might have forgiven me. He wasn't the type of man who needed credit. But a failed operation? A missed opportunity? Let's just say I wasn't expecting an invitation to Easter dinner at the Dekker estate. Of course, I was still angry with him as well, but I was kidding myself if I believed our motives were equally noble. The only bright spot keeping me from burrowing under a blanket was that Agent Thornfield wasn't upset with my false tip. In fact, he didn't think it was false at all. He'd checked with the New York branch of the DEA, and their intel matched the possibility that The Blue Lagoon was a runner.

Runners were notoriously difficult to catch, Agent Thornfield assured me. In the hierarchy, from leader to dealer, they took on the least amount of risk, only having drugs in their possession for a few hours. A bit longer for flights, but maritime travel would always be limited. And since land smuggling was far and away the most popular choice those days, boats didn't get a lot of attention. The occasional submarine might make the news because of novelty, but your run-of-the-mill speedboat—or in this case, sunset cruiser—wasn't making the papers. If the drugs were wrapped carefully and no longer on board when the dogs arrived, they'd never get caught. The Blue Lagoon could continue operation for years. Cover stories weren't generally so elaborate, actually open for business five days a week. I suspected Leeza genuinely believed that her husband's fishing excursions paid their mortgage. Maybe he hoped they would someday, that he could pass along an above-board family business to their daughter.

If The Blue Lagoon was really trafficking—and that seemed likely—I should be bummed that the bust failed, right? Guilt over Barrera aside, I should admit that every part of an operation was complicit. There were parts of the business runners never saw. They could ignore the intimidation techniques, the acid baths and shallow graves, not to mention the addictions. The lives ruined from somebody needing one more fix.

When Dolly sauntered out, my attention finally focused on the stage. He was wearing an off-white gown that resembled a wedding dress but somehow managed to look appropriate. The whistles and applause started immediately, and when he twirled, I looked around for possible swooners. He only wore one wig these days, a flattering bob that Vondya had created especially to hide the scar on his forehead. That night, he'd donned a small, Windsor-ready hat and elbow-length gloves. I admired their sparkle until the pianist started playing the opening bars of "Candle in the Wind." Fake breasts, but the voice? The sound lilted and dodged, flew up into the stage lights and sauntered out into the audience like honey on summer strawberries, ripe for picking.

The music soothed me, and when I finally crashed on Dolly's couch, I had more clarity than I expected. I'd been so distracted by the day's events that I hadn't thought about Tabor very much. But now I wondered if I'd been too quick to dismiss a link between The Blue Lagoon and my super's death. At the very least, he must have known that the tourist attraction had some illegal side dealings. Why else send workers without paperwork there? I needed more intel, and I wasn't going to get it poking around the bare-bones office. I wanted to get back on that boat.

CHAPTER 25

Lonnie Almy was what my mother would have called a "piece of work," what Meeza would call a jha-taka—a word she used rarely but with purpose—and what Thornfield would have called a "real son of a bitch." Hank may have been a handful, but his brother was a bully. By the time I'd booted up the office computer, he'd called me stupid for dropping the mail, mocked my new favorite sweatshirt, and left pee on the toilet seat. My resolve to venture into the middle of ocean with this clown wavered, but I wanted a closer look below deck. I mentioned that Hank sometimes let me go out on the afternoon cruise, and Lonnie answered with a string of expletives about freeloaders. That route unavailable, I switched to espionage, planting myself at the Manny's Catch window on my lunch break.

From my perch, I could watch The Blue Lagoon as I picked at some fried cod. The restaurant wasn't exactly bustling, but it was busy enough for my tarrying to go unnoticed, or at least unremarked upon. I made sure to sip my Diet Coke, so that the waitress didn't have to return too often, leaving her to complain about the family of six that kept dropping their silverware and needing new forks.

The next tour didn't depart until four, so there

weren't any customers milling around the docks. I'd sold a few tickets that morning, more than usual, but those patrons wouldn't think it was strange that I loitered anyway. It was mainly Lonnie who I wanted to avoid, though being caught snooping by any workers could spell disaster. Real runners wouldn't waltz into the Atlantic unarmed. True, runners didn't often get their hands dirty. Their role was specialized, and it saved them some trouble. Watching too many late-night episodes of *Miami Vice* might convince people that they knew how to handle fiberglass on open waters, but it's a skill, some might even say a talent. Of course, this wasn't your typical speedboat operation. The new cartels insisted on a breed called super speedboats, Picudas, that were fast enough to escape Coast Guard detection. If The Blue Lagoon was playing this game, it was using different rules. Hiding in plain sight, so to speak. And, of course, Hank had made sure to tell me that the company was his alone. If Lonnie was involved, his role was discreet since I hadn't seen him before. Basically, Hank had arranged the pieces in such a way that only he would be knocked down if the DEA found a shipment aboard. Noble, in a certain shady light.

I squinted at one of the workers on deck, thinking it was Diego, though it could have been his quiet friend, John G. The sound of an engine revving caught my attention, and I turned to see Esmeralda slipping behind the wheel of her boat. Even if she glanced my way, she wouldn't recognize me from that distance, but there was only one hairdo that big in Coney Island. The sequins on her blouse caught the light and twinkled. Her logo was memorable, too—a giant fish with eyelashes and lipsticked mouth. I guessed she didn't always rely on boy toys to drive.

Lonnie disappeared below deck, and I smiled at the waitress, who rolled her eyes at me when a customer demanded more tartar sauce. The place reeked of vinegar, and the floors boasted a charming combination of spilled beer and grease. With entrées starting at ten dollars, I sympathized with anyone who relied on the tips here to pay their rent. While I waited for my window of opportunity, I kept an eye on the noisy family, willing them to leave more than a couple of bucks in their wake.

When Lonnie emerged, I almost missed him, but he shouted something to Diego or John G., and they stomped down the gangplank, disappearing in the general direction of The Blue Lagoon office. I knew Lonnie would be irate if he was looking for me, but, fingers crossed, I would only be yelled out for taking an extended lunch. I signaled for my check and paid in cash, leaving extra with the hope that the patron saint of terrible jobs would be kind to me.

Resisting the urge to glance behind, I strode purposely onto The Blue Lagoon and headed straight down the stairs. Plywood crates were still stacked up, but I knew they weren't empty. The fish smell wasn't overpowering, but it was present, a day-old perhaps, though my expertise did not extend to tuna rot. I peeked inside to be sure and was greeted by rows of glass eyes and slit bellies. Worried that they might squirm to life from some residual poisons in my system, I waited until I thought they would behave. I slipped my hands underneath and between the bodies, giving the cadavers a pat down they didn't deserve. We're innocent in all this, they insisted with their sad mouths, and I agreed. The first crate didn't contain anything suspicious, so I closed the lid, pulse beating a bit faster. I wasn't sure how I could explain my prying, and Lonnie wasn't a small man.

The second crate yielded the same discouraging results, and I moved as quickly as possible over to the third, hoping that it was the charm. After my search finished, I rocked back on my heels, scanning the area for any other possible containers. The boat clearly wasn't carrying tons of cocaine, which couldn't be hidden in such a small space. What was I missing?

"Help a lady out," I whispered to the fish heads, and they seemed to consider the request. Before I could second-guess myself, I pushed my sleeves up and plunged my hand into one of their bellies, forcing my fingers to explore their guts. Forcing myself not to gag, more accurately, I moved onto others, trying to be both speedy and thorough. It was one thing to explain away curiosity, quite another blood up to my elbows. On my sixth fish, I got lucky, extracting a vacuum-sealed pouch that looked all too familiar. My excitement quickly turned to disappointment, though, as I took in the size. A couple of ounces, I estimated, or two thousand dollars give or take the buyer. Not exactly proof of a smuggling operation. Hank might be dealing, but an amount like this could as easily be a personal stash. Meaning it seemed possible that I'd sicced the DEA on a man with a habit, not an operation.

The footsteps on the stairs jolted the thrill of discovery away in an instant, and I stuffed the drugs back where I found them, praying that the skin wouldn't bulge unnaturally. There was still the little problem of having blood on my actual hands, so I used my sweatshirt to open the bathroom door and darted inside.

"Trespassers are shot on sight," Lonnie shouted, his voice sounding nearer than possible. He hovered right outside the door, as I tried to figure out how to first get the stains off my skin, then get it out of my clothes. When he laughed and called me "stupid bitch," I realized that he must have spotted me board The Blue Lagoon and tried to fib my way out of the situation. I flushed the toilet to buy time, settling on the easiest excuse.

"Sorry, bad fish at Manny's," I said as meekly as possible, then made dry heaving noises that sounded pretty realistic to my ears. Then again, I was feeling nauseous. Adrenaline pumped through my veins, mixing unpleasantly with the boat's rocking.

I couldn't hear what Lonnie muttered, but I bet the insults weren't ones I wanted to memorize anyway. When his footsteps receded, I turned on the sink and washed with Lady MacBeth-worthy fury, using toilet paper to wipe up anything that fell on the floor. The blood on my shirt was more difficult, but with a healthy amount of soap, I managed to create a basketball-sized wet spot that camouflaged the stains. It would have to do. I splashed my face and hair, too, going for full-blown sick, and when I stepped into the sun, Lonnie and Diego seemed convinced. At the very least, they stayed as far away from me as possible.

I slunk down the ramp, planning to head back to the office in defeat. My gratitude for not being shot was short-lived. A week's worth of work, and I had nothing to show for my efforts. Every line slipped out of my hands before it led anywhere. And with a lethal Magrelli deadline hanging over my head, my time was limited. It didn't seem like I was going to be any use to Tabor's memory, never mind helping Agent Thornfield or Ellis in a meaningful way. Perhaps if I told Ellis that he was wasting his time with The Blue Lagoon, he could use his department's resources on another case. Would he believe me, though? I doubted he would trust my instincts as much as he trusted his own.

I waved at Esmeralda as she returned to shore, and she took a hand off the wheel to beckon me toward her. With a fake smile, I approached, impressed by how she cut the engine and glided into her small slip. Compared to the yachts around her, the motorboat looked like a kid's plastic model. It was in mint condition, though, in stark contrast to the tour vessels and shrimpers.

"You sure keep her clean," I said, offering a hand to Esmeralda as she jumped onto the dock. I was glad to see that she was wearing a lifejacket now, and not only because it hid the sequins and kept the glare away. I'd been out on those waters and knew that even an experienced driver could get hurt.

"Thanks, baby. Take pride in everything, I always say."

She checked her hair, tucking a few unruly strands back into the nest, then zipped out of her safety equipment, tossing it casually on board where the jacket landed with a thunk. Squeezing my arm, she told me that she'd asked around for me, and there might be an opening at Manny's.

The way my luck was going, I might need that job and doubted I would be let anywhere near the floor. They'd probably have me scaling fish on the overnight shift. With these cheerful thoughts, I headed back to The Pink Parrot and asked Dolly if he had some secret way to get blood out of beloved sweatshirts. He didn't, or at least he swore baking soda wouldn't work and threw my "I ♥ NY" advertising into the trash.

CHAPTER 26

I heard the baby before I pushed open the door to The Blue Lagoon offices. The screaming bundle stared up at Esmeralda, who made noises that were supposed to be coos but sounded like a penguin in distress. Motherly she was not, and I suspected the child was as pleased with the honking sounds as she was with the woman's scratchy chiffon top. There was also the matter of perfume, filling the small space with the scent of begonias and something like chili powder. Even with a newborn, somehow, Esmeralda managed to steal the spotlight, and I nodded at her as I went to congratulate the mother. Leesa's cheeks had busted blood vessels, and a banana clip held her unwashed hair, but at least one myth about motherhood was true—she glowed. Uncle Lonnie was less impressed, scowling from the corner, but I ignored him and mouthed my best wishes over the wailing.

"Isn't she something?" Esmeralda said, passing over Baby Chaya before I'd even dropped my bag. I was caught off guard but managed to tuck the tiny head into the cradle of my elbow the way I'd seen on television. I'd never actually held an infant before, and I pushed my panic down. Surely the odds of me breaking her with so many adults around was small. She yelled one last time, then settled, sticking her fingers in her perfect red mouth and staring up at me with curiosity. Her almond-shaped eyes looked somehow familiar, and I figured my long-buried biological clock played tricks on me. I didn't feel like weeping or running out the door with the little one, but she was pretty cute.

"And she smells like heaven. They weren't lying about that," Leesa said, seeing my blissed-out expression and feeling some well-deserved pride. I agreed, but a kernel of an idea took root in my mind. It struck me as odd that mom and baby weren't at home. Wasn't it dangerous to take such a young child out into the public? There must be concern about germs or—I tightened my grip ever so slightly—clumsy PIs.

"Chaya is a lovely name," I said after I'd let the silence stretch on too long. "Where's it from?"

"Not from our family, I can tell you that damn much."

Lonnie's near-shouting voice jostled Chaya out of her calm, and she started screaming again. I glared at the man, wishing this ogre wasn't her relative. He acted as if she were an intruder, not the newest member of his bloodline. I thought grown men melted at the sight of their kin in miniature form, calloused palms and hairy knuckles gingerly touching fingers and toes. Lonnie didn't seem under Chaya's spell, though, and I doubted that would change. If the magic baby smell that kept fathers—and presumably uncles—from eating their young wasn't working, toddler tantrums wouldn't have much of an effect. Leesa blushed from her brother-in-law's reaction, and I smiled again, trying to soothe over the awkward situation. My presence only made the situation worse, though, an outsider encroaching on family business. When Lonnie finally stormed out, mumbling something about washing the deck, general relief flooded the small space. I handed Chaya back as gently as possible.

Leesa sank into the office chair, rubbing her hand lightly over the baby's head, soothing her. The mother looked content for a moment, but a flash of worry took over her face. She seemed to forget that she had company, and Esmeralda waved her goodbye, slipping outside. Not wanting to disturb Leesa, I watched her quietly, considering whether her anxiety was normal new motherhood or something else. Why was she at work instead of enjoying her maternity leave? Introducing the child to her uncle didn't seem like it warranted a trip, and I was a nobody to her.

I tried to think of an appropriate conversation topic, running through possibilities and rejecting them one by one. What did women talk about at baby showers? Did I know anything about diapers? The commercials with the blue liquid made me gag, but that didn't seem like a fun tidbit.

"Does she have any cousins?" I finally asked, blurting out the question too loudly. Chaya's eyes fluttered opened, then closed again when Leesa kissed her nose. The mother then closed her own eyes and leaned back. She was silent for so long that I thought she's gone to sleep, and I walked toward the blinds to lower them.

"Hank has a sister with twins," Leesa said, and I jumped, not so much at the words as at the tears in her voice. When she didn't elaborate, I made a comment about how much fun that would be for Chaya. Pool parties and slumber parties. Leesa nodded, but didn't look at me.

"Should I call someone for you?" I asked, sensing that Leesa wanted to be alone, though I wasn't sure that was a good idea. I'd heard of postpartum depression and thought it might look like this, a glowing woman with tears on her cheeks, shutting her eyes to the perfect baby in her arms. My heart started thudding in my ears, but Leesa shook her head. When she looked at me, her eyes were shining, but she smiled.

"She'll have me," she said. "That will be enough."

"What about Hank?" I asked. I pictured the box of doughnuts he'd bought on my first morning at The Blue Lagoon, how sweet he'd been with his wife. But I knew as well as anyone that he had another side, too, perhaps a temper that Leesa didn't want around her daughter. Maybe a drug problem that altered his personality.

Not from our family, I can tell you that damn much. Lonnie's words echoed in my head, and I knew why Chaya's eye looked familiar. I'd seen them recently, staring vacantly up at me from the face of a dead man.

Confessing to Leesa that I was really a private investigator went as well as could be expected, and she told me she was happy somebody cared enough about Tabor to investigate. While she didn't admit to an affair, she was quick to assure me that Hank had been home with her the night Tabor plummeted from the George Washington Bridge. After that, she wrapped Chaya and hurried out.

I tried to piece together what I knew of the Almy family. While Leesa had seemed over being pregnant when we first met, motherhood suited her. There was no denying her googly-eyed love. This was a wanted child at least by one parent. Why would Hank object, unless—as I now suspected—Chaya wasn't his biological child? A tumble with charming, handsome Tabor could have taken place on any number of visits. According to Esmeralda, Tabor sniffed around frequently, and maybe his purpose wasn't just checking on his workers. From what I'd learned about him, he was something of a ladies' man, not to mention opportunistic. Could he have been using himself as a stud horse? Luna's guilt suddenly made a lot more sense. She wasn't worried about God finding out about her superstition; she was worried about her very human husband finding out about her very human solution to their problems.

The Viagra was a decoy of sorts. Perhaps it treated impotence, or perhaps it just encouraged a little randiness. When a baby resulted nine months later, there was no suspicion. Unless that baby's eyes had almond-shaped, caramel eyes. And maybe Tabor hadn't been as discreet as he imagined. How difficult would it be to lure a friend to the top of the bridge, I wondered. Probably not that hard. It would be a private place to have a mano a mano talk. Was there a French term for that? Oh, right. Préméditation.

The subway ride back to the Heights had never seemed longer. The above-ground stops let in warm air, and instead of being grateful for the spring weather, I was angry. Angry at Tabor for letting me believe he was one of the good guys this whole time. Finding jobs for the downtrodden. Giving art away to lonely wives. Oh, he'd been giving something away alright. I thought of Señora Amador and her grandson, trying to remember if the child bore any resemblance to his super. How many little Tabor Campions were there in New York? How many enraged cuckolds? I had more questions than answers, and the biggest one was which husband had taken matters into his own hands. Leesa could be protecting her husband, making amends by providing an alibi.

By the time we got to Atlantic Avenue, my anger had turned to fear. A man capable of pushing a friend— even a deceitful one—to his death was capable of hurting his wife as well. Was that why Leesa was at The Blue Lagoon office? Was she hiding? When the conductor announced the stop for Union Square, I wondered if I should jump off, head back toward Coney Island. I was halfway between Luna and Leesa, and I had to make a choice. I thought of Hank's surly attitude, how he stomped around the boat, his frustration visible to anyone who dared to board. Then switched to Dante, his bashful excitement over becoming a father. But what would happen to that emotion if he suddenly found out that he'd been mistaken? What could such a large man do in range? I stayed in my seat, praying for no track fires or sick passengers to create delays.

I transferred at 145th Street, sprinting toward the elevator and not even minding the crush of people as we ascended toward the A train. On the platform, I had time to catch my breath, wondering if the city's favorite motto was "Rush and Wait." We were always doing one or the other. When the train finally roared into the station, I stepped back to let the passengers off, then slipped inside, second-guessing myself again. Should I get off to call Ellis? Or would that waste too much time? The NYPD wasn't even investigating Tabor's death. The door shut, settling the issue for me, and I hung onto the pole as we moved farther uptown.

When I was finally above ground, I sprinted again, plan-less but with direction at least. If I could just get Luna somewhere safe, I would have time to think, make the right decision. The entry to her building was still unlatched, and I raced to the fourth floor, ignoring the pain in my side. I tried to knock normally, but adrenaline pushed through my veins and my hands pounded of their own accord. When the door yanked open, it wasn't Luna that greeted me. And Dante didn't look happy to see me.

CHAPTER 27

When he grabbed my shoulder, I winced, knowing that I would have bruises in the morning if I survived that long. The gentle, aw-shucks man I'd met at the bar was gone, replaced by a ball of energy that started shaking me. My teeth slammed together and I twisted my arm, trying to get out of his grasp, but he tightened his grip. I was good and caught.

"Where is she?" he said, and tears sprung to my eyes from the pain. I'd noticed how big Dante was before, but now he seemed mammoth, towering over me as I kicked out. He dodged my foot easily and pulled me into the hallway. "Where is my wife?"

I blinked, clearing my vision, and tried to say that I didn't know, but he cut me off, dragging me toward the stairs. I dug in my heels, worried that he was going to throw me over the railing. Four stories might not be a six-hundred-foot bridge, but I doubted I would survive all the same. My efforts didn't help me much, and my knees slammed into the ground before I was hauled up again. I whimpered, the bruises from the boat making my fall sting even more.

"She's gone," I whispered, hoping to distract my attacker at least. It worked better than I expected, and he let go of my arm. I stumbled at the sudden freedom, falling against the railing and feeling myself tip over into space. The concrete floor below swam toward me, and I tried to scream, the sound more of a gurgle than a full-throated yell. Then I was pulled back to safety by Dante. When I landed, relief flooded my system, and for a moment I let myself sink down.

"We don't have time," Dante said, jerking me up again, and I realized that he wasn't hurting me on purpose. Luna was missing and he was genuinely panicked, worried about his wife, the one he rarely let out of his sight. I wasn't bad at finding people, and I ignored the aches in my arm and knees as I tried to think of the first steps for a missing person case.

"Does she have a best friend?" I asked. "How about family?"

Dante took the steps down two at a time. I followed as quickly as I could, now as worried as he was. It was surprisingly clear now that she wasn't well when I'd last seen her. What I thought was fatigue—those haunted, dark circles around her eyes—was really guilt, and that emotion could make you desperate. Would she hurt herself? Dante clearly thought she was capable of that dark frame of mind. I hurried after him into the bright afternoon. We both squinted, looking up and down the busy street as if we might see her taking out the trash or chatting with a neighbor. Kids had knocked the cap off of a fire hydrant, and they ran through the cold sprays. A few parents gossiped nearby, but the children were mostly left to their own games, supervised but loosely. When Dante saw them, he started to cry, collapsing onto the sidewalk like old birthday streamers.

"I knew she didn't love him," he mumbled, staring at his large hands. "She just wanted a baby. So did I."

"Friends and family," I tried again, but Dante didn't hear me, or couldn't. He'd given up, convinced his wife had left him or worse. I tried not to dwell on the "worse" and asked him if Tabor's fall had been an accident. I rubbed my shoulder where he had gripped it, suspecting that he hadn't known he was hurting me. This man could do a lot of damage in a fit of rage, but Dante shook his head at my easy way out. He rejected my excuse for him outright.

"No accident. I was doing what had to be done. When a man fucks—sleeps with your wife," he amended quietly. "But he wasn't some man, was he? He was a friend."

Dante stopped crying, but his calm acceptance concerned me more. Here was a love triangle that deserved the name. Except Luna didn't love Tabor. Dante loved his friend. He loved his wife, too, and it had been too much for him. A few of the neighborhood women pointed at us, and I sat down beside this broken man, wondering if he'd repeat his confession at the precinct or if it would be his word against mine. My practical thought embarrassed me, but I'd been burned by confessions before. Somehow, I couldn't imagine Dante changing his tune, though. This seemed like the end of the story. I only wish that had turned out to be true.

"I told her what I'd done," he said quietly, and I resisted the urge to slap him. His attack of conscience made my job easier, but why would he burden his wife with such a confession? Luna was sure to feel as if the blame was hers. If she'd had more faith, if she'd had more patience, more acceptance that not everyone got to be a mother. I'd seen enough murderers to know that the guilty party is usually the one with blood on his hands, but it's easy to blame yourself. I let my anger at Dante pull me to my feet, tugging on his collar.

"Where are her favorite places? Where does she go to be alone?"

He mumbled something about not knowing his wife at all, and I yanked on his clothing harder, forcing him to look at me.

"You can sail down this pity river another day. We need to find Luna." His eyes were slick and I doubted he could see me. He looked lost, and I needed him to find some focus. "You still want this family, right? You've got to fight for them."

He let his head drop into his hands and froze, statue-still. It was hard to tell if he was even breathing, and I struggled to find some words of motivation. It wasn't every day I tried to team up with a killer, but to be fair, it wasn't the first time either. I screamed in frustration, and a few children stopped their playing to stare at me. They giggled behind their hands, and Dante lifted his head to stare back at them. He nodded, coming to a decision, and I hoped it was the right one.

"My Luna. She asked me for forgiveness," he said.

"And do you forgive her?"

As if a starting gun had fired, Dante took off

sprinting down the street, and I ran after him, trying to keep up. There was a possibility that he was running away, but I believed he was running toward his wife, trying to save what could be saved. When he turned on 181st Street, the George Washington Bride loomed in front of us as we dodged bikes and people to reach the pedestrian entrance. The ramp was steep, and I was winded but pushed through the stinging in my lungs. Dante started shouting his wife's name, crying out in distress. The few bystanders stood out of our way as we raced upward.

Traffic crawled along, and it was hard to hear over the collective engines and occasional honking, but the people path wasn't crowded. This was no Brooklyn Bridge, popular with tourists and locals alike. This expanse offered an equally pretty panorama of the city, but it was too remote, didn't lead to ice cream parlors and carousels. When it shook, the sensation made me feel as if I were sinking, instant vertigo. There was no time to slow down, though, as Dante and I ran out over the water.

The scene was hard to decipher at first, but I knew the guard wasn't where he was supposed to be. He wasn't inside his observation booth. Instead, he gripped the railing of the bridge, his eyes wide in panic. I followed his gaze to see that Luna had climbed over and was straddling a beam of the east tower, a good sixty stories above the Hudson. Her long skirt billowed in the wind and swirled to match the currents below. One hand held on while the other cupped her belly. She murmured what could have been prayers, but she was too far away to tell. I grabbed Dante's arm, shaking my head when he cupped hands around his mouth to yell.

"Don't startle her," I said, panting out the words. The guard approached us, asking us to stand back. His tone was cautious, almost a question, and I suspected that his training hadn't prepared him for the reality of jumpers. Statistics, fine. But a woman who'd escaped his notice as she stepped out into the sky? He'd imagined peaceful mornings, maybe the occasional graffiti artist who needed to be turned toward another outlet. Not an expectant mother ready to give up on life. It must have been difficult for her to climb out onto the tower. Jumping from the middle of the bridge would have been easier, and if she'd been one hundred percent determined to die, she would have let go already. There must have been some doubt, and I held onto that conclusion like a lifeline.

"Can you climb out to her?" I asked Dante, who backed away from my request. I turned toward the guard, but he was waving "No" with his arms and saying something about protocol.

"Call for help. Precinct 19. Tell them Kathleen Stone—" I said, then stopped, not sure how to describe what I was about to try. I let the sentence fall and swung a leg over the rail, swallowing the bile that rose into my throat. Luna had chosen the Manhattan facing side, and the skyline loomed in the distance, postcard-ready. The bridge shook again as a tractor trailer passed besides us, and I used both hands to steady myself. My fingers vibrated in fear, but I hardly noticed, not sure if I could make myself complete this task. I looked up again at the two men behind me. The guard watched, but Dante had covered his eyes. With no other option, I swung over my other leg and lowered myself, facing away from Luna. I could see land and water below my feet, and my vision blurred for a second. When it cleared, I made myself turn, keeping my focus on the woman's back and trying not to glance toward the dull horn of a tugboat. I could crawl out to Luna if I didn't look down again. That was the trick, not looking back down.

Letting go of the railing created a surge of panic, but I managed to drop to my knees, white knuckling the beam. The metal was hot, and flakes of gray paint bit into my palms. I began to inch forward, estimating that the distance was only six feet—the longest six feet I'd ever seen, much less travelled. Sirens wailed in the distance, but I knew I couldn't wait for them and live with the consequences. Luna could let go, become another name in a list of suicides on a Wikipedia page.

Convinced that losing my concentration for even a second would bring on more dizziness, I kept my attention on Luna's hair. If she had been a sculpture instead of a living and breathing woman, I might have thought the color was pretty, sunlight creating white highlights in the black curls. In that moment, the vision seemed sinister, as if small snakes slithered over her head, controlling her mind. That's just the crazy talking, I told myself, and they vanished, hallucinations saved for another day. When I got close enough to touch Luna, she finally noticed me, and yelped, raising a hand to her mouth and swaying. I reached out to grab her arm, but one of my knees slipped off, swinging off into space.

Luna's yelp turned to a scream, and I hooked my other leg around the beam. I had only fallen a couple of inches, but my heart slammed inside my chest, warning me. I straddled the metal and gasped until the panic ebbed into something I could handle. When I looked up at Luna, her eyes were full of concern, and despite the odds, I smiled. She didn't smile back, but she didn't leap to her death either. I forced myself to crawl the last few inches until I could perch beside her. We sat quietly, contemplating the view, how we could be such small pieces in a grand city. I knew the little red lighthouse was directly below us, but I didn't look. It would still be there when we got to the ground. And we were going to get there, weren't we?

"Tabor was a good man," she said, and I nodded. I'd heard that before, several times, in fact, and I wanted to believe her faith in him wasn't misplaced. It's true that he didn't seem like the average philanderer. His dalliances had a purpose. But wouldn't a friend suggest Luna talk to her husband? Infertility wasn't the end of the world. A more accurate view would have him as neither the hero nor the villain, someone making choices just like the rest of us. And who was I to judge anyway? I'd never dreamed of having a family of my own, never doodled little girl names and little boy names in a notebook. Maybe Margaret, I thought. And she could go by

Molly or Maggie or Meg.

"Are you finished with your goodbyes?" I asked, pushing away the image of pale blue eyes blinking up at me from a bassinet.

"Yes. Ni con Dios ni con el Diablo," she said, looking out over the river.

Not with God or the Devil. I could relate.

CHAPTER 28

Dante had to be cuffed, but Ellis put the zip tie in the front so that he could hold Luna. The couple leaned against a police cruiser, and I knew that officers would take Dante away soon. He wouldn't see his baby—Tabor's baby—being born, but at least the girl would be born. At least she would grow up with a mother who'd chosen hope over guilt, some kind of future over a grave. I wondered what they would tell her when she was old enough to notice her missing parent. How did you explain to a child that she'd lost two fathers? Ellis caught me staring wistfully at Luna and headed toward me. His stern expression never wavered, and I expected a lecture on the risks of neck-breaking heights. Or, a favorite of his, good guys versus bad guys and never forgetting which side was which. He'd always found the divide easy to locate. I never had that talent, and a small part of me believed I knew best, in this one area at least, though I hoped Ellis never came to the same conclusion. I liked his clarity. To be fair, I liked everything about him, but did I dare to dream of a future with Ellis? It seemed like a longshot even on a good day. Maybe today was a good day, though.

When Ellis got close, I put up a hand to ward off his speeches. He took off his glasses and rubbed his eyes. I'd been making him tired for years, but he could have left me alone. Especially after I'd emerged from my undercover assignment, hellbent on avoiding anyone I used to know, including him. Yet here he was, working a case that wasn't his because I'd called him. Never mind that he thought there was some sort of vice angle. If Luna could forgive Dante and Dante could forgive Luna, Ellis and I could see past our little differences. I was having this logical but unemotional talk in my head when he turned his pale blue eyes on me, and my heart stopped. Maybe it was the residual adrenaline or maybe it was the way he took my hand, but either way, it wasn't really my fault when I stepped into him and pressed my lips against his. I pulled away, shocked at myself, but he wrapped an arm around me and pulled me closer. I was a woman possessed, and he kissed me back with a decade of longing. We only stopped when the whistles started.

When had Sammy been relieved from desk duty? was my first, unromantic thought. The portly man was making obscene gestures with his hands, and I figured his release wouldn't last long. He wasn't exactly the face of the NYPD.

"Right," Ellis said, and I looked up at him, not sure what to expect. He was almost grinning, but someone calling for Detective Dekker made the expression snap closed. He nodded at me and turned toward the officer who needed him.

"Right," I said to myself.

The NYPD had blocked a lane of traffic, and

commuters shouted as they passed, unimpressed that we'd saved a woman's life. Their honking sounded as if it were coming from overhead speakers, not fully attached to the congestion. I was moon-eyed and unready to return to reality. But if Ellis could turn his emotions on and off, so could I. To prove the point, I turned toward the closest cop, asking if I could give my statement.

"Of course, Miss Stein," said the baby-faced officer, reaching for his notebook.

"Stone," I said, spelling my name to make sure the record got it right for once. He noted the correction, then asked me to start from the beginning, as if that were a simple place to find. The sooner I recited the facts as I knew them, though, the sooner I could climb up the stairs to my apartment and collapse on my bed. My days at The Pink Parrot were over, one way or another. The note I'd sent to Salvatore Magrelli had suggested a meeting, and that wasn't an appointment I was willing to miss. If I could climb out onto a two-foot-wide beam hundreds of feet in the air—not to mention kiss my best friend like a drowning woman—I could face a sadistic kingpin. He was a business man, and I had a business offer to make.

*

The stingray stared at me through the new acrylic, circling in a graceful backflip to come near me again. His skin sparkled in the artificial lights, and it was easy to miss the scars near his spine. Had he always been an aquarium attraction, or had he once called the Atlantic home? He seemed less interested in the tuskfish that swam nearby than he was by the humans who'd come to call. Admirers trickled by, stopping to stare for a moment then moving on to the next exhibit. Elsewhere, I knew there was a petting pool for his smaller kin. Kids could use two fingers to feel the slick hide. I'd pass on that particular experience, and not just because I wasn't a kid anymore.

When Salvatore Magrelli walked up beside me, I didn't turn toward him right away, though my whole body knew he was there and told me to flee. I let him watch the animals, too, grateful the dark lights would disguise my discomfort. I'd started sweating even before I arrived, and I knew that I looked like a narc. That was a persona who specialized in getting her throat slit. Not my favorite.

"They all survived Hurricane Sandy," I said, ignoring how my voice cracked on "all." Salvatore didn't respond, but I wasn't ready to look the devil in the face yet. I nodded as if he had asked a question. "Every last one. Even though the place was devastated. Water pouring in from ducts."

I gestured above me toward the air conditioner vent, but Salvatore didn't follow my arm. Even in my periphery, I knew I was being watched, evaluated. He was deciding if I was wired, and my voice quaked even more as I described how an eel had survived in the staff showers, moving around in three inches of water. That detail had stuck with me long past the news reports, how much effort it took to survive sometimes, how hard we had to fight. I doubted Magrelli wanted a history lesson, but it was all I could think to talk about. The flooding had damaged every corner of the New York Aquarium, yet all those creatures made it through. Sea horses, eels, a giant lobster.

"There was an orphaned walrus," I said, and stopped. Magrelli turned toward me and patted under my arms. I froze, horrified by his touch, but unwilling to object when he moved his hands inside my legs. He was efficient, but I still shuddered when he moved over the four-inch scar he'd given me. When he lifted my shirt, I didn't have time to react before he pulled the fabric back into place. If other guests thought it was odd that a woman was being frisked in plain sight, they didn't say anything. When Salvatore stepped back, I let out the breath I had been holding. I wasn't wired. I wasn't even wearing the ear canal device Agent Thornfield had suggested. I was on my own, and that felt all too familiar.

"Not all, Miss Stone," Salvatore said, his voice a sort of rumble. I noticed that nobody stopped to see the exhibit now, their hackles raised whether they recognized the feeling or not.

"Excuse me?"

Salvatore put his hand on the tank as the stingray returned, our only witness. One unlikely to help me in case of emergency.

"One hundred and fifty koi were killed. The ones in the pools outside. All dead," Salvatore said. I started to object, then stopped. No, he was right; I remembered the story now. They'd been forgotten or abandoned in their temporary space. "We're better off inside where people care for us. Wouldn't you agree, Miss Stone?"

"What if you don't like that particular brand of caring?"

Salvatore shrugged, and I finally faced him. There'd been a brief period of time when I thought his power was attractive. At twenty-two, I had felt myself pulled to him, like all of my neighbors did. He wasn't handsome exactly—his nose broken then healed without being set, his lips thin and pale—but he was impressive. Even standing next to him, I couldn't be sure if he was six feet or eight. I knew that I felt dwarfed beside him, and I had to force myself to stand still, to not run. I'd been running long enough. The kind of protection he offered me wasn't without a cost, and that cost was too high, even if I could have swallowed my disdain for his operation. As it was, my morals were on shaky ground, and I knew that Ellis wouldn't approve of why I'd come. Then he'd better not find out, I said to myself before I made my offer.

I'd come into some information about a rival cartel that might be useful. Not the kind of intel that would shut them down from top to bottom, mind you. More like taking out a knee. Runners were valuable, and I knew where to find one. I kept my speech brief, explaining that in exchange for having a runner shut down, I wanted to be left alone.

It hadn't dawned at me all at once that Esmeralda was sneaking cocaine into the harbor through her parasailing company. No, I'd been too distracted by her glitz and glitter to imagine a criminal lurked beneath. But the sound of that lifejacket hitting the floor of her boat couldn't be denied. If every cushion was actually a brick, as I suspected, she'd brought in a million dollars' worth of goods in one haul. Single-handedly, though I suspected her boy toys were actually paid muscle. Body guards, not eye candy. Or, at least not only eye candy. I tried not to be impressed, but I failed. That I genuinely liked Esmeralda made my betrayal worse. She'd told me to take pride in everything, but I couldn't take pride in this step. Even so, I knew it was my only move. Not exactly checkmate, but not lights out either.

I didn't share the company's name or location, of course, while trying to gauge Magrelli's interest from how many times he glanced away from me and at the water. There was no other change in him that I noticed, and I'd been taught to read people. More than analyze his movements, I prayed silently, hoping that what I knew could be exchanged for something that felt like freedom. I doubted I would ever drop completely from Salvatore's radar. There would always be some monitoring; I'd realized too late that nobody simply walked away from the Magrellis.

The thought of sailing Esmeralda up the river, as it were, didn't make me hesitate as much as it would have when I was younger. I'd given up idealistic, come through cynical, and found realistic waiting for me like a second skin. Like an identity I could face in the mirror at least, if I didn't have to look at her every day.

Magrelli carried a 9mm in his boot, and I found my gaze drifting toward it as I finished my pitch. I'd take my knowledge to an inside contact at the DEA, and the runner would be out of business within a week. I didn't know which cartel Esmeralda worked for, but they wouldn't be happy about the interruption. Supplies would be short. Customers would look for a new supplier. I would have preferred taking the Magrelli cartel down to giving them more business, but I'd tried before and failed. The best I could hope for now was saving my own neck. Not the devil or God, I thought as I waited for my fate to be decided.

A small, unremarkable fish bumped against the plastic in front of me, and its scales flattened then reformed when it passed. Another made the same move, scales flattening then springing back, and they made the transformation look easy. As if we could be changed and somehow return to ourselves. But each step I'd taken toward my pre-undercover life had taken me deeper into the ocean, not certain I could recognize myself in the dark. I'd given up being a saint years ago, but this betrayal of Esmeralda felt different. If this was the real Kathleen Stone when all the disguises were stripped away, I wasn't sure I liked her. But I could live with her, and that was the point.

Salvatore reached into his pocket, and I froze, wondering if he'd risk killing me in a public place. I'd picked the aquarium for strategic reasons, not because the fish were nice to look at. Instead of a weapon, though, he pulled out two masks. One I'd given him—

I'd recognize that grimace anywhere. The other was blue and more square than oval, not Tin Man's work. I didn't want them, but neither did I want to be at this family-friendly spot with a murderer. I'd rather be strolling through the latest displays, wondering if it was true that more people died from coconuts than sharks.

"Do we have a deal?" I said, and Magrelli paused before handing me the blue mask. He tucked the other one into his pocket, then mock-bowed. I watched him exit the space, kids instinctively scurrying out of his way. I ran my hand over the face, noting that this one seemed manufactured rather than hand-painted. The lines were too even, the gloss too bright. My appraisal was a form of stalling, but I was worried about the message I might find inside. My fingers trembled as I tried to open the hidden compartment, and in my clumsiness, I cracked the cheap wood. A paper the size of a fortune drifted toward the floor, and I couched down next to it, not bothering to touch the slip since it had landed face up. In neat, tiny letters, it simply read, "Yes."

*

The text from Ellis was even briefer. Somehow, Hi made me feel light-headed, and I texted back Hi before I could chicken out. My relief at escaping from Salvatore unharmed was tinged with unease, but I couldn't confess to Ellis. Agent Thornfield hadn't asked a lot of questions when I told him about Esmeralda's operation, that perhaps The Blue Lagoon intel was misdirected. A local operative found her lifejacket in a small, on-board safe, and the bust had been easy. Esmeralda was smart enough to lawyer up, and part of me hoped she'd get a plea deal. The more practical part hoped I'd never see her again. It was almost too easy, this slippery slope. I flipped open my disposal phone again to read Ellis's message. Nobody was going to get rich publishing our love letters, but even poets had to start somewhere.

I knew that I'd only negotiated a ceasefire and not a treaty with Salvatore Magrelli, but I felt lighter as I tromped toward the lighthouse. It was fully spring, and the stubborn patches of snow had melted. The path was clear if not exactly dry. The warmer weather meant I wasn't making my pilgrimage alone this time, and I stayed near the shoulder in case any kamikaze bikers wanted to pass. The trail wound through Fort Washington Park, the bridge appearing then disappearing as if playing a game of tag with me. And why not? The giant had never been at fault.

When I finally arrived at the lighthouse, I could see that the lock had been replaced. A familiar wild-haired park ranger sat inside the acrylic booth, watching families set up lunch on the picnic tables. I'd been looking for solitude—not bothering to tell anyone where I was headed—but this was better. The shrieks of kids dodging bees colluded with the roars of jet skis to create a soundtrack of change. Only the historical landmarks stayed the same. The rest of us found a way to make peace with our past selves, say hello to the ones currently living. I'd been given a lot of advice lately, but I trusted a children's book more than I trusted most people: "The little red lighthouse still had work to do. And it was glad." I could be glad, too, I decided, climbing onto the rocks for a better view of the river. A few seagulls flew away as I approached, and I heard their squawks of protest. It was a bright, clear day that would be warm by mid-afternoon. For now, though, a breeze held off the heat, doing its best to hold off my regrets as well. I shielded my eyes for a last look at the bridge, happy to be looking up instead of down or even back.

ACKNOWLEDGMENTS

On the morning of February 12, 2006, I woke to the sight of my fire escape enveloped in snow. The forecasted blizzard had not disappointed, and New York City was in the last hours of receiving nearly 30 inches. The typically dismal view outside my window—a shared alley for trash—was transformed. It downright glittered, and my neighbors Ricardo Maldonado and Matthew Pennock were already calling. I dug out my warmest coat and boots, heading out into the winter wonderland. I met my friends on Pinehurst Avenue, our cheeks flushed as much from the joy of missing a day's work as from the cold. From there, we trekked into Fort Washington Park, the George Washington Bridge looming above but nearly obscured by the swirling snow. The Jeffrey's Hook Lighthouse was easy to find, though, its cheerful red façade beckoning us. We were the only visitors.

I'd lived in New York City for many years before discovering the lighthouse and surrounding picnic area, what would soon become my favorite spot. I have a used copy of *The Little Red Lighthouse* and the *Great Gray Bridge*, written by Hildegarde H. Swift and illustrated by Lynd Ward. I'm grateful that this children's book helped save its titular landmark. Even better, it was reissued in 2003 for a new generation to enjoy. I never intended to set a murder in the park, and part of me still feels a bit guilty about my fictional blood splatters. In reality, it would be difficult for someone jumping from the bridge to land atop the lighthouse, so I've taken some creative license. Moreover, a tall fence now helps prevent suicide, but that wasn't constructed until 2017 and this story is set a few years earlier.

Most of the research I find gets cut during the revision process as I strive for believability. I don't want Kat to suddenly have an encyclopedic knowledge of Manhattan history or current affairs. She's street smart and aware, but not a policy expert. Nonetheless, I do want to mention a few sources that helped me with the novel and the important topic of immigration. I wrote this book under a different administration, naively imagining that we would find a humane and fair way to treat people looking for a better way of life in the United States. I am indebted to the excellent reporting of Ginger Thompson and Sarah Cohen in *The New York Times* for providing me with much-needed context. Lauren Hilgers's "The Kitchen Network" from *The New Yorker* was eye-opening. On a lighter note, I was delighted to find Mike Peed's "Fish Story" (also in *The New Yorker*), so that people besides my college roommate would believe me when I talked about seeing a pet shark in a West Village apartment. And for all of my Kat Stone novels, I've relied on crime statistics made publicly available by the FBI. I also want to confess that I played a little fast and loose with the jellyfish. While there are jellyfish that cause hallucinations, these species do not reside off the coast of New York.

I am incredibly blessed to have such supportive friends and family members. Ricky (of snowstorm fame above) provided invaluable guidance on this manuscript. It is a much better book—as is all of my writing—because of him. The feedback I received from Rosie Jonker was equally helpful and I am grateful to her and everyone at the Ann Rittenberg Literary Agency. It is a privilege to work with Ann whose fierce support of her authors makes me believe this crazy writing life is possible. Working with Jason Pinter has also been a dream. He has created something truly special with Polis Books, and I am honored to be part of a noir lineup that includes Alex Segura and Steph Post. I'd also like to thank Kristen Linton, Toral Shah, Katie Meadows, Tayt Harlin, Emily Mitchell, and Matt (also of snowstorm fame). My parents Kevin and Paula Wright have given me unwavering support. None of this would be possible without them. Finally, my husband Adam Province makes the journey worthwhile—and a lot more fun.

About the Author

Erica Wright's debut crime novel *The Red Chameleon* was one of *O Magazine's* Best Books of Summer 2014. *The Granite Moth* was called "brisk, dark, slinky" by *USA Today* and was a 2016 Silver Falchion Award Finalist. She is also the author of two poetry collections, *Instructions for Killing the Jackal* and *All the Bayou Stories End with Drowned*. She is a senior editor at *Guernica Magazine* as well as a former editorial board member for Alice James Books. She grew up in Wartrace, TN and received her B.A. from New York University and her M.F.A. from Columbia University. She now lives in Washington, DC.

Visit her online at www.ericawright.org or on Twitter at @eawright.